Lady Elect

Lady Elect

Nikita Lynnette Nichols

URBAN
CHRISTIAN

www.urbanchristianonline.com

Urban Books, LLC
78 East Industry Court
Deer Park, NY 11729

ISBN 13: 978-1-60162-833-6
ISBN 10: 1-60162-833-1

First Printing June 2012
Printed in the United States of America

10 9 8 7 6 5 4 3 2 1

Distributed by Kensington Corp.
Submit Wholesale Orders to:
Kensington Publishing Corp.
C/O Penguin Group (USA) Inc.
Attention: Order Processing
405 Murray Hill Parkway
East Rutherford, NJ 07073-2316
Phone: 1-800-526-0275
Fax: 1-800-227-9604

Lady Elect

by

Nikita Lynnette Nichols

Also by Nikita Lynnette Nichols

None But The Righteous

A Man's Worth

Amaryllis

A Woman's Worth

Crossroads

The poem entitled "Ain't Goin' Nowhere" was written specifically for this book by Jamia Ray.

Dedication

I wish to dedicate this book to all of the preachers' wives. I know there may be times when you wanna act a fool and can't. You have to always smile. Well, this book is for you. I give you permission to live vicariously through my character, Lady Elect Arykah Miles-Howell.

Acknowledgments

Well, Father, you did it again. You showed up in this book, and you showed out. Until now, my novel *A Man's Worth* had always been my personal favorite. But, Father, because of your infinite wisdom, I can truly say that this book, *Lady Elect*, is my best to date. I had an absolute ball writing this book.

I must acknowledge my readers, my fans, and my supporters. You are all, without a doubt, the wind beneath my wings. I appreciate the encouragement you gave me when writing this book. Many of you reached out to me daily with words of kindness, pushing me all the way to the last page. I can no longer call you my fans, but I must now acknowledge you as my sisters and my brothers. You are family to me.

My parents, William and Victoria, all I can say is, "Wow."

Raymond and Theresa, my brother and sister, I'm blessed to have you both in my life.

Rafael, in *Crossroads* you shined big time. Thanks for all of your suggestions that are *always* keepers. When you say to me, "Sweetie, that doesn't sound right. How about this?" and then you give me exactly what my books need, I can't help but to give you your props. You, Rafael, are undoubtedly the best.

Chapter 1

Arykah Miles-Howell and her best friend, Monique Lynnette Morrison-Cortland, along with Monique's cousin, Amaryllis Price, and Amaryllis's best friend, Bridgette Nelson, sang and danced to the music of R&B group Kool & The Gang.

"Oh yes, it's ladies night and the feeling's right. Oh yes, it's ladies night; oh, what a night," the ladies sang.

For the past four months the full-figured beauties had rotated each other's livingrooms, on every third Saturday evening, for their monthly "fat girl" party. This particular evening the living room in a five-bedroom, six-and-a-half bath estate, in Covington, a subdivision in Oakbrook Terrace, was filled with joy and laughter.

Hostess Arykah changed CDs and led her girlfriends in the electric slide as each of them held flutes filled with virgin Bahama Mamas.

"Come on, sistas. Step it to the left, now rock it to the right, take it on back, now jump two times. Uh-huh, uh-huh, now jump again. Now swing it all around and take it to the ground," Arykah instructed along with the CD.

Collectively, the ladies would tip a scale at nearly nine hundred pounds. A lavish buffet table consisting of honey barbeque buffalo wings, taco salad, a tray of rolled salami and ham slices, and fresh baked Hawaiian bread sat front and center in the home's two-story foyer.

"Ain't no party like a fat girl party," Bridgette, a size fourteen and the smallest of the group, said as her bulging eyes roamed over the food. Two dozen Krispy Kreme doughnuts was the first of the feast to catch the ladies' eyes when they had entered Arykah's front door earlier that evening.

Sweating to the music, Monique was the first to sit down on the plush white Berber carpet to catch her breath. She let her head fall backward on the cushion of the custom-made, ivory-colored Nicolette suede chair.

"Come on, cousin. I know you ain't tired yet. This is only the second song,"Amaryllis teased.

Monique absorbed the sweat beads on the tip of her nose into a Kleenex tissue. She had become a newlywed just four months ago and her then size twenty figure had grown bigger, to a size twenty-two W. "I ain't as thin as I used to be. I can't do all of that bending and twisting and jumping. And I told Arykah that I was on a diet. If she was a true friend, she wouldn't have served all that fat food."

Arykah took a sip of her exotic drink while keeping up with the dance movements.

"It's a fat girl party, Monique. You know how we do it. Did you expect me to serve a lettuce, tomato, and cucumber salad? What the heck were you thinking?"

Monique inserted the tissue in her blouse to soak up the wetness in her cleavage.

"Well, now that you've mentioned it, a salad with fat-free dressing would have been a nice change."

Arykah stopped dancing and placed her hand on her right hip. She then shifted all of her weight onto her right leg. "What, are we rabbits now? I think there's a bag of carrots in the fridge. You want me to get you some? Keep in mind, Monique, you've inhaled four doughnuts and just about ate all of the salami. And

don't even go there about bending, twisting, and jumping, because you ain't got a problem with bending,
twisting, and jumping for that superfine husband of
yours."

Monique chuckled. "That's because Adonis under-
stands that ten good minutes is all I'm good for. And
when my ten minutes are up, he does all the work with
my two hundred forty-seven pounds."

Bridgette, Amaryllis, and Arykah burst into laughter.

"Does he work it, girl?" Bridgette asked.

"Adonis works it so good, I think he had Energizer
batteries implanted," Monique added.

Amaryllis snapped her fingers in the shape of the
capitol letter Z. Over the past year, she had allowed
herself to balloon from a petite figure eight to a size sixteen. Amaryllis blamed her emotional eating binge on
two bad relationships. "All right, cousin, I ain't mad."

"I know that's right," Bridgette said.

Arykah was out of breath. She collapsed on the floor
next to Monique, panting for air. "Do you remember
where we were only four months ago? I was doing my
realty thing and wasn't even thinking about a man,"
she said to Monique.

Monique wiped sweat from around her neck. She
thought back to the mistake she had almost made with
her ex-boyfriend, Boris Cortland, who just happens to
be her husband's cousin. "And I was about to destroy
my life. Marrying Boris would have been like commit-
ting suicide."

Bridgette and Amaryllis joined Monique and Arykah
on the floor. "I remember it like it was just yesterday,"
Amaryllis said.

"Me too," Bridgette added.

Arykah shook her head from side to side in disbelief. "Monique, when you called out Adonis's name at

the altar, I almost fainted. Even though he and I had planned and hoped that things would turn out the way they had, I was stunned that it actually did. I was so happy when you called from Jamaica, and told me that Adonis had proposed to you in midair. You said you needed a maid of honor, and I begged Lance to come to Jamaica with me."

"Who would've thought that Lance would propose to you only minutes before Monique walked down that sandy aisle?" Bridgette asked Arykah.

"And who would've thought the two of you would have a double wedding?"Amaryllis added.

Arykah looked at them both with a gleam in her eyes. "God thought it."

Two hours after the sun had risen over Lake Michigan, Pastor Lance Howell lay in the middle of his California king-sized bed. He was waiting for his wife to emerge from their massive walk-in closet. Sunday mornings were fashion show time in the Howell household. Arykah appeared in the closet doorway. She was dressed in a navy Dolce & Gabbana silk sarong dress that tied on the left side of her waist and hugged every curve of her plus-size figure.

"Okay, Bishop, tell me what you think of this one," Arykah said.

Lance exhaled loudly and extended his arms behind his head. "Cheeks, why do you make me go through this torture every Sunday morning? I think it's lovely on you, just like the other nine outfits you tried on prior to that one."

"What about the length of this dress? My knees are showing."

"So, what?"

"You don't think it's inappropriate for the first lady to show her knees in church?"

Lance got up from the bed and walked over to Arykah. He wrapped his arms around her wide waist and snuggled her neck. "Why don't you just go to church naked so I can watch your butt cheeks jiggle when you walk? You know I like that."

Arykah chuckled. "You need to get saved. If your congregation could hear half of the things that roll off of your tongue, they would vote you out of the pulpit."

Lance playfully tapped his wife's behind on his way to the shower. Arykah's backside was his favorite area on her body. And he'd nicknamed her accordingly.

"Cheeks, they can do whatever they want. It won't change the fact that I am in love with my wife."

Arykah took off the dress and laid it on the bed, among the other outfits she had modeled for Lance that morning. She slipped into her bathrobe, then followed him into the master bath. She sat at her vanity, next to their his-and-her marble sinks, where she applied moisturizer to her face.

"So, you and I have a deal, right?" Lance asked from the shower.

Arykah rolled her eyes into the air. She knew what he was referring to, but asked the question anyway. "What deal are you talking about?"

"I'm talking about you allowing Mother Pansie Bowak to sit in on your counseling session with Sister Darlita Evans after morning service."

"Lance, Darlita asked if I would meet with her to discuss how she should handle her husband's third adulterous affair. It's a private issue, and I think it would be wrong to add a third party to the session. Besides, Mother Pansie doesn't like me."

Arykah faced opposition the moment Lance announced to his congregation that he had married a woman who wasn't a member of the Freedom Temple Church Of God. Lance knew the rules of the church; that it was forbidden for the pastor to marry outside of the immediate church family. Though he was raised to believe that rule, Lance chose to follow his heart.

When Lance asked Arykah to stand and he introduced her as Lady Elect Arykah Miles-Howell, few people clapped or offered a smile of congratulations. Mother Pansie, along with the entire Mothers Board, stormed into his office immediately after the benediction to express their disapproval. The mothers pleaded with their pastor to see that it wasn't fair to the hundreds of single women sitting under his nose, Sunday after Sunday. Surely, he could have chosen a more traditional lady, unlike Arykah Miles, who was much too bold, very outspoken, short tempered, and not likely to be controlled.

"Pastor, think about your reputation. She's not first-lady material."

Lance embraced each mother. He thanked them for caring about his well-being, then ushered them, one by one, from his office. Truth be told, Lance was in love with the too bold, very outspoken, short tempered, and not likely to be controlled, Arykah Miles.

"What makes you think Mother Pansie doesn't like you, Cheeks?" he asked from the shower.

"She told me so."

"Maybe you misunderstood her. What were her exact words?"

"She said, 'I don't like you.' I wanted to tell her to kiss my behind, but I know I must respect my elders, no matter how old and wrinkled they may be. Plus, I promised God that I would stop cursing."

Lance didn't respond right away. He rinsed the soap-suds from his body, then lathered the sponge again. He knew Arykah wasn't exaggerating; Mother Pansie had openly expressed her dislike for his wife on many occasions.

"Bishop, her skirts are too short and her lipstick is too red. Bishop, you shouldn't allow her to wear high heels that tie up around her ankles with diamonds on them. It draws too much attention to her legs. Bishop, first ladies should not be seen with blond streaks in their hair. Bishop, why do you allow her to wear her arms out in the sanctuary? Bishop, why did you allow that woman to keep her maiden name? She's openly disrespecting you when she doesn't carry your name and your name alone."

"As church mother, Pansie Bowak has been counseling the women for years. But I would like for you, as my wife, to take over that responsibility. Just think of it as a training session. I only ask that you allow Mother Pansie to sit in on a couple of marital counseling sessions so that you can get a feel on how troubled marriages should be handled."

Arykah applied Johnson & Johnson's baby oil gel to her elbows and the heels of her feet. "Humph, I already know how troubled marriages should be handled. I believe that if a husband or wife cheats, it's up to the injured spouse to decide if they want to stay in the marriage. There is absolutely no excuse for adultery. But if the marriage is strong enough to survive it, then to God be the glory. But this Negro has stepped out on Darlita three times. And I'm well aware that the morally correct advice that I should give her is to turn the other cheek. But heck, Darlita only has two cheeks, Lance. And she's already turned them both."

Lance stepped from the shower and wrapped a towel around his waist. He stood behind Arykah and placed his hands on her shoulders. "I'm worried about how you'll handle this situation with Darlita. Remember that God hates divorce."

Arykah was about to cut a hangnail when she stopped abruptly and looked in the mirror up at her husband's reflection. A serious expression was displayed on her face.

"And He hates adultery too."

What was Lance to do? He married a woman who was headstrong and sugarcoats nothing. He imagined Arykah advising Darlita to set the house on fire with her husband in it.

Lance stood Arykah up and turned her around to face him. "I know it's a struggle adjusting to the role as the first lady, but when you're giving advice to the women, you must always refer to the scriptures. You can't give advice based on your personal feelings on a matter. I don't want to see every woman who is dealing with infidelity leave your office with a made up mind to divorce her husband. That's why I think it's important to have Mother Pansie sit in on a couple of sessions."

Arykah turned her head away from Lance. He cupped her behind and squeezed.

"Please, Cheeks. Do this for me."

Arykah smiled even though she knew what she was up against. Mother Pansie was old school and from the South. She believed that women were inferior to men and a dutiful wife should always do what she's told.

After the benediction two Sundays ago, a young lady confided in Arykah that she was troubled in her marriage. She confessed that she had been a punching bag for her husband's stress relief method for the past eight months. She told Arykah what Mother Pansie had told her; that if her husband didn't beat her, he didn't love her.

Hot under the collar, Arykah marched the young lady straight to Lance's office. "Bishop, we have a problem."

Behind closed doors, Lance listened as the young lady revealed that her husband was facing a layoff. Their mortgage was being threatened, and her husband wouldn't seek counseling to deal with his emotions. She had become subjected to rape and beatings on a daily basis.

Lance looked at his wife and discerned her spirit. The expression on Arykah's face was horrifying. He had married a firecracker and knew without a shadow of a doubt that Arykah wanted to advise the young lady to drug her husband, wait until he fell asleep, then cut off his private member and arms. That was a sure way to cease the torture she was going through.

Lance could've counseled the young lady himself but wanted to afford Arykah the opportunity to step in as his wife, as his right hand, and as the first lady, to become a mentor to the women in the church. Arykah was from the streets. She hustled for years to get to where she was. But Lance still saw signs of Arykah's roots taunting her. Though she wanted very much to be delivered from her abusive past relationships, Lance knew he had to continue to cover his wife in prayer and work through her struggles and insecurities with her.

But Arykah was now a pastor's wife. Lance silently prayed for God to write on her tongue. He cleared his throat and loosened his necktie in preparation for damage control.

Once he gave Arykah the go-ahead, there would be no telling what would come flying out of her mouth.

"First Lady, what do you advise this sister to do?" he nervously asked.

Both Arykah and the young lady sat in chairs opposite of Lance. Arykah held the young lady's hands in her own. "I want you to know that God loves you, and He didn't create you to be anyone's punching bag. You are fearfully and wonderfully made. It is unacceptable for a man, any man, to put his hands on you in anger. If Mother Pansie told you that your husband loved you while beating and raping you, she was mistaken.

"Your body is the Lord's temple, and no one, not even your husband, should be allowed to abuse and destroy it. If he isn't willing to seek counseling for his abusive behavior, then you should pack your things and leave. Because the next time he lays unholy hands on you, you may not survive it. And you should seek professional help from an abuse therapist for yourself. It isn't normal behavior for you to have accepted your husband's fury for so long. Ask the therapist to help you find out why you willingly tolerated his mood swings.

"And you have to learn who you are in God. My husband taught me that women must realize their worth and own it. Because if we don't own it, we become vulnerable. And vulnerability is a pathway for the devil to destroy us, often through the very ones who claim they love us."

Lance was well pleased with Arykah's Christ-like attitude. Maybe he could go ahead and sit Mother Pansie down after all. He'd have to wait and see. He tightened his tie around his neck and leaned back in his chair while he watched God work through his wife.

Arykah dabbed the young lady's tears with a Kleenex tissue that she had pulled from a box on Lance's desk. *"And you have to always protect your gates. Gates are openings that lead to your soul. Through our eye gates we may have seen our parents become victims of spousal abuse. And because we see it, our souls accept it as normal behavior.*

"That's a trick of the enemy. Our ear gates can become flooded with damaging words spoken to us through verbal abuse.

"I once dated a man who constantly told me that I was too fat, that I wasn't pretty, that I was unattractive, and that I would never be loved by a man. And I believed that lie for years before Bishop Howell deposited a word of release into me. I tolerated that man's behavior because it was what I had become used to.

"And we have to protect our vagina gates also. Mother Pansie may have told you that it was impossible for a husband to rape his wife, but that was absolutely not true. How do you feel when your husband forces himself on you for sex?"

The young lady sniffed and wiped her eyes. "I feel violated because he's so rough with me. He never kisses me. Never asks how I feel or if I'm in the mood for sex. He just tells me what he wants, and then takes it from me and demands that I do things I don't want to do. And sometimes he bites my breasts until they bleed. And after he's done, he calls me dirty names."

Arykah was flabbergasted, and Lance was appalled. But he sat silent and let Arykah do her thing that she was doing so well.

Arykah knew all too well what it felt like to be in the arms of a man that didn't love her. Listening to the young lady's story brought tears to Arykah's own eyes. She squeezed the woman's hands for comfort. "When I'm with my husband, I feel safe and secure. I feel protected and adored. He cares what my feelings are. There's no dirty name-calling. There's no hurt or pain. Only love, comfort, and security. When a man takes his wife's body by force and inflicts sexual pain upon her, he's raping her. And what you must do is start loving yourself and get out of this relationship because it's not holy, which means it's not of God."

Arykah looked across the desk at Lance to see, through his facial expression, if she had crossed any lines. Lance softly smiled at his wife and nodded his head in agreement with everything she had said. He was well pleased.

"Bishop Howell and I will always be here for you, and we want you to feel free to come to us for anything. We are your spiritual parents, and we'll do all that we can to encourage you and keep you strong in the Lord," Arykah assured the young lady.

Lance stood and encouraged the young lady to follow Lady Arykah's advice. He assigned certain scriptures pertaining to strength, courage, and peace for her to study.

He led the three of them in prayer for the young lady's strength and peace of mind.

The young lady hugged and thanked them both, then walked out of Lance's office and closed the door behind her.

Arykah looked at Lance. "You need to deal with Mother Pansie."

That meeting was still fresh in Arykah's mind as she and Lance stood in the middle of their master bath. "Lance, you know what happened the last time Mother Pansie counseled a young lady, but if you want her to sit in on the session with Darlita and me, then so be it."

"Thank you."

"You don't have to thank me, we're a team."

Lance kissed Arykah passionately and guided her back to the bed.

"Do we have time for this before church, Bishop? Don't you have to preach in a couple of hours?" she asked, wanting Lance just as much as he wanted her.

Lance removed Arykah's bathrobe. He let his towel slip from his waist. "This will help me preach real good." He enjoyed his wife in between the Egyptian cotton sheets.

Later that morning, on the South side of Chicago, the sanctuary at Freedom Temple Church Of God was filled to capacity. Every seat, approximately five hundred of them, was spoken for. The congregation was in high praise when Lance and Arykah appeared in the doorway entrance to the center aisle.

The praise and worship leader signaled to Adonis Cortland, the head musician, to lower the organ's pitch while she announced their pastor and first lady. "Please stand and receive Bishop Lance and Lady Elect Arykah Miles Howell."

With Arykah standing on his right, Lance passionately placed his open palm on the small of her back. Arykah wrapped her left arm around Lance's waist, and they walked confidently as husband and wife down the center aisle. As he did Sunday after Sunday with a smile on his face, Lance escorted Arykah to the first pew and greeted Monique, Arykah's personal assistant, with a peck on the cheek.

Four months ago when Lance walked into the sanctuary for the first time as a married man, he moved his ten deacons from the front left pew to the front right pew. He reserved the front left pew for Arykah, her guests, and Monique. Arykah was now in Lance's full view.

Mother Pansie hadn't taken that rearrangement too kindly. It had been tradition that the mothers sat behind the deacons on the left side of the church. But with the deacons sitting across the aisle, Mother Pansie had to constantly look at Arykah's back side.

Lance sat in the pulpit among his assistant pastor, Minister Carlton Weeks, to his left. The associates sat on the right side of Lance. Minister Darryl Polk, Minister Tyrone Williams, and nineteen-year-old Minister Alfonzo (Fonzie) Kyles, whom Lance was leaning toward promoting to youth pastor, each shook Lance's hand and gave him a hearty, "God bless you, Bishop."

Lance looked at Arykah, then winked his eye and smiled. She returned the gesture.

Monique nudged Arykah with her elbow and whispered, "I saw that, First Lady. You and the bishop should know better than to partake in foreplay in the sanctuary."

Arykah chuckled and leaned into Monique for privacy. "If you would've been in our bedroom two hours ago, you would've seen some *real* foreplay."

Monique gasped, and it caused a few heads to turn their way. She met Arykah's lean and kept her whisper, "On a Sunday morning?"

On the pew behind them, Mother Pansie tried desperately to hear Arykah and Monique's conversation. She saw the wink Lance had given his wife. And because Arykah and Monique were leaning into each other whispering and gasping, Mother Pansie concluded that their conversation may not have been appropriate for the sanctuary. She tapped Mother Gussie Hughes, who sat on the right of her, on the knee and nodded her head in Arykah and Monique's direction.

Mother Gussie, affectionately known as "Momma G," hadn't liked Arykah since the day she had first called the church asking to speak to Bishop Howell. As the church's secretary, she had interrogated Arykah about why she was calling. Once Arykah revealed that she wasn't a member but just a friend of Bishop Howell, Mother Gussie felt she was just another single lady all too eager for the pastor to place a ring on her finger.

Mother Gussie had had her own plans for Lance's future. As soon as her granddaughter would have gotten paroled and delivered her third child, Mother Gussie had planned to bring her to the church and introduce her to the pastor. But only weeks after she had answered Arykah's phone call, Bishop Howell introduced her as his wife.

Mother Pansie and Mother Gussie both turned their noses up at the form-fitting, crimson-red, knee-length crochet dress Arykah had decided to wear to church that morning. They couldn't help but notice the three-carat diamond platinum studs shining in Arykah's ears. Her lobes were completely hidden. Arykah's hair was pulled back into an elegant ponytail that revealed the matching six-carat diamond teardrop necklace around her neck. As Arykah giggled and whispered in Monique's ear, the mothers saw her bright red lip gloss. Her perfectly decorated eyelids were adorned with false eyelashes.

Arykah felt their stares. She purposely placed her left hand on Monique's right shoulder to give the mothers something to really be hot about. When Mother Pansie and Mother Gussie caught a glimpse of the massive diamond ring, coupled with the diamond tennis bracelet on the first lady's wedding finger and wrist, their breaths caught in their throats.

Arykah heard the gasping sounds and turned around with a smile. "Hello, Mothers. It is so good to see you both on this fine Sunday morning."

The looks on the mothers' faces confirmed to Arykah what she already knew. They didn't like her and preferred she didn't speak to them. But Arykah didn't wait for a response. She knew it wasn't forthcoming anyhow.

When her mission had been accomplished, Arykah turned back around and found Lance's eyes staring into her own. He gave her a half smile and slowly shook his head from side to side, indicating to Arykah that she should be ashamed of herself for meddling with the mothers. She winked her eye at Lance. He smiled broadly, then turned his head to focus on the choir rendering in song.

The mothers hadn't seen Arykah's feet yet. She felt Mother Pansie and Mother Gussie would probably have a heart attack if they saw her red stilettos that were adorned with Swarovski crystals.

Many congregants approached the altar for prayer after Bishop Howell had preached a lengthy sermon on prosperity. The associate ministers came from the pulpit to assist their pastor with laying holy hands on the people. Lance called for Arykah to stand by him when he ministered to women. That was new for Arykah. She hadn't understood what Lance wanted her to do at that time. When he ministered to a woman, he'd ask Arykah to give her an encouraging hug. Arykah felt honored to be in ministry with her husband. It was exhilarating.

The last woman Lance instructed Arykah to hug was Darlita, the woman she was to counsel after morning service. She stood before Arykah with a tear-stained face.

Because Arykah knew Darlita's story, she immediately pulled her into her arms and began praying for Darlita's strength and sanity. Arykah was the first to pull away when she had finished praying, but Darlita didn't let go. She held on to Arykah as if she was in a safety zone. It was as if Darlita felt that if she let go, her world would collapse.

"Come on, sweetie, let's go to my office," Arykah said.

Monique saw Arykah guide Darlita from the sanctuary and knew that was her cue to grab Arykah's things and follow them. Mother Pansie also saw Arykah leaving the sanctuary with Darlita. As soon as Monique stood to leave, so did she.

Upstairs in Arykah's office, that was adjacent to Lance's and just as large, Monique placed Arykah's Bible and purse on top of the desk and stated that she was going back down to the sanctuary to pay her tithes and offerings.

Soon after Monique had left Arykah's office, Mother Pansie burst into the room. She was out of breath from rushing up two flights of stairs. "First Lady, the bishop asked me to sit in on this meeting you're having."

Arykah wanted to curse, but remembered her surroundings and the promise she had made to God. "That's fine, Mother Pansie, come on in." Arykah placed two chairs on the opposite side of her desk for Darlita and Mother Pansie, but Mother Pansie had positioned herself comfortably in Arykah's chair behind the cherry oak wood desk.

"That's *my* seat, Mother." Arykah made the statement as calmly as she possibly could, but Mother Pansie was already working on her last nerve. When Mother Pansie had taken her rightful seat, Arykah told Darlita that Pastor Howell had requested that Mother Pansie, the president of the Mothers Board, sit in on the counseling session.

Before Arykah started the meeting, she silently prayed that the Lord would help her control her emotions, but came to the conclusion that if anything popped off between her and Mother Pansie, it would be her husband's fault.

She opened her right desk drawer to briefly glance at a poem she had written for herself shortly after some of the women at Freedom Temple revealed their true feelings about her position as the pastor's wife. The poem was for her own self-encouragement whenever the enemy came upon her to eat of her flesh.

Ain't Goin' Nowhere

Me in my high heels and short skirts
Decorated in things that sparkle and shine
That's right, ladies
Pastor Howell is all mines

He chose me because I am the cream of the crop
Looking at y'all, humph, do you even shop?
Take a long, wide glimpse of your today
Give it up, haters, because I'm here to stay

Don't need to explain nothing to you
Only to the one I'm married to
I see you looking, can't help yourselves
Compared to me, you're like bookends on a shelf

Trying to be a nice woman to you in church
Having to bite my tongue is hurting me so much
My girl, Monique, got my back with her raw words
To make all you wannabes run like a charging herd

So, keep on whispering, talking, pointing, and looking

I promise you, I don't care
Whether you accept me or not
I ain't goin' nowhere

Arykah shut the drawer and kicked off her stilettos under her desk. "Mother Pansie, Sister Darlita is here seeking counsel. Her husband has committed adultery a third time. He isn't a member of this church, and according to Darlita, he doesn't want to give marital counseling a chance."

The first thing that came out of Mother Pansie's mouth to Darlita was, "It's *your* own fault that your husband is unfaithful."

"How in the heck is it *her* fault?" The words flew out of Arykah's mouth at the speed of lightning before she had a chance to catch them, not that she really wanted to.

Mother Pansie looked at Arykah with raised eyebrows. *"Excuse me?"*

Arykah swiveled her high-back leather chair in Mother Pansie's direction. "What do you mean it's Darlita's fault that her husband is unfaithful? What is *his* responsibility to the marriage? Surely you're not suggesting that Darlita forced her husband to put his shaboinka inside of another woman."

Mother Pansie's eyes bucked out of her head. She placed her hand over her heart as if she was going to pass out. She wished Bishop Howell could have been there to witness his wife's outspokenness. "With all due respect, First Lady of *only* four months, if a woman keeps her house and takes care of her husband's needs, he wouldn't stray. And it would be wise for *you* to take heed to this advice I'm giving."

It hadn't bothered Arykah when Mother Pansie reminded her of how long she'd been the pastor's wife. Whether she'd been married for four months or forty years, she would not sit there and allow Mother Pansie to make Darlita think that her husband's infidelity was her fault.

The enemy got the best of Arykah. She forgot that she was there to counsel Darlita.

She set her gaze on Mother Pansie. "First of all, my marriage is on point. And you will not sit in my office, in my presence, and convince this sister to accept the blame for her cheating husband. The devil *is* a liar."

Mother Pansie was vested; she had put in her time. She had been the church mother for over thirty-five years. More than half of the women in the church, she helped raise from infants. She refused to let some fat heifer from the street walk into the church and take over her position and teach the women to be disrespectful and rude. She scooted forward in the chair and pointed her finger at Arykah. "Now see, I don' told the bishop that you weren't first-lady material. You need to show some respect. You only been married a short while. What do you know about being a wife? Sometimes a woman's gotta go through—"

Arykah stood up from her desk and raised her voice. She wouldn't let Mother Pansie complete her sentence. "I don't give a rat's behind how long I've been married! And as far as respect goes, old woman, you've got to give it to get it."

Darlita sat still. She didn't know what to do.

Mother Pansie stood up. She breathed in hot coals and exhaled fire. She raised her pitch to match Arykah's. "Just who in the heck do you think you're talking to, li'l girl? You ain't nothing but a two-bit tramp that latched on to the bishop. Ever since you been here, you ain't done nothing but walk around here like you're better than everybody else.

"I don't care how bright your bracelets and earrings shine or what you're driving. You're still trailer trash, and you need to crawl back under the rock you came from."

Arykah instantly felt herself being drawn into a zone. She was so mad that she literally felt her head spin three hundred sixty degrees around on her shoulders. The little girl from the movie *The Exorcist* had nothing on Arykah. Arykah was possessed and fully under the devil's command. She stepped out of herself to watch herself perform a scene from *The Matrix* movie. Arykah had never performed a back bend in her entire life, but at that moment, she was as flexible as a rubber band. In a circular slow motion, she bent backward and was getting ready to leap forward over the desk.

"That's enough, Mother!" Lance stood in the doorway to Arykah's office with an expression on his face that she had never seen before. Someone was in trouble. Arykah didn't know whether it was her, Mother Pansie, or the both of them.

"You see, Bishop? Do you see what happened now that you've brought this floozy into this church?" Mother Pansie asked Lance.

Arykah was fit to be tied. "Floozy? Who are you calling a floozy?"

Mother Pansie stood her ground. "I didn't stutter. I called *you* a floozy with your fishnet stockings and fake hair. You ain't got no business—"

Lance slammed the door behind him, which cut Mother Pansie's words off. "I said that's enough! I can hear the two of you way down the hall."

Mother Pansie looked at Lance. "That's because your wife doesn't know her place."

Arykah was getting ready to comment, but Lance held up his palm to silence her.

"Have you finished your session?" he asked Arykah.

"No, I haven't."

Lance spoke to his wife but focused on Mother Pansie's eyes. "Take Sister Darlita to my office and finish your session."

Arykah hastily grabbed her Bible from her desk and escorted Darlita across the hall to Lance's office.

Lance mentally calmed himself before he spoke to Mother Pansie. "Never again are you to speak to my wife in that manner."

"But, Bishop, she—"

"Never again, Mother. Is that understood? Arykah is my wife and whatever she does, she does it under my authority. I won't stand for you, or anyone else, to disrespect her.

"And effective immediately, *she* will be overseeing the women in marital counseling—alone."

Lance may as well have slapped Mother Pansie across her face. She snapped her head back in disgust. *"What?"*

"It's time, Mother. You've held the ball long enough. I have a wife now, and I trust that she can do the job."

Without saying another word, Mother Pansie opened the door and stormed out. Lance would soon realize that he had just declared war.

Chapter 2

Later Sunday afternoon, Lance sat next to Arykah, and Adonis sat next to Monique.

The two couples shared a booth as they dined at Leona's Italian Restaurant on West Ninety-fifth Street in Chicago Ridge, Illinois.

"The choir sounded great today, Adonis. I see a major improvement since you came on board," Lance complimented before inserting a hefty forkful of lasagna in his mouth.

It wasn't often that the friends dined out after morning service. Sunday afternoons were usually dedicated to Lance and Arykah's formal dining room. Lance was gifted in the pulpit, but his passion was standing in front of his stove where he mastered his culinary skills.

Adonis savored a bite of warm, seasoned Italian bread. "Well, Bishop, I thank you for the opportunity. Truth be told, I didn't know what we were gonna do after the honeymoon. Since Monique and I are now married, I knew that going back to Morning Glory wouldn't have been good for either of us. I love the church and the choir, but with Boris being there, it would've created an uncomfortable situation for us all."

On the airplane ride back to Chicago, after their double wedding in Jamaica, Adonis shared his concern with Lance that he and Monique couldn't return to Morning Glory Missionary Baptist Church in good faith. It had been his cousin Boris's church home, where he was the head musician, for many years before Adonis had joined and became a member of the musician staff.

Monique and Boris had been engaged when Adonis moved into their basement. He was a witness to Boris's infidelities and total disrespect toward Monique. One morning, after hearing a spat between Boris and Monique, Adonis confronted his cousin.

"Cuz, why you gotta talk to her like that?" he asked Boris.

"Look, man, Monique ain't perfect. She needs to know her place," Boris replied.

It wasn't long after when Adonis began sending Monique flowers to cheer her up after she and Boris had gotten into heated arguments. Having suffered from neglect, rejection, and plenty of verbal abuse at Boris's hands for two years, it wasn't difficult for Monique to fall into Adonis's arms. And because Adonis had married Monique, Boris refused to speak to either of them.

After swallowing from her glass of raspberry lemonade, Arykah wiped the corners of her mouth with a white linen napkin. It was no secret that she didn't care for Boris. She knew he was a cheater and hated every moment when her best friend was living with him.

"Ain't nobody thinkin' about Boris. It was his own dumb fault that he couldn't hold on to a good woman. But hey, when you snooze, you lose."

"Well, don't hold anything back, First Lady. Tell us how you *really* feel," Lance chuckled.

"I'm just saying that there was no love lost between Boris and me. Humph, after the hell he put Monique through, I wouldn't spit on that fool if he was on fire. She's much better off without his trifling behind."

Monique noticed the conversation at the table carried on as if she weren't present.

"Uh, hello? I *am* sitting here." She was eager to change the subject. Her ex-fiancé was nowhere on her radar, and Monique wanted to keep it that way. "So, uh, what happened in the counseling session?" she asked Arykah.

Arykah leaned forward, set her elbow on the table, placed her palm over her forehead, and exhaled loudly. "Oh my God. Mother Pansie has some serious issues. That old biddie is gonna make me catch a case for real. I thought she was gonna pull out a gun and shoot me."

Adonis chuckled. "For real?"

Lance looked at Arykah. "Oh, come on. It wasn't that bad."

Arykah looked at her husband with raised eyebrows. "Lance, please. Don't even *try* to act like she wasn't out of control. You know what you walked in on, and you heard what she said to me."

Monique forgot about her grilled chicken Caesar salad. "Girl, what did Mother Pansie say?"

"She said it didn't matter how much my jewelry cost, I'm *still* trailer trash."

"*What?*" Adonis and Monique exclaimed at the same time.

"I'm telling y'all that if Lance hadn't walked in when he did, something would have popped off."

"Something like what?" Monique instigated.

"Don't answer that," Lance said to Arykah. He knew Monique was trying to get her riled up. Arykah's tongue was still in church training, and she was failing the course miserably.

Arykah looked at her husband. "What happened in my office was *your* fault. You know that, don't you?"

"Why is it *my* fault?" Lance asked her.

"Because at home this morning, I told you that Mother Pansie didn't like me and I didn't want her in the counseling session with me and Darlita. I knew it would get out of control. My views and Mother Pansie's views on marriage are totally different."

Lance couldn't argue with that. "What can I say? When you're right, you're right."

"Spoken like a man who wants to keep his marriage a happy one," Adonis teased.

Lance looked at Adonis. He nodded his head and winked his eye to let Adonis know that he was correct. Arykah was his first priority. The church came in second. If Lance kept his wife happy, then their home was happy.

"I informed Mother Pansie that you alone would be conducting marital counseling with the women from now on," Lance said to Arykah.

"Humph," was the only comment Arykah made as she sampled her dessert. Tiramisu was her favorite.

"Wow, I can only imagine how Mother Pansie absorbed that," Monique said.

Lance exhaled. "I would think that by the way she stormed out of the office, she didn't take it well."

"Uh-oh. You better watch your back, First Lady," Adonis joked.

"That's *my* job," Monique said protectively. She looked at her best friend. "We may just have to go to jail."

Lance and Adonis connected eyeballs and raised their eyebrows. They knew Monique and Arykah were tight like Krazy Glue, and if anyone in the church came up against one, they'd have to come up against the other as well. And with both of them weighing over two hundred pounds each and carrying attitudes that were just as heavy, it wouldn't be long before the folks at Freedom Temple Church Of God In Christ realized that Lady Elect Arykah and her sidekick were the new sheriffs in town.

Later that night after Arykah had put her husband to sleep in his favorite way, she went into her walk-in closet and lay on her dressing divan. She closed her eyes and exhaled. "Lord, I want to apologize for my behavior today. I'm trying with all of my might to be the wife and first lady you want me to be. I'm aware that the enemy is constantly pulling at me, taunting me, and practically begging me to act a fool."

Arykah recalled how she let Mother Pansie get under her skin and regretted it. She sat up on the edge of the divan and covered her face with her hands and started rocking back and forth. "Father, please help me. I want to be pleasing in Your sight. I want to stop cussin', and I want my husband to be proud of me. I don't want him to hesitate to use me in ministry. Please, God, please strengthen me to walk among my enemies and not give in to the temptation of saying things that'll have me in here repenting every night."

Chapter 3

Bright and early Monday morning, Mother Gussie Hughes was sitting at her post outside of Lance's office with her cellular phone held up to her ear. "Pansie, we have to come up with a plan to get that broad out of this church. We just can't sit back and let her think she's running thangs around here. And it ain't no use in tryin' to talk some sense into the bishop. She's got his nose so wide open, all he can see is her big wide butt in those short, skintight skirts." She saw Lance approaching and quickly ended her call.

"Okay, thanks for calling. I'll talk to you soon."

"Praise the Lord, Mother," Lance greeted as he passed her desk on the way to his office.

A pregnant pause presented itself before Mother Gussie responded. "Praise the Lord, Bishop."

Lance noticed she had delayed her response and stopped in his tracks. "How are you feeling this morning?"

She exhaled heavily. "I'm still in the land of the living. I guess that's a good thang."

The last time Lance asked Mother Gussie how she was feeling, she wasn't nearly as chipper. *"My left foot is in the grave, and my right foot is on a banana peel."*

Lance proceeded to his office and sat behind his desk. Mother Gussie prepared his coffee with two teaspoons of cream and four individual packets of Splenda. It was hot, light, and sweet; just the way he liked it. She set the mug on Lance's desk and placed herself in a chair across from him.

She took notice of Lance's attire. Since he'd been married, he'd traded his conservative dress code from crisp white button-down shirts, an occasional necktie, and slacks, to T-shirts and blue jeans. Lance always wanted to look professional just in case he was called out to minister to someone. He had never wanted to look too casual. Mother Gussie wondered if he still felt that way. There was no doubt in her mind that Arykah was responsible for Lance's carelessness. To Mother Gussie, the black turtleneck sweater and black denim jeans Lance was wearing made him look more like a regular member of the church than a conservative pastor. She hadn't yet seen the new black cowboy boots Lance had decorated his feet with. They were a Christmas gift from Arykah.

"Bishop, you know who Brother Jackson Cartwright is, don't you?" Mother Gussie asked.

Lance logged on to his desktop. With about five hundred members on the roll, he tried to jog his memory. "Brother Cartwright, Brother Cartwright. No, I can't say that I do. Is he active in the church?"

"No, he's not active, but he does attend church every Sunday, and he is a faithful tither," Mother Gussie answered. "You eulogized his wife, Justine, last May when she was killed in a hit-and-run car accident."

"Oh, yeah, yeah, yeah, now I remember Brother Cartwright. How is he doing?"

"Not too well, I'm afraid. He called the church this morning and said his only son, Justin, had been found dead late last night."

Lance sat straight up in his chair. "My God. What happened?"

It was then, when Lance made the sudden movement, that Mother Gussie noticed his shiny Rolex
watch peeking from beneath the long sleeve of his
sweater. She'd never seen Lance wear jewelry that
flashy before. It too had been a Christmas gift from his
wife.

"According to Brother Cartwright, Justin had been
strung out on dope for years. Before Justin's death, the
Cartwrights always had their son's name on the special
prayer request list."

"Was Justin a member of this church?" Lance asked.

"No. But he had been here a few times. I'm sure it
was just to please his parents. Justin could never get
into the service. He would just sit there and space out.
Brother Cartwright said Justin wasn't saved."

That bit of information saddened Lance. "Oh, wow.
That's a shame. Does Brother Cartwright know exactly
how his son died?"

"The only thing he knows is that when Justin was
found, he had been lying in an alley next to a dumpster
only a few blocks away from home. There was a needle
stuck in his arm. The police are calling it an accidental
drug overdose."

Lance shook his head from side to side. "Poor Cartwright. First his wife, and now his only son," he said
regretfully.

"You have a decision to make, Bishop," Mother
Gussie informed him. "The church policy always had
been that if someone died who wasn't a member, they
can't be eulogized here. I didn't want to say that to
Brother Cartwright. I wanted to get your take on it.
Brother Cartwright isn't active in the church, but like I
said, he's one of our biggest tithers. I can't see Freedom
Temple turning its back on Brother Cartwright in his
time of need. And I don't think he's completely healed

from his wife's death. It's only been a year." Mother Gussie shrugged her shoulders. "I mean, do we tell Brother Cartwright that he has to take his son's body to a funeral home?"

Lance intertwined his fingers and placed his elbows on top of his desk and thought about Brother Cartwright and all that he must be going through.

"No, Mother, that won't be necessary. We'll accommodate Brother Cartwright and his family with whatever their needs are. He's more than welcome to have his son's funeral here at the church."

Mother Gussie smiled. "You're such a softie, Bishop. But you know you're gonna hear flack from the deacons about this. They are extremely strict when it comes to following the church's guidelines."

Lance picked up his mug, sipped his coffee, and swallowed. "I'm the pastor of this church, am I not? If I say that Brother Cartwright can have his son's funeral here, then that's what will happen. If the deacons give you any grief about it, direct them to my office."

"Yes, sir," Mother Gussie said as she stood up to leave Lance's office.

"Also, Mother," Lance stopped her from leaving his office, "please contact my wife at the realtor's office and tell her about Brother Cartwright's son. Let her know that I want her to accompany me to visit the family this morning."

The last thing Mother Gussie wanted to do was contact Arykah about anything. She faked a smile. "Of course, Bishop. I'll get on it right away, but don't you have a meeting with a major land developer at the construction company at ten o'clock this morning?"

Lance looked confused. "No. That meeting is tomorrow morning."

"I don't think so. I'll check your date planner, but I'm pretty sure the meeting is *this* morning, Bishop."

Mother Gussie retrieved Lance's date planner from her desk. She walked back into his office and set the date planner on his desk. She opened it to the month of February.

Lance read in big bold letters, *Monday, February 4th, 2012, meeting with Mr. Ysi Shyuang from Hiroshima Technologies, Japan, ten A.M.*

"Oh, my goodness," Lance said. He quickly shut his desktop down and rushed out of his office. On his way out, Lance said, "Mother, get a hold of Lady Arykah. Tell her about Brother Cartwright's son's death. Inform her that I have a meeting that I absolutely can't miss. I need her to go in my place to pray with the family."

Lance had exactly one hour to fight his way through rush-hour traffic, toward the north side of the city, to Howell Construction.

Mother Gussie called Brother Cartwright at home and informed him of Bishop Howell's condolences, then relayed his apologies and explained why he couldn't be present to pray with him and his family. She said that Lady Arykah would be more than happy to attend to his family's needs. She asked Brother Cartwright what would be a good time for the first lady to come by. Moments later, Mother Gussie dialed Arykah's number and extension at Bowen Realty.

"Praise the Lord, First Lady. This is Mother Gussie from the church. How are you?"

The telephone call caught Arykah completely off guard. She remembered that the last telephone call she received from Mother Gussie hadn't gone so well. It happened when Arykah called the church the morning after her first date with Lance. When Arykah arrived to work, she saw roses waiting for her at her desk. She knew they had been sent from Lance.

Arykah called Freedom Temple to thank him. When Mother Gussie answered Arykah's call, she grilled her about who she was and wanted to know why she was calling the single pastor.

"Who is this?" Mother Gussie had asked Arykah.

Arykah could've sworn she was speaking with a jealous wife. "My name is Arykah Miles."

"Is the pastor expecting your call?"

"No, but I—" Arykah couldn't get a word in edge-wise.

"Well, he's in a marital counseling session and can't be disturbed."

"Oh, I don't want to disturb him," Arykah said. "May I leave a message for him?"

"What's the message?"

"Will you please ask Bishop Lance to call me when he becomes avail—"

"Is this for a counseling session?"

"No, I just—"

"Well, what's the reason for your call?"

"The reason I'm call—"

"Are you a member of this church?"

"No, I'm a friend." Finally, Arykah was able to give a complete answer.

"What kind of friend?" Mother Gussie asked nastily.

That telephone call five months ago was the reason Arykah never called the church when she wanted to reach Lance. To avoid another interrogation, she simply dialed his cellular phone.

Arykah knew Mother Pansie and Mother Gussie were good friends that cackled like two hens locked up in a chicken coop. And she was sure that Mother Gussie shared with Mother Pansie the event that went on in Arykah's office at church the day before.

"I'm blessed and highly favored of the Lord," Mother Gussie said most assuredly.

Arykah rolled her eyes in the air and silently exhaled a long sigh. *Yeah, whateeeveeerrr.*

"What can I do for you, Mother?"

"I'm calling to let you know that one of our members, Brother Cartwright, lost his son, Justin, last night."

Arykah sat at her desk at the realtor's office going over her scheduled appointments for the day. "Oh my. I'm sorry to hear that. I don't think I know Brother Cartwright personally. What do he and his wife do at the church?"

This was the first death in the church since Arykah had married Lance. She wasn't sure what her response should have been or what her duties as the pastor's wife were when a member died.

"Brother Cartwright is a widower; we buried his wife last summer. He isn't active in the church and his son, Justin, wasn't a member."

"How old was Justin and was his death tragic?" Arykah asked.

"Justin was twenty-seven years old and according to the police report, he died from a drug overdose."

"Oh my God. How awful. Brother Cartwright must be devastated. Have you informed the bishop?"

"Yes, and that's why I'm calling," Mother Gussie said. "Whenever there's a death in the church, Bishop Howell goes to the family home and prays with them. But this morning, he has a meeting with a developer from Japan at ten o'clock. The meeting was scheduled three weeks ago and since the client came all the way from Japan, the bishop felt he shouldn't cancel. He asked that I call you to see if you were willing to go in his place to console the Cartwright family."

What? Arykah's eyes bucked out of her head, and her heart dropped from her chest to the pit of her stomach. What did she know about consoling a church member and his family? Aside from saying "I'm sorry about your loss," Arykah didn't know what to do.

How dare Lance throw her to the wolves to fend for herself? Couldn't he get one of the associate ministers to do this good deed?

And what about the deacons? Aren't they the ones who are supposed to go out and console families in a crisis, like tending to the widows? Can't they tend to the widowers too?

Arykah began to sweat, but she didn't want to give Mother Gussie and her cackling hen-friend the satisfaction of thinking that she couldn't handle the situation. She quickly pulled herself together. "Of course, Mother. I would be more than happy to represent my husband," she lied. "What is Brother Cartwright's address and what time is the family expecting me?"

Arykah jotted down the information she needed.

"I will call Brother Cartwright and let him know to expect you at one o'clock this afternoon," Mother Gussie informed Arykah.

"Thank you, Mother," Arykah said and hung up the phone. She looked at her schedule of appointments and saw that she was supposed to show a 7,400 square foot home in the southwest suburb of Warrenville. The estate listed for 2.5 million and Arykah was elated that the listing had landed in her lap a week ago. The potential buyer was in the NFL. When Arykah learned that the wide receiver of the New York Giants would be flying in to Chicago for only a few hours to house hunt for a home for his mother, a Chicago resident, Arykah became excited. The agent of the football player was adamant that the realtor be on time at one P.M.

Arykah was torn. This could be her biggest sale to date. That is what she had worked so hard for. She couldn't risk not showing up for her appointment and losing the largest commission check that she'll probably ever receive. And she certainly couldn't ignore Lance's request to represent him and Freedom Temple at Brother Cartwright's home. By marriage, Arykah knew she was obligated to honor her husband. She hung her head, closed her eyes, and exhaled. She was frustrated, but Arykah had no choice but to pass along the listing to someone else.

At WGOD radio station, Monique's secretary informed her that Arykah was holding.

Monique picked up line three. "Hey, First Lady. What's poppin'?"

"I feel like pulling my weave out. I didn't sign up for this."

Just like many times before, by the sound of her voice, Monique knew that Arykah was fit to be tied about something, and it was always a church issue. Monique turned away from her computer, crossed her left leg over her right knee, then gave her best friend her full, undivided attention. "Okay, what happened now?"

"That cow from the church just called me," Arykah said.

Monique frowned. "Who?"

"The broad that sits outside of Lance's office."

"Oh, you're talking about Mother Gussie?"

"Yeah, *that* cow," Arykah said nastily.

"You shouldn't call Mother Gussie a cow, Arykah," Monique reasoned. "You are the pastor's wife. What if someone else hears you?"

Monique couldn't see Arykah shrug her shoulders.

"I don't care," Arykah confessed.

"Well you *should* care. I keep telling you that you must watch your mouth at all times, even when you're away from the church."

"I'll watch my mouth when she and that other cow, Pansie, watch theirs. Shoot, why am I the only one who has to put on a front?"

"Because that's what preachers' wives do. They front." Monique realized that there was no use in trying to reason with Arykah. It was like talking to a brick wall. "Just tell me why Mother Gussie called you."

"The son of Brother Cartwright, a member of the church, was found dead last night. And apparently Lance always visits the family when someone dies. Well, the cow called to inform me that Lance has clients from Japan visiting the construction company today and he can't go to console the Cartwright family. So, he asked that I go in his place."

"Is that what has you so mad?" Monique asked. She didn't see the big deal.

Arykah raised her voice. "I'm mad because I have to miss out on showing a mansion worth over two million dollars. And I'm mad because I don't know a thing about consoling a family. I mean, I don't see why one of the deacons weren't called to do this. I don't even know Brother Cartwright." Arykah repeated her previous statement. "I didn't sign up for this."

"Well, what did you think the duties of a pastor's wife were?" Monique asked.

Arykah shrugged her shoulders again. "Heck, I don't know. How about sittin' on the front pew looking extra fly in big beautiful hats and wearing lots of bling. What else is there to do?"

Monique chuckled. It was time for her friend to grow up. "I hate to burst your bubble, sis, but as a preacher's wife, your duties are the same as Lance's. So, I suggest you get your behind out of that office and over to Brother Cartwheel's house and start consoling."

"His name is Cartwright, and am I supposed to take a bucket of fried chicken with me?"

Monique laughed. "You are *so* ghetto."

At Freedom Temple, Mother Gussie dialed Brother Cartwright's home and informed him that Lady Arykah would be arriving at 11:00 A.M., the exact time he requested. She knew that by giving Arykah the wrong time to be at Brother Cartwright's house would set off a bomb and Mother Gussie was looking forward to the explosion.

At twelve fifty-five, Arykah stood on Brother Cartwright's front porch. She continually rang the doorbell without getting an answer. Then she walked to the bay window to peek through the vertical blinds and lace curtains. There was no movement inside the living room. Arykah looked toward the driveway and noticed that it was empty of cars. A cold breeze whipped across Arykah's face and neck. She pulled the collar of her full-length Chinchilla up around her neck, then checked her diamond Cartier wristwatch and saw that it was just about 1:00 P.M. She was right on time.

Arykah rang the bell again. When she didn't get an answer, she reached inside her purse for her cellular telephone and dialed the church. Maybe she had jotted the wrong address down when Mother Gussie had given it to her.

"Good afternoon and thank you for calling Praise Temple. How may I help you?"

Mother Gussie greeted cheerfully. She was extra happy to answer that particular call.

Thanks to caller ID, Mother Gussie recognized Arykah's cellular number and was anxiously waiting for her to call. It was showtime.

"It's Arykah." It wasn't a good afternoon for Arykah; therefore, she wasn't about to return Mother Gussie's greeting.

"Yes, First Lady. What can I do for you?"

"What address did you give me for Brother Cartwright?" Arykah asked.

Mother Gussie confirmed that the address that Arykah had jotted down was correct.

"Well, I'm here, and it seems like no one is home," Arykah stated.

"I didn't think anyone would be there at this hour. The family has arrangements to make."

Arykah became irritated. "Well, didn't you inform Brother Cartwright that I'd be here at one o'clock?"

Mother Gussie was having a wonderful day. "One o'clock? You were expected hours ago, at eleven this morning."

"What the f—" Arykah had to catch herself and calm down. She had almost cursed. She didn't want to lose her temper. She took a moment to inhale and exhale. She reminded herself that she was the first lady of a church.

The day before she married Lance in Jamaica, Arykah and Monique had pampered themselves at the hotel's spa at the Rui Resort in Montego Bay. Arykah's face was facing downward in the opening of the pillow as a man massaged her back and shoulders.

Arykah thought about the worldly things she'd be giving up once she said "I do."

One thing Arykah was known for was not holding back her tongue. Often she'd let curse words flow freely from her lips without caring who she said them to or how the recipient received them. As long as she got her point across, Arykah didn't care. She felt liberated whenever she cursed. When it dawned on her that the next day she'd become a pastor's wife and she could no longer express herself the way she wanted, she opened her mouth and gave herself a treat. Profanity rolled off her tongue like never before.

Monique was lying on the massage table adjacent to Arykah. She looked up and over at her friend. The expression on Monique's face was a Kodak moment. She looked like a deer that had been caught in head-lights. "Arykah, what is wrong with you?"

Both masseuses stopped. They couldn't speak Eng-lish but could tell by the way Arykah was rolling her neck from side to side and bobbing her head up and down that something was wrong.

Every curse word that Monique had ever heard in her entire life spouted from Arykah's mouth. Four-letter words, five-letter words, six-letter words, and some words that had too many letters to count were let loose into the atmosphere. She kept on and on.

"Arykah!" Monique shouted.

Arykah stopped cursing and looked at her best friend. "I had to get that out of my system. Today is the last day that I can curse." Arykah grabbed the masseuse's hand and put it on her back. "You can con-tinue now." She placed her face back down in the hole of the pillow.

"Mother Gussie, you told me to be here at one o'clock. I wrote the time down next to Brother Cartwright's ad-dress that you gave me."

It hadn't gone over Mother Gussie's head that Arykah had almost cursed. Arykah's careless slip of the tongue proved what Mother Gussie had thought all along; the pastor's wife was incompetent and wasn't fit to hold the position as first lady.

"I'm sorry, Lady Arykah, but you're mistaken. I specifically remember telling you that the Cartwright family expected you at eleven. I guess they got tired of waiting."

With her free hand, Arykah massaged her temple. She felt a migraine coming on. "I know what you told me, Mother Gussie."

"Humph, apparently you don't. The bishop won't be too happy to hear about this here mistake you made." With that being said, Arykah heard a click in her ear.

She walked down Brother Cartwright's front steps, went back to her car, and sat in the driver's seat. Finally, she started the engine, turned the heat up to its highest setting, switched the gear to drive, and pulled away from the curb.

Arykah was livid. There was no doubt that Mother Gussie had set her up to fail. She had been tricked by the enemy. Arykah knew that her next step had to be a call to Lance's construction company. She would bet money that Mother Gussie was calling Lance as well. On her cellular telephone, she quickly pressed the number on speed dial.

"Howell Construction. Vivian speaking."

"Vivian, it's Arykah. How are you?"

"I'm fine, Arykah. And you?"

Vivian and Arykah got along very well. There wasn't a time when Arykah had visited the construction company or simply called when Vivian hadn't treated her with respect.

"I'll be doing much better once I speak with Lance," Arykah said. "Is he available?"

"He's behind closed doors in the conference room with his guests from Japan. They just sat down to lunch. I can put your call through if you like."

The last thing Arykah wanted to do was interrupt Lance with her complaint about his secretary at church, but at least Mother Gussie hadn't gotten to him either. "That won't be necessary, Vivian. It can wait 'til later."

"Are you sure?" Vivian asked. "Mr. Howell told me to always put your calls through to him, no matter what he was doing. I don't wanna be in the hot seat when he finds out that you called, and I didn't put your call through to him."

Arykah smiled at Vivian's words. They proved what Lance had been telling her since the day they married; that he'd always make time for her. "You have nothing to worry about, Vivian. I don't want to disturb Lance, and neither you nor I have to mention that I called."

There was a celebration taking place when Arykah arrived back at the realtor's office.

When she walked in, she saw fellow agents surrounding the agent that Arykah had passed the million-dollar listing to. The word "congratulations" was flowing throughout the office.

Without saying a word, Arykah turned back around, got in her car, and started the engine.

She sat behind the wheel with tears flooding her eyes. That two-million-dollar sale was hers. It was hers before Mother Gussie threw a monkey wrench in her plans. Arykah reached in her glove compartment for a Kleenex tissue. She blew her nose and dried her tears before starting her car and driving away.

Moments later, she reached in her purse for her cellular phone and called WGOD radio station and was told that Monique was in a meeting. If there was ever a time when Arykah needed her friend it was right then.

Her emotions were all over the place, and she needed Monique to talk her down. Monique was gifted in that area. Whenever Arykah was about to fly off the deep end or do something that would eventually come back to haunt her, Monique was there to calm her down and talk sense into Arykah's ears. Today was one of those days when Arykah could benefit from one of Monique's pep talks. She wanted to drive to the church and give Mother Gussie a piece of her mind. There was no doubt that Mother Gussie had set her up.

To calm herself down, Arykah got on the Dan Ryan Expressway and drove for two hours. She needed to collect herself. She felt comfort in knowing that Lance would have Mother Gussie's hide when he learned of the trick she pulled. Just as he did when he sat Mother Pansie down and checked her when she had called Arykah trailer trash.

Arykah was thankful that she could count on her husband to have her back.

After driving for two hours, she headed home. Lance should be there by now, and Arykah couldn't wait to fall into his loving arms.

When Arykah entered the kitchen from the garage, she found Lance standing at the stove adding the finishing touches to a pan of meatloaf and potatoes before placing it in the oven.

"Good evening, sunshine," Arykah greeted him.

"Good evening," Lance responded without making eye contact with her. His words were quick.

Arykah knew that Mother Gussie had gotten to Lance. She could tell by his mannerisms.

Lance always greeted Arykah with open arms and a kiss, but not that evening. But Arykah hadn't spoken with Lance yet. So far he had only heard one side of the story, and there was no telling what Mother Gussie had said to him. Once he heard her side of the story, she was sure Lance's coldness toward her would thaw.

Arykah walked further into the kitchen and set her briefcase, purse, and keys on the center island. Then she stepped to Lance and tried to kiss his lips, but he turned away from her and Arykah caught the corner of his mouth.

"Is something wrong?" she asked him.

Lance rinsed his hands in the sink, dried them with the dish towel, then laid the towel on the counter. He leaned back against the sink, folded his arms across his chest, and looked at his wife. "I don't ask you for much, Arykah. And because I don't ask you for much, I expect that you'd be more dedicated and committed to whatever my needs are."

"Is this about Brother Cartwright?"

"What do you *think* this is about?" he returned sarcastically.

For the second time in one day, Arykah had to catch herself from losing her cool. Yes, Lance was indeed her husband and head of their household. But speaking to Arykah as though he were scolding a rebellious teenager, Lance was *not* going to do.

"Okay. Before this conversation goes any further, you better change your tone. Don't you dare speak to me like I'm a child, Lance."

Lance cocked his head to the side and raised his eyebrows. "I *better* change my tone?" His tilted head and arched eyebrows didn't intimidate Arykah one bit. If Lance thought he was going to place blame where it didn't belong, he was in for a rude awakening.

"Yes, you better." Arykah placed the ball in Lance's court. If he wanted to talk the issue out calmly, she was willing. There were no other options.

"I don't appreciate you telling me what I better do, *wife*." Lance put special emphasis on the word "wife" to remind Arykah who was in charge.

Arykah caught the emphasis, and it made her chuckle. "Oh, you must not know about me."

"What is that supposed to mean?" he asked her.

Arykah mimicked Lance and folded her arms across her chest. "It means that I am *not* the one. Okay? I ain't the one, *husband*."

They stared at each other like a lion and a hyena ready to battle. Truth be told, Lance was caught off guard by Arykah's straightforwardness. When Mother Gussie informed him that Arykah had failed to represent him at Brother Cartwright's house, Lance was all set to come home and demand an explanation. However, he wasn't prepared for Arykah to stand toe-to-toe with him.

"Can you please explain to me what happened today?" His voice was calm.

Now that her point was made, Arykah began massaging her temples again. The migraine was trying to make a comeback. "Look, Lance, I don't know what to tell you. I went to Brother Cartwright's house at one o'clock, the exact time Mother Gussie told me to be there. She tricked me."

Lance looked at Arykah like she was from another planet. "What do you mean, she tricked you? Do you realize how ridiculous that sounds? Why would Mother Gussie purposely give you the wrong time to go and comfort the Cartwrights? It doesn't make sense."

Arykah was stunned. She was totally expecting Lance to see that she had clearly been set up. After all, he was well aware of the dislike the mothers of the church had for her.

Arykah took a step backward and looked into her husband's eyes. The same husband who promised to love and cherish her forever. The same husband who vowed to honor and respect her at all times. The same husband who had convinced her that he'd protect her from the lions, tigers, and the two barracudas at Freedom Temple.

"Wow. I didn't see *that* coming."

"You didn't see what coming?" Lance asked her.

"I never would've thought that you wouldn't back me up. Because of your secretary, I missed out on a huge deal this afternoon, but I guess that means nothing to you, huh?"

"I spoke to Mother Gussie and—"

"Of course you did."

Arykah's interruption told Lance that she was highly upset, but so was he. "I spoke with Mother Gussie, and she assured me that she told you to be at the Cartwrights at eleven."

Arykah chuckled. "And that's what you're banking on, her assurance?"

"She's been my secretary for years, Cheeks. And not one time have I ever missed or been late for an appointment. It's because of Mother Gussie that I didn't blow a major deal with Hiroshima Technologies this morning."

"So, what are you saying, Lance? You think I'm lying on your faithful church secretary?"

"I'm not saying that anyone is lying."

Arykah's voice raised an octave. "Oh, somebody is *definitely* lying."

"Look, maybe with your house-showing appointments, it's possible that you got your times mixed up. You're a busy woman. It could happen."

Don't curse, Arykah told herself. *Don't curse.* "And it's *not* possible that Mother Gussie set me up? That could *never* happen, right?"

Lance didn't respond.

"Think about it, Lance. Just yesterday you fired Mother Pansie and put me in her place. You know that she and Mother Gussie are tight, and they both loathe me. Why is it so difficult for you to comprehend that Mother Gussie gave me the wrong time? She is avenging her friend, and they are in this together. And this whole thing is playing out exactly how they planned. You're upset with me. Their mission was accomplished."

"Cheeks, that's ridiculous." Lance just couldn't see the logic in Arykah's accusation.

It took every ounce of energy she had for Arykah not to call her husband a dumb, stupid fool. She picked up her purse and briefcase from the center island. "Okay, I can clearly see who won this battle. I guess this is the first of many." She turned and headed out of the kitchen. "Be sure and congratulate Mother Gussie in the morning," she said over her shoulder.

During dinner, Arykah refused to make eye contact with Lance. They sat and ate in silence until Lance couldn't take it anymore.

"You're giving me the silent treatment?" he asked Arykah. He noticed she was not eating but only picking at her meatloaf.

"What do you want me to say?" she replied without looking at him.

"Tell me about your day."

Arykah almost dropped her fork. She looked across the table at Lance. "Are you serious? I mean, really, are you serious, Lance? You know exactly how my day went, but since you want to hear it step-by-step, here it goes." Arykah laid her fork down on the table next to her plate. "I had an appointment to show a two-million-dollar estate this afternoon at one o'clock. But Mother Gussie called to tell me that Brother Cartwright had lost his son and you needed me to take your place to go and console the family."

Arykah made quotation signs with her fingers to quote Lance's words to her. "So, because I *am* 'dedicated and committed to your needs,' I had no choice but to pass the listing to another agent.

"I arrived at Brother Cartwright's house at one o'clock, the exact time that Mother Gussie told me to be there, only to find that no one was home. I called the church to tell Mother Gussie that I was at the Cartwrights'. That's when she told me that I was two hours too late. Then I pulled the piece of paper out of my purse that I had jotted the address and time on. I saw that I had written down one o'clock and went back and forth with Mother Gussie about the time she'd given me and she had the gall to hang up on me.

"Because of her, I missed out on a two-million-dollar sale, I never got to comfort the Cartwrights, and I returned to my office to find the entire staff congratulating the agent who inherited my listing."

"So, because Mother Gussie is still pissed at you for marrying me, she became pissed with me also. And you get pissed with me when she pisses *on* me. And while all of this pissing is going on, I'm pissed with *you* because you're not pissed at the right person."

Arykah stood up from the table, threw her linen napkin on her plate, and stormed out of the kitchen.

A half hour later after Lance had cleaned the dinner dishes, he walked into the master bath and found Arykah soaking by candlelight in the oversized jetted tub. Fred Hammond's "Give Me A Clean Heart" was playing on her iPod that lay on the ledge of the tub close to her ear.

Lance sat on the ledge of the tub. He dipped his entire left hand in the hot water and created a rippled effect by moving his hand toward Arykah's upper torso. "A penny for your thoughts," he said to her.

Arykah looked up at her husband. "Oh, honey, you don't wanna know what I'm thinking. Trust me on that, Bishop."

Lance looked at the bubbles dancing in the water. "Is there room for two?"

It was Arykah's expression that answered Lance. He saw tears on the verge of falling from her eyes.

"Why the tears?"

"You wouldn't understand, Lance."

"Try me."

A single tear fell from her right eye onto her cheek. "I did."

"I'm over the Cartwright situation."

"Well, I'm *not* over it!" Arykah snapped. "I know what time Mother Gussie told me to be there. I'm not stupid, Lance."

Lance reached forward and wiped her tear away. "No one said you were. You're making a mountain out of a molehill."

Arykah's neck began to dance. "Well, excuse the heck out of me for trying to get you to see my side of the story. I'll tell you what; I'll just shut my darn mouth. How about that?"

"Your behavior is not called for," Lance said as he stood and left Arykah to her bath.

She could have easily said something that would've given Lance just cause to set all of her belongings outside and have the county sheriff serve her with divorce papers.

Who the heck was Lance to tell her that her attitude was uncalled for? Perhaps taking one of his golf clubs and going upside his head, then driving across town to Mother Gussie's house and going upside her head may be uncalled for, but Arykah would've felt justified.

Before bed, Arykah was in her closet on her knees. "Father, I let You down today. I don't know if I'm cut out for this first-lady role. I just don't think that I can do it. I tried real hard not to cuss today, Lord. I bit down on the inside of my mouth so hard that my tongue is raw. But I almost let that broad get the best of me. And, Lord, sometimes men can be dumb as heck. I mean, why did You make them so dumb, Lord? I pray that You deposit some common sense into Lance real soon because I'm almost at my breaking point."

Lance turned over and found himself in bed alone. The digital clock on his nightstand read 2:38 A.M. He got out of bed and searched the master bath for Arykah.

When he didn't find her there, Lance walked up the spiral staircase and found her asleep in one of their guest bedrooms. He tapped her lightly on the shoulder. "Cheeks, get up and come to your own bed."

Arykah stirred. "I am in my own bed," she responded without looking at Lance. The bed she was sleeping in had been her bed in the townhome she owned before she moved into Lance's estate.

Lance exhaled. "You're behaving very silly, and I'm not gonna play this game with you. Come to bed."

Arykah was facing away from Lance. She looked over her shoulder at him. "And what if I don't? What are you gonna do? Make me?"

"If I'm forced to," Lance answered.

Arykah giggled sarcastically. "Humph, I'd like to see you try. That'll be the day."

Her giggle may have been a sarcastic one, but Lance also heard a little playful daring in her voice. Since he and Arykah had been married, they'd never slept in separate beds. Lance needed to establish some ground rules in his household. The first rule? Argument or no argument, there will be no going to bed angry, and the guest bedrooms were for guests only.

"Don't play with me, Arykah," he said while placing his hands on his waist wondering just how he would pick her up out of the bed.

The day they had returned from their honeymoon in Jamaica, Lance tried to carry Arykah over the threshold. But he let out a loud groan when he hoisted her in his arms, and Arykah felt pity for her new husband.

"Put me down, honey. I can walk through the door myself. I need you to save your strength for other things."

Arykah turned her back to Lance and pulled the sheets up to her neck. If Lance couldn't carry her over the threshold four months ago, he sure as heck couldn't pick her up now. She'd gained at least ten pounds since she'd vowed to love and cherish him.

Lance was a skillful chef, and his nightly home cooked meals added more weight on to Arykah's scale. Sometimes Arykah didn't know if Lance's gift in the kitchen was a blessing or a curse.

His wife had challenged him. He needed to show Arykah that he wasn't a punk. She may have outweighed him by seventy pounds, but he was still head of his household, and he would maintain that position by any means necessary. He took a deep breath, his feet placed apart at shoulder width, and squatted down. In a single motion, Lance scooped Arykah in his arms and lifted her up, sheets and all, out of the bed.

The same groaning noise Arykah heard the day he tried to carry her into their home for the first time she heard again.

The bishop took her by surprise. "Lance, what—?"

"Hush!" he demanded as he turned from the bed and carried Arykah out of the guest bedroom and down the spiral staircase. By the time he reached the bottom step, he was panting like a cheetah that had just run one hundred miles at ninety miles an hour.

As he turned toward their bedroom, Arykah felt Lance's arms weaken. She let out a giggle knowing that Lance was struggling to prove his point. His knees bent, and he almost dropped Arykah, but he managed to hold on to her. He slowed his pace as sweat beads popped out on his forehead.

"Oh God, my back. My knees. Oh, my knees," he moaned.

Arykah couldn't help but to laugh out loud. She played every bit of the damsel in distress as she placed her head against Lance's shoulder. When he had made it to the doorway of their bedroom, Lance looked like the Hunchback of Notre Dame. He was bent over forward with Arykah almost resting on his knees. But he was only a few feet away from their king-size bed, and when he saw that he was in the home stretch, Lance went for it. He mustered enough strength to hoist Arykah up in his arms, placed one foot ahead of the other, and charged toward their bed. He made it just in time before his arms gave out and he dropped Arykah on the mattress.

She laughed out loud when Lance collapsed on the bed next to her. He rolled onto his back and panted for air.

"See, that's what you get for trying to be the boss," Arykah teased. "You darn near gave yourself a heart attack."

Lance wiped sweat from his moist forehead. He could barely get his words out without losing his breath. "That's . . . okay. I . . . pay . . . the . . . cost . . . to . . . be . . . the . . . boss."

Arykah looked into her husband's face. She found Lance to be kind of sexy lying helplessly on his back without an ounce of strength. She sat up on the bed and straddled her husband. With her weight, she pinned him down on the mattress, and she heard all of the wind leave his lungs.

"Am I too heavy for you?"

He placed his hands on Arykah's waist, straining to get his words out. "Didn't . . . I . . . just . . . prove . . . that . . . you . . . weren't?"

"What you just proved was that you're nuts."

Lance looked into Arykah's eyes. "What I just proved was that we'll never go to bed angry or separately."

"Well, I'm still angry," Arykah said.

In one move, Lance miraculously flipped Arykah over and changed positions with her.

He kissed her lips and neck seductively. "You still angry?"

Arykah's eyes rolled to the back of her head when Lance's tongue tickled her cleavage.

She purred like a kitten. "Angry about what?"

Chapter 4

Mid-Tuesday morning, Mother Gussie sat at her post. She could hardly keep still in her chair. Lance was extremely late getting to the church. She was anxious to find out how he dealt with his incompetent wife yesterday. If given the opportunity, Mother Gussie would have sacrificed the activity of her limbs for a chance to be a fly on the wall when Lance confronted Arykah.

Mother Pansie had already called the church three times that morning, dying to find out how much hot water their first lady was in. Mother Gussie's plan couldn't have gone any better, and she couldn't wait to speak to Lance. It was 11:40 A.M. when Lance approached her desk for his messages.

"Good morning, Bishop," Mother Gussie greeted. "It's almost noon. I didn't think you were coming to church today. You're always here before nine."

"Morning, Mother. How are things?" Lance retrieved his mail and messages from the "in" basket that sat on the left-hand corner of Mother Gussie's desk, then proceeded to his office.

Mother Gussie rose from her seat and followed him. She couldn't tell by his expression or demeanor if Lance was angry or not. He seemed normal. His greeting was casual. But Mother Gussie did take notice that Lance didn't offer her an explanation why he was tardy.

"Mother, I wished that I'd listened to you and Mother Pansie when you tried to warn me about Arykah.

She's bossy, way too outspoken, and I can't rely on her for anything.

She dresses provocatively and spends too much money on material things. I've decided to speak with my attorney about getting our marriage annulled."

"Mother?"

Mother Gussie snapped out of her daydream. "Yes, Bishop?"

Lance chuckled. "Where were you just now? You were smiling up at the ceiling."

Mother Gussie blushed. "Oh, um, I was just thinking about something that Pansie told me. Would you like some coffee? I just put on a fresh pot."

Lance sat behind his desk. "No, thanks. I've already had my caffeine fix for the day."

"You stopped off at Starbucks?" She knew that every now and then Lance liked to indulge in Starbuck's white chocolate mocha flavored coffee.

Lance logged on to his computer. "No. My beautiful wife treated me to a breakfast date at the Pancake House this morning. Have the arrangements for the Cartwright funeral been finalized?"

Errrrrrrr. Mother Gussie heard screeching tires coming to a halt. *Wait a minute. What?* She couldn't absorb the question that Lance had just asked her. Her brain was trying to process the words he stated before he asked her the question about the funeral.

What did the bishop mean that his wife treated him to breakfast? Why did he call it a date? Only people who enjoy being in each other's company go on dates. Why wasn't he angry that his wife didn't carry out the task he'd asked of her? Something wasn't right. What the heck happened?

When Mother Gussie had informed Lance that Arykah didn't make it to the Cartwrights' in time to console the family and tend to their needs, Lance was hot under the collar. He told Mother Gussie that he'd be sure to speak with his wife.

Being the loud mouthed and independent woman that Mother Gussie knew her first lady to be, she assumed that when Lance had spoken with Arykah, fireworks had popped off. Now Mother Gussie knew that the fireworks had apparently taken place in their bedroom. But how could Lance go from one extreme to the next? Yesterday, he was clearly upset. But now, he's behaving as if nothing happened.

Mother Gussie wouldn't put it past Arykah to have been naked when Lance arrived home yesterday. *That fat cow seduced him. That had to be it.*

"Mother?" Lance snapped her out of her thoughts a second time.

She blinked twice and looked at him. "I'm sorry, Bishop, what did you say?"

"I asked about the Cartwright funeral. Have the arrangements been finalized?"

Mother Gussie was messed up. Discombobulated. She couldn't gather her thoughts.

She looked at Lance like she was seeing two of him. "Huh?"

"Mother, are you feeling all right?"

She blinked twice again to combine the two Lances into one. "Um, yeah, uh, what was your question again?"

Lance had never seen Mother Gussie that out of sorts. He became concerned. "Sit down, Mother."

Mother Gussie's equilibrium was off. Slowly she sat down on the edge of the chair across from Lance's desk with one butt cheek on the seat and the other hanging off the side. It took a few moments for her to compose herself.

"Can I get you a glass of water?" Lance asked.

Mother Gussie composed herself and sat up straight in the chair. "No, Bishop. I'm fine." She felt a hot flash coming on. "The, um, services for Justin will take place on this coming Saturday morning. The wake is at nine and the funeral is at ten."

Lance had been jotting down the information when he looked up at her. "And the burial site?"

"Is at the Restvale Cemetery. The last car in the procession must have passed through the cemetery gates before one P.M., or the cemetery will charge Brother Cartwright an additional three hundred dollars."

Lance nodded his head and completed his notes. He looked up at Mother Gussie and smiled. "Fine, Mother."

She stood and proceeded to exit his office when Lance called out to her. "Mother, will you get me the number to that flower shop that's located on South Ashland Avenue?"

"I've already taken care of the wreaths and flowers for the funeral, Bishop."

"Okay, great. But I want to send Lady Arykah two dozen roses to the realtor's office. She didn't have a good day yesterday. Hopefully the flowers will help to make today better for her."

Mother Gussie's feet were glued to the floor. What in the world was going on? She was sure she'd heard disappointment in Lance's voice when she told him that Arykah had missed her appointment with the Cartwrights. "This is unacceptable," she remembered him saying.

Maybe if she reminded Lance about his wife's short-comings, he'd rethink the flower order. "About yesterday, Bishop, I'm so sorry that Lady Arykah failed to do what you asked of her. I know how particular you are, and when you ask that a task be carried out, you expect it to be done. A careless mistake like that on Lady Arykah's behalf is a bad reflection on you and this church as a whole. Maybe you should—"

"All is well, Mother. Can you get me that number?" He and Arykah had worked past the Cartwright situation. It was no longer an issue.

"I just don't see how she could've gotten the time wrong. I mean, because of her mistake, the Cartwright family may feel that the church isn't sympathetic about their loss."

Sssssssssss.

Lance's spiritual ear discerned a rattlesnake slithering in his presence. He watched Mother Gussie's lips move.

Sssssssssss. "If your wife isn't capable of handling the simple things that a first lady should, then maybe you should rethink . . ." *Sssssssssss.*

Lance realized that Arykah had told the truth. She had been set up to fail. But he didn't want to deal with Mother Gussie right then. Lance needed to wait for just the right moment to set her straight. Truth be told, Lance wanted to give Mother Gussie more rope to hang herself. The most important thing was that he and Arykah were now on the same page.

"The Cartwrights are fine, Mother. At breakfast this morning, Cheeks, uh, Arykah came up with the perfect resolution. She thought it would be good if she and I both went to the Cartwrights and bring them breakfast for the entire family, and so we did. So, you can relax about the Cartwrights. They are good. Now, can you please get me the number to that flower shop?"

At the same time Lance was on the phone placing Arykah's flower order for delivery, Mother Gussie was at her desk, on the phone, whispering, "Pansie, you ain't gonna believe this."

Chapter 5

"**Okay**, what is so important that you couldn't tell me over the telephone?" Monique asked Arykah as soon as she joined her in a booth at J. Alexander's Restaurant. Arykah called Monique that morning and told her what Mother Gussie had done. Arykah had begged Monique to meet after work for dinner because Mother Gussie was getting on her last nerve and she needed to talk.

"Do you realize that it's rush hour and the traffic on the Dan Ryan and Eisenhower Expressway are no joke?"

"Well, hello to you too, Ms. Thang. I ordered you a raspberry iced tea. The waiter will bring it in a minute." Arykah looked at Monique's turquoise Donna Karan blouse. "You look fab, dahling." They had been shopping in Logan Square when Monique saw it hanging in a showcase window. Monique didn't even blink at the $130 price tag attached to the sleeve. She had to have it.

Monique adjusted herself comfortably in the booth, set her cellular phone on the vibrate mode, then laid it on the table. "I'm always fab. Adonis sends his love. When I told him that you were dragging me from the south side just to talk, he made a joke about us having Mother Gussie and Mother Pansie kidnapped."

Arykah didn't respond to the joke. She was staring out of the window at a family of geese crossing the restaurant's parking lot.

"Uh, hello? I just sat in traffic for an hour at your request," Monique fussed. "The very least you can do is talk to me."

Arykah looked at her. "That's not a bad idea. I should've thought of it myself."

Monique frowned. "Am I supposed to know what you're talking about? 'Cause I don't."

"Kidnapping them."

Monique leaned back against the cushion. "You do know that was a joke, right?"

Tears spilled out of Arykah's eyes. Before Monique could address the tears, the waiter approached their table with their drinks and set them down. "Here you go, ladies." He withdrew a notepad and pen from his apron pocket. "Can I get you started with an appetizer?"

"Can you give us a few more minutes?" Monique asked.

"Sure thing," the waiter said, then excused himself.

Monique opened her purse and pulled out a Kleenex tissue, then held it across the table for Arykah to take. "I know this is about what Mother Gussie did to you yesterday. Did you and Lance fall out over it?"

Arykah took the tissue and dabbed the corners of her eyes. "We had words."

"Did he believe your story?"

"I tried to convince Lance that she set me up, but he told me that I was being ridiculous. He said that he'd been relying on Mother Gussie for years, and she'd never let him down. One word led to another, and I just walked away from him."

"Wow. How did the two of you resolve things?"

Just thinking about how Lance had struggled to carry her down the stairs last night made Arykah chuckle. "We ended on a good note. Lance wouldn't let me go to bed angry. He distracted me from my anger."

Monique knew what that meant. "He flipped you over?" Monique asked smiling.

"Literally."

Monique cocked her head to the side. "Okay, then why are you crying? Everything is good, right?"

Arykah exhaled. "No. Everything is not good, Monique. Just because we had sex doesn't mean that Lance believed me over Mother Gussie. All he did was move past the issue. He swept it under the rug. That doesn't cut it with me. That b*#@h lied, and I want Lance to know it."

Monique gasped, and her eyes bucked out of her head. She looked around to see if anyone else was within earshot of what Arykah had just said. Two Caucasian women sat three booths over. They were into their own conversation. It was early evening, and the restaurant was nearly empty. Monique leaned her torso over the table. "Look, I know you're mad, but you gotta watch your loose lips. If a church member had been sitting at a nearby table and heard—"

"Monique, do you really think I give a rat's behind what a church member might hear me say? I ain't sitting in Sunday service or Bible class. I'm on my own time." Arykah rolled her eyes. "Heck, I can say whatever I wanna say."

"No, you can't," Monique corrected her. "I tell you time and time again that you have to be aware of your surroundings. You have to always be on guard, especially when you're in public. And speaking of Bible class, why aren't you there?" Although Monique was a faithful attendee at Sunday School, she wasn't a regular member at Bible class. But she believed it was Arykah's duty as the first lady of the church to be there.

Arykah picked up her menu from the table and glanced at the entrees. "Girl, please. I wasn't about to walk in the church and play nice. I'm tired of playing nice. It doesn't benefit me at all."

"It *does* benefit you, Arykah. No one needs to see their first lady showing her behind."

"Humph. We're dealing with black folks, and the majority of us only understand harsh language. I'll only have to flip my weave one good time for those old broads to leave me alone."

The waiter was back at their table. "Have you decided?"

Monique ordered a half roasted chicken with garlic mash potatoes while Arykah opted for a full slab of barbecue ribs, french fries, and coleslaw. They both ordered slices of J. Alexander's famous key lime pie and told the waiter to bring the dessert right away. The two of them were in the habit of eating their desserts before their main course was served.

The waiter was back in two minutes with their pie.

Monique inserted a forkful of pie in her mouth and moaned at how good it tasted.

"This is why we're fat, Arykah. Who besides us eats dessert first?"

Arykah savored the delicious treat. "What difference does it make if we eat the pie now or after dinner? It's still gonna land on our hips and thighs."

"I've gained ten pounds since we've been married," Monique confessed.

"And I've probably gain more than that. What's your point?"

"My point is that spring is approaching. It's time to shed these pounds."

"Humph, you go ahead and do what you gotta do. I'm married to a chef and I like to eat, so I ain't worried about it. You bought those Tae Bo exercise DVDs. Go home and work out."

Monique belched. "Chile, please. When I get through eating the only thing I wanna do is Tae Adonis."

The two best friends finished their meal making small talk about planning their next vacation before heading home to their husbands.

Arykah was lying across the bed watching a movie on the Lifetime Channel when Lance entered the bedroom undoing his necktie. "Hey, Cheeks."

"Hi."

He walked to her side of the bed and knelt down to kiss his wife. Arykah connected her lips with his and got a whiff of his cologne. "You smell yummy."

"I missed you at Bible class," Lance said as he turned toward his closet. "Did you have appointments this evening?"

Arykah turned to lie on her back. "No. Monique and I met for dinner. I needed to vent."

Lance poked his head out of the closet and looked at her. "Vent about what? Did something happen at the realtor's office today?"

Arykah rolled her eyes. *He's so dumb, Lord. I asked You to change that.* "I wanted to talk with her about what happened yesterday."

"Yesterday? You mean the Cartwright issue? Cheeks, I thought we got past that."

"Why? Because we made love last night? Lance, sex doesn't change the fact that Mother Gussie lied, and you did nothing about it. I feel like I have to compete with your church members."

He raised his eyebrows. *"My* church members?"

Arykah mimicked Lance and raised her eyebrows as well. "Well, heck, no one at Freedom Temple has accepted me as their first lady. They're *your* members, Lance."

Lance didn't want to inform Arykah just yet regarding his revelation about Mother Gussie earlier that day. He knew that Arykah would demand that she'd be fired from her position as church secretary, but Lance had a plan for both Mother Gussie and Mother Pansie. For now, Lance knew the best thing to do, at the moment, was to keep his wife's enemies close. Eventually whatever the mothers were planning would blow up in both of their faces. He had to lay low and watch the snakes slither just a little bit longer.

"Well, Cheeks, you haven't exactly shown the congregation that you're approachable. Every Sunday before the benediction is given, you and Monique grab your things and leave the sanctuary. In the four months that we've been married you have yet to stand with me to shake hands and fellowship with the people when they leave the sanctuary. You know I do that every Sunday."

Arykah knew that Lance was speaking the gospel truth. And it wasn't that Arykah didn't want to stand at her husband's side and greet the members when service was over, but Arykah didn't believe that she'd be welcomed. Oftentimes Arykah had walked through the church doors and saw members talking among themselves. When she spoke, she wasn't acknowledged so she decided "to heck with them" then. She wouldn't waste her breath or go out of her way to get anyone to talk to her. And it wasn't the men who shunned Arykah; only the women. But right now talking with Lance, Arykah had an epiphany. She decided that she'd kill the ladies at Freedom Temple with kindness.

"You know, honey. You're right. You're absolutely right about me not making myself approachable and friendly. So, from now on, I'll stand with you after morning service and greet the people. And I'll think of a perfect way to melt the ladies' hearts."

Lance was pleased. "That's great, Cheeks."

Arykah was sure that Mother Pansie and Mother Gussie had tainted her image with the women at Freedom Temple. But come Sunday morning, Arykah would change that. She'd be more engaged and be more inviting. She'd introduce herself to the women she had yet to meet. She'd follow Monique's advice and put on a front. Arykah would stand next to her husband with a forced smile on her face and pretend as though she's loving the moment like a dutiful first lady should.

Chapter 6

Saturday was upon Lance before he knew it. The morning of Justin Cartwright's funeral, Lance sat behind his desk at the church wondering how he would eulogize him. Lance had never met Justin, and the only thing he knew of him was that he was a drug addict that had been found dead of an apparent overdose.

With dead saints, Lance could celebrate the fact that they've gone on to be with the Lord in his eulogy. When Lance and Arykah visited the Cartwrights on Tuesday, Brother Cartwright had informed Lance that Justin held no interest in God whatsoever and lived the fast life earning fast money.

To Lance, it was easy to preach about a dead person when they were saved and lived the life of a saint, but what could he say about a nonbelieving drug addict? Lance would just have to wing it and talk about the happy times of Justin's life that Brother Cartwright shared with him.

This would be a first for Lance. He had eulogized many people during his pastoral ministry, but they'd all been church members. As he sat behind his desk, he prayed that when he stepped behind the podium, God would write on his tongue.

"It's open," Lance responded when he heard a soft knock on his office door.

Carlton Weeks, one of the associate ministers, poked his head inside. "Bishop, may I speak with you?"

"Sure, Carlton. Come on in."

Carlton entered Lance's office and closed the door behind him. He sat in a chair across from Lance's desk with a weird expression on his face. "There's something funky going on downstairs in the sanctuary, Bishop."

Lance frowned. "Funky how? Have the Cartwright family arrived?"

Carlton twitched in his seat. "Um, yeah, um, see, Bishop, that's what I came to talk to you about. The Cartwrights are here, but there are other people here too."

"Friends of Justin's?"

As if his necktie had been tied too tightly around his neck, Carlton pulled at it to loosen it up. He then pulled his handkerchief from his jacket pocket and dabbed at sweat beads that had begun to form on his forehead. "Yeah, I guess you could say that. Um, Bishop, how much do you know about Justin Cartwright?"

Lance shrugged his shoulders while frowning at Carlton's uneasiness. Carlton appeared to be on the verge of a stroke or heart attack.

"Not much. I never met him," Lance said. "Carlton, what is the matter with you? You're losing all of the color in your face. Do you want me to call an ambulance?"

Carlton wiped more sweat from his forehead and neck as well. "Nah, Bishop, I'm cool. But I gotta warn you about something before we head downstairs."

Lance was becoming impatient. "Well, spit it out."

Carlton searched for delicate words but couldn't find any to describe the scene in the sanctuary. "There are men dressed as women sitting on the opposite side of the Cartwright family." He rushed the words from his lips.

Lance's eyebrows rose; then he frowned. Carlton had spoken so fast, Lance was sure he hadn't heard him correctly. He turned his left ear toward Carlton and connected eyes with him. "Say what?"

"Apparently Brother Cartwright had kept Justin's other life a secret. Having the drag queens in the sanctuary won't be a problem as long as they are respectful. But the late Sister Justine Cartwright's side of the family is here as well and her youngest brother, Isaiah, Justin's uncle. They are very disturbed by the drag queens' presence and wants to open up a can of whoop-you-know-what on them."

Lance hung his head and shook it from side to side. "Oh my Lord."

Carlton wasn't finished delivering bad news. "And, Bishop, the deacons are fit to be tied. They wanna open up a can of whoop-you-know-what on *you*."

Lance repeated his previous statement. "Oh my Lord."

The choir was rendering in song when Lance and Carlton walked down the center aisle toward the pulpit. Lance saw the Cartwright family sitting on the right side of the sanctuary. To his left, he saw the backs of heads with long hair taking up the second through the eighth pews. It took every ounce of Lance's self-control not to look at the faces of the people sitting opposite of the Cartwrights when he passed them by.

As he walked up the three steps into the pulpit, Lance glanced at Adonis sitting behind the organ. Adonis was doing his best to keep his spiritual composure and concentrate on the choir, but he had to smirk at the way Lance was trying to control his own body. Adonis knew by Lance's stiff neck and the way he coordinated his upper torso that the bishop was fighting with himself not to look into the faces of the people sitting behind the deacons.

When Lance had reached his seat in the pulpit, he looked at the deacons sitting on the front pew, now on his right. All three deacons scowled at him. They were angry, and Lance knew he was in trouble. *"I'm the pastor of this church, and if I say that Brother Cartwright can have his son's funeral here, then that's what will happen. If the deacons give you any grief about it, direct them to my office."* His own words had come back to haunt him. Lance wished he could prolong the funeral forever just so that he wouldn't have to face the wrath of the deacons.

A situation like that was exactly why rules had been set up. Surely the deacons would be waiting in Lance's office after the funeral. Lance will have to take his butt whooping like a man and learn from this experience. He closed his eyes and listened to the choir.

"Swing low, sweet chariot. Coming forth to carry me home."

The choir's words were exactly what Lance wished for at that moment. He wished for a chariot to whisk him away and take him home.

Lance couldn't fight the urge any longer. His eyeballs were winning the battle. He gave in to temptation and allowed his eyes to roam over the figures sitting behind the deacons.

Oh my Heavenly Master, Lance thought. If Carlton hadn't warned Lance ahead of time, he never would've believed that the women he was looking at were actually men.

About fifty of the most beautiful drag queens in the world were sitting in the sanctuary of Freedom Temple Church of God in Christ.

Wigs, sewn in weaves, natural hair that had been processed, pressed, and flat ironed were on top of heads of faces that Lance thought should grace the covers of *Ebony*, *Essence*, and *Jet* magazines.

Perfectly arched eyebrows and eyelids adorned with various colors of eye shadow blended to compliment light, medium, and dark skin tones brought Lance's attention to false eyelashes. He saw petite noses above full painted lips. There wasn't a mustache or beard in sight. Though he tried his best not to stare, Lance didn't see one Adam's apple.

He was blown away. Pink, yellow, lilac, orange, and mint-green skirt suits and dresses, some with hats to match, reminded Lance of a roll of Sweet Tarts candy. They looked more like they were attending Easter Sunday service on the first day of spring, rather than a funeral near the end of winter.

Freshly painted manicured fingernails dangled over the sides of the pews down the center aisle. Because they were seated, Lance could only view the drag queens from the waist up but guessed that many a stiletto were in the house.

When the choir finished singing, Minister Weeks stepped to the podium and invited to the altar anyone who wished to say a few words in Justin's remembrance; then he sat down and waited.

No one from the Cartwright family stood. A full thirty seconds had passed when Lance saw one of the drag queens stand from the fourth pew, excuse himself as he passed the others still seated, and walk seductively toward the altar. He stood next to Justin's closed casket.

Carlton nudged Lance to look at Uncle Isaiah's red face. He was so angry Lance could see his chest heaving up and down as he breathed.

"Good morning, everyone." The drag queen stood about six feet four.

With such a soft and sultry voice, Lance found it hard to believe that the tone was coming from a man.

"My name is Peaches," he continued. "I just want to take a few minutes and say what a wonderful person Pinkie was."

Uncle Isaiah jumped up. "Who in the heck is Pinkie? His name is Justin. Sit your faggot behind down!"

"Who are you calling a faggot?" another drag queen sitting opposite the Cartwrights yelled out.

Uncle Isaiah didn't know who asked him the question, but he turned to face all of the drag queens. "I'm calling *all* y'all faggots."

Every drag queen in the sanctuary stood, with heights resembling a basketball team, and began yelling obscenities at Uncle Isaiah. The men in the Cartwright family came to Uncle Isaiah's defense and met the obscenities, word for word. Brother Cartwright hung his head in shame.

Lance quickly stood and approached the podium. "Quiet in the church!"

The deacons on the front row had moved themselves out of the drag queens' way as they moved slowly but surely in the direction of the Cartwrights.

"Quiet in this church! Quiet in this church!" Lance's words couldn't be heard over the yelling and shouting.

Carlton stepped next to Lance and grabbed the microphone. "Everyone, calm down and take your seats. Please be seated."

Someone from the Cartwright side of the church threw the first punch and the brawl was on. The event happening at Freedom Temple Church Of God In Christ was a shame before the Lord.

Wigs were snatched from heads and thrown across the sanctuary. Punches, jabs, scratches, and kicks, along with plenty of profanity, filled the church. Pandemonium had erupted.

Lance and Carlton witnessed Peaches pick up Uncle Isaiah and fling him toward the front of the church. He landed against Justin's casket, and it slid off the riser and tumbled to the floor along with flower arrangements and wreaths that sat upon pedestals. Brother Cartwright saw his son's casket fall. He started crying openly, but he didn't move from his seat.

"Deacons, get order in this church!" Lance demanded.

"This is *your* mess, Bishop. *You* get order!" one of the deacons yelled back.

It was a scene from a horror movie. The Cartwrights and the drag queens fought like cats and dogs.

Lance stood flatfooted in the pulpit and yelled into the microphone. "Everybody get out! The funeral is over. Leave the sanctuary now!"

He laid the microphone down on the podium and ran out of the pulpit toward the fight. Carlton and Adonis were on his heels. The three of them began pushing and shoving anyone and everyone out of the sanctuary. Between the three of them, it took a half hour for them to clear the sanctuary. When the last member of the brawl was shoved outside, Lance locked the church doors and leaned against them, out of breath.

"Call the police," he said to Carlton.

The fighting continued outside until the Chicago police had arrived. Thirteen arrests were made and Uncle Isaiah was the first to be put in handcuffs.

Four pallbearers were allowed back into the sanctuary to pick up Justin's casket and carry it out to the waiting hearse. There was no telling what position Justin's body lay in at that time.

Lance examined the mess the Cartwrights and drag queens had left behind in the sanctuary. Hundreds of flower petals were scattered near the altar. Eyelashes and press-on fingernails lay about the center aisle. Individual micro-braids took up residence on the pews. Lance looked down at a sparkling gold tooth on the floor.

Adonis and Carlton came and stood next to him. "Are you all right, Bishop?" Adonis asked.

He looked at them both. "How in the world could this have happened?"

Carlton chuckled. "That's what the deacons wanna know. They're waiting for you upstairs in your office."

It was time for Lance to face the fire. "Weeks, I want you to handle the burial. Are you prepared?"

"You taught us to always be prepared, Bishop."

Lance patted Carlton on the back. "Thanks, Weeks. I appreciate it."

Carlton proceeded to his car to follow the hearse to the cemetery, and Lance slowly climbed the stairs to his office.

Adonis saw that Lance wasn't in a hurry. "You want some backup, Bishop?"

He stopped and looked back at Adonis. "Yeah, I do, but this is one whooping I deserve. I'll see you in the morning."

On his way out of the church, Adonis peeked into the sanctuary and saw the cleanup crew hard at work.

The deacons were seated around Lance's desk when he walked into his office. He disrobed, loosened his tie, and sat behind his desk. Without looking into anyone's face, Lance said, "Deacons, I made a mistake. I tried to help a member, but from here on out, I will abide by the rules of the church."

Chancellor Wells, the eldest of the deacons, spoke. "And that's all that we ask, Bishop. See, you're a young cat, but we've been around much longer than you, and we know that the church can't help everybody. There are reasons why we established certain rules, and most of them are for the protection of our pastor."

Lance accepted the rebuke like a man and shook each deacon's hand. He was grateful for the slap on the wrist and appreciative that they hadn't thrown him out of the church for bringing such shame on them.

Never in all of her life had Arykah laughed at something so hard. Listening to Lance describe the funeral had her mouth wide open and her head thrown back screaming and laughing at the same time. Tears ran down her face, and her abdomen ached, but she couldn't stop. She was practically rolling on the living-room floor.

"I'm glad you're getting a big kick out of this, Cheeks. Had you been there, you wouldn't have laughed."

"Don't be so sure of that. It's a good thing I didn't go to the funeral. As soon as Justin's uncle told that man to sit his faggot behind down, I would've hollered."

Lance shook his head, turned away, and walked toward the kitchen. "I'm hungry. I'm gonna cook."

The telephone on the end table next to the sofa rang as Lance was walking by, and he saw Adonis's name and home number on the caller ID. "It's for you, Cheeks." He knew it was Monique calling to gossip with Arykah about what Adonis shared with her about what had happened at the funeral. When Lance set a wok on top of the stove, he heard Arykah scream in laughter. For half an hour, she and Monique had a good time laughing at Lance's expense.

When Arykah sat down at the kitchen table opposite of Lance, she still couldn't stop laughing. "According to Adonis, the drag queens came in their own limousines."

"Well, I wouldn't know about that," Lance said. "I wasn't in the pulpit five minutes before all heck broke loose. When we shoved everybody outside, I wasn't interested in looking to see who was riding in what."

"So, are you gonna address what happened at the funeral when you get to church tomorrow morning?"

"I wish I didn't have to, but I know I should say something. I know it's hot gossip right now. I'm sure every member already knows what happened."

Arykah chuckled. "Well, I bet the next time the deacons say that you can't eulogize somebody, you'll listen."

Lance agreed. "You got that right."

Chapter 7

The fire alarm jolted Lance's body awake. In a panic, he sat straight up in the bed.

His nostrils inhaled smoke. When Lance looked to his left and didn't see Arykah, he threw the covers from his body, jumped out of bed, and ran from the bedroom. "Cheeks! Cheeks! Where are you?"

Arykah heard Lance call out to her. She was in the kitchen fanning flames over the stove with a dish towel. The black smoke filled her lungs. She was coughing and gasping for air at the same time. "I'm in the kitchen," she managed to say.

Lance arrived at the archway of the kitchen. The smoke was thick, and the alarm was screaming. Through the black cloud in the kitchen he could see Arykah's silhouette. He saw her waving a white cloth over orange flames at the stove. "Oh my God," Lance exclaimed. He ran to the pantry for the fire extinguisher, then rushed to Arykah's side. The flames were dancing about twelve inches high above the stove. "Move back, Cheeks."

Lance pushed Arykah out of his way and extinguished the fire. It took about fifteen seconds for the entire fire to cease. When the last flame was blown out, he turned to his wife. "What happened?"

Arykah stood in the middle of the kitchen in a short pink sheer teddy. It was her intent to prepare breakfast for her husband and serve it to him in bed. Arykah wasn't a professional cook. Frying chicken, making spaghetti, and boiling hot dogs, she could handle with no problem. She really didn't think that frying bacon and scrambling eggs would be very difficult.

"I don't know how the fire started. One moment I was frying bacon, and the next moment, flames shot up from the skillet."

Lance opened the kitchen windows and the door to the patio to let fresh air inside.

Soon after, the fire department was banging on their front door. Lance quickly made his way to the front door and yanked it opened just as a fireman was getting ready to use his big ax to gain entry.

"Is everything okay here?" a fireman asked Lance as he rushed inside, followed by three more firemen carrying a huge fire hose.

"Yes. The fire is out, but there is a lot of smoke in the kitchen," Lance stated.

"Bring the fans inside," the lead fireman yelled over his shoulder to his crew. When he arrived in the kitchen, the fireman saw Arykah placing a burnt frying pan in the sink.

"Ma'am, are you all right?"

"Yes, I'm fine," Arykah said. Her statement wasn't the truth. She was embarrassed at her failed attempt to seduce her husband with breakfast in bed.

The lead fireman instructed his team to place three huge fans near the patio door to direct the thick smoke outside. He noticed the damage to the stove and the backsplash.

"Someone trying to cook?" he asked.

"Well, I—" Arykah started.

"I was careless," Lance interrupted her.

Arykah wasn't aware that Lance had returned to the kitchen. She saw him standing in the archway of the kitchen. "Huh?"

Lance walked further into the kitchen and stood next to Arykah. "If my mother told me once, she told me a thousand times to never place a dish towel on top of the stove."

"You know," the fireman started as he positioned one of the blowing fans closer to the patio door, "dish towels left on top of stoves are the leading cause of kitchen fires."

"I guess I gotta be more careful the next time I try to surprise my beautiful wife with pancakes in bed." Lance kissed Arykah on the cheek.

Arykah was speechless. Lance had just taken the rap for her mistake.

As the smoke made its way outside, the kitchen became brighter. Lance noticed that one of the firemen was focused on Arykah's attire. Her short sheer teddy left nothing to anyone's imagination. Her every body part was visible. But her private body parts were for Lance's eyes only. He spoke softly in Arykah's ear. "You trying to get me locked up?"

Arykah didn't have a clue what Lance was talking about. "What?"

"You want me to go to jail?"

"Lance, what are you talking about?"

"Can you please put some clothes on before I catch a case?"

Arykah looked down at what she was wearing. In the midst of all the commotion, she had forgotten she was practically nude. Without another word, she scurried away. As she exited the kitchen, Arykah tried to cover her backside with her hands. But her backside was large. She couldn't cover it all. The fireman didn't take his eyes off of her. He got a good look at her voluptuous assets until she was out of his view.

Lance cleared his throat and crossed his arms over his chest. The fireman connected his eyes with Lance's and knew that he'd better be about the business at hand. He shut the fans off and prepared to leave.

After the firemen had packed up their gear and left, Lance found Arykah in the shower. "Is there room for me?" he asked her.

"Absolutely," she smiled.

Lance stripped from his pajama bottoms and joined his wife in the shower.

Arykah lathered her soap sponge with body wash and ran the sponge across Lance's chest. "So, how much damage did I cause?"

"Not much," Lance stated. "It shouldn't cost a bundle to replace the stove, hood, and backsplash. It's not even worth getting our home owners insurance involved."

Arykah turned Lance around to face away from her. She lathered the sponge again and massaged his back and shoulders with it. "Why did you tell the fireman that you started the fire?"

"Because I could tell that you were a bit embarrassed."

"Humph, that's an understatement. I wanted to make breakfast and surprise you in bed."

Lance turned around, wrapped his arms around Arykah, and pulled her body into his.

"Well, I appreciate the effort. You get an A for that."

"But I destroyed your favorite spot in the house," she whined.

"Obviously you don't know where my favorite spot in the house is. Let's rinse these suds off and I'll show it to you." Five minutes later, Lance brought Arykah to their bed and pointed at it. "*This* is my favorite spot in the house."

After Mr. and Mrs. Howell enjoyed each other at Lance's favorite spot in the house, Arykah started her fashion show for him. Her first choice to wear to Sunday service was a burnt-orange wool two-piece skirt suit with Swarovski crystals decorating the collar and cuffs around the wrists.

Lance lay in bed with his arms extended behind his head. "That's beautiful, Cheeks. You're showing your knees. You know I like that."

Arykah's next choice was a winter-white sweater dress she found at Macy's. "It's a little snug but SPANX will take care of that. I'll sport my winter-white boots with this dress."

"Yikes," Lance commented. The dress, a size twenty-two W, hugged Arykah's curves in all the right places. And the boots she spoke of were a favorite of Lance's. Arykah's legs were plump and round. Lance thought his wife to be extremely sexy when she wore boots because they fit her thick legs like a glove. "I like the dress better than the suit," he said.

"Girl, smoke was everywhere," Arykah said to Monique. They were in Arykah's office at the church.

Monique sat in a chair across from Arykah's desk. "That's what you get," Monique chuckled. "You know you ain't got no business trying to cook anything. Name one time when you actually put a meal together that was edible. That's why God blessed you with Lance. He knows you can't burn." Monique thought about what she just said. "Well, obviously you *can* burn."

Both women were laughing when Lance knocked on Arykah's closed door.

"It's open," Arykah spoke.

Lance opened the door and poked his head inside. "It's time to head down to the sanctuary."

That was the part of Sunday morning service that Arykah loved the most. Walking into the sanctuary with all eyes on her and Lance as they walked hand in hand down the center aisle was what Arykah looked forward to. She rose from her desk and walked around to where Lance stood.

"Arykah!"

She turned to see why Monique had screamed her name. "What?"

The expression on Monique's face was horrifying. *"Your dress,"* she shrieked again.

Arykah looked down at her dress. "What about my dress?"

Monique walked to her and studied the stain on the back of her winter-white dress.

"You're bleeding right through it."

"What are you talking about?" Arykah asked Monique, already pulling Lance into the office so that she could check herself in the full-length mirror that hung on the back of the door. She saw a huge red stain just below the buttocks area of her dress. "Oh my God. What the heck is that?"

Lance studied the stain. "Didn't you just have your cycle three weeks ago, Cheeks? You're having it again?"

"Didn't we get freaky this morning?" she answered Lance with a question. "You know that I'm not on my period." The presence of Monique never kept Arykah from speaking her mind. Arykah felt comfortable discussing personal matters with Lance in front of her best friend. Arykah focused on the stain. "I don't know what this is."

"Well you must've sat on something," Monique said.

Lance walked to Arykah's chair and saw a small puddle of red liquid in the middle of the leather seat. "What the heck?"

Both Arykah and Monique approached Lance and saw the stain on the chair. "What *is* that?" Monique inquired.

Arykah dabbed her index finger in the suspicious liquid and looked at it closely. "This is red ink."

Lance frowned. "Ink? How did red ink get on your chair?"

Arykah looked at Lance with a scowl on her face. She knew exactly who was responsible. "Those b#@&*es."

Because Arykah had referred to the mothers by that name on other occasions, Monique knew exactly who she was referring to. "You think the mothers did this?" Monique asked Arykah.

"I *know* they did."

Lance knew Arykah was hot. And it was very possible that Mother Gussie and Mother Pansie were behind the prank, but he had no proof and neither did Arykah. "Hold on now. There is no proof the mothers are behind this."

Arykah exploded. "Don't you dare defend them, Lance. Don't you *dare* defend them."

"This is jacked up," Monique said. She was just as angry as Arykah.

If Lance didn't calm both of them down, he'd have a second fire to extinguish. "I'm not defending anyone, and I'm not blaming anyone. But we gotta have proof before we can point fingers."

Arykah was so hot, her earlobes were burning. "Little girls point fingers, Lance. I'm a grown woman, a grown *black* woman, and I don't point fingers. What I'm getting ready to point is my .357 magnum. Three holes each. When I get through capping off, those old broads' heads will look like bowling balls."

Lance's eyes bucked out of his head, and his mouth fell open. This was the first he's heard of Arykah speak of owning a gun. "Cheeks, you own a gun?" They had been married four months and dated only for three weeks prior to the wedding. Lance was smitten from the moment he first laid his eyes on Arykah. And when she confessed to Lance that she was ghetto when he cooked dinner for her, he became more intrigued with her. Lance grew up at Freedom Temple, where the women were always so perfect and controlled. The fact that Arykah was headstrong and outspoken turned him on. She was different. The total opposite of what he'd be expected to marry.

Arykah always stood her ground and never seem to back down from anyone. She was strong, confident, and could hold her own. Lance knew Arykah was a pistol, but he had no clue that she owned one and knew how to shoot it.

Monique spoke. "She owns a gun, a machete, and stun gun. We both do."

"Oh my Lord," Lance said. Who did he marry, a vigilante? Lance wondered if Adonis knew that his wife was packing.

"You *better* call on the Lord," Arykah said to Lance as she moved toward the office door.

Lance blocked her from leaving the office. "Cheeks, we have no proof."

"The mothers hate me, Lance. What more proof do you need? Look at my dress. They jacked up my dress." Arykah opened the door. "I'm getting ready to whoop some . . ."

Arykah's vow to stop cursing was long forgotten.

Lance shoved the door shut. "What are you doing? You can't go down to the sanctuary and cause a scene."

"Why not?" The question came from Monique.

"Because she can't." Lance grimaced at her. "And I could use a little help from you."

Monique folded her arms across her chest. "Humph."

"Let me out of this office, Lance," Arykah demanded while pulling on the doorknob.

Lance stood with his back against the door. Arykah's request wasn't an option. There was no way he would allow her and her ghetto friend to leave the office. "Cheeks, please calm down. Remember where you are right now."

"Screw that," Arykah said. "Did they remember where they were when they put the ink on my chair?" She pulled on the doorknob again. "Let me out of here!" she demanded.

"No, I'm not letting you out of this office until you calm down."

"This *is* calm," Arykah confirmed. "But you just wait 'til I get downstairs."

"You know we can take you, right?" Monique addressed Lance while slowly moving toward him.

The two of them combined outweighed Lance by more than two hundred pounds. If they double-teamed him, he wouldn't have a chance. Lance had to think quickly.

"I think he's in the first lady's office," Lance heard Minister Carlton Weeks say from the other side of the door. Lance forcefully removed Arykah's hand from the doorknob, then opened it and poked his head out. He saw that Carlton was about to knock.

"Oh, there you are, Bishop. It's time for you and Lady Arykah to make your way downstairs," he said.

Carlton couldn't see Arykah and Monique on the other side of the door tugging at Lance, trying to move him out of the way.

"Weeks, you gotta preach for me this morning."

Carlton could tell that Lance was disturbed. And he noticed Lance couldn't keep still.

The way Lance twitched from side to side, it appeared he had to go to the bathroom.

"You all right, Bishop?" Carlton asked.

Lance was losing the battle. With Arykah and Monique shoving him, he had to end the conversation with Carlton quickly and shut the door. "Yeah, um, something just came up with Lady Arykah. She's not feeling well, so I'm gonna take her back home."

Lance quickly shut the door, then opened it again. "And Weeks? Get Brother Adonis up here, right now." He needed backup.

"Bishop, Adonis is on the organ."

"Now, Weeks. Get him up here *now*. Stop the service if you have to, but get him up here." Lance didn't wait for a response from Carlton. He quickly shut the door and leaned against it. He was almost out of breath from fighting against Arykah and Monique.

"Both of you stop it right now!" he said sternly.

Arykah and Monique took a step back from Lance, but they were still too close for his comfort.

"I want to get to the bottom of this just as much as you do," he said to Arykah. "Just let me figure this out, okay?"

"The cards are faceup on the table, Lance. What's to figure?" Arykah asked.

Now was not the time to tell Arykah. It was too soon. But Lance had no choice.

"Okay, listen." As he spoke, Arykah and Monique were still standing toe-to-toe with him. "Can you both please back up?"

Monique took three steps back to give Lance room.

Arykah folded her arms across her chest and stood her ground. "I'm not moving."

Lance kept his back against the door and looked into his wife's eyes. "I believe the mothers put the ink in your chair. If they didn't do it themselves, I think they put someone up to it. And I believe that Mother Gussie purposely gave you the wrong time to be at Brother Cartwright's house last week."

Arykah unfolded her arms and placed her hands on her waist. "Well, if you believe that, then why won't you let me do what I gotta do?"

"Because we're gonna beat them at their own game," Lance said.

"We?" Monique asked.

There was a knock on the door. Lance opened it and allowed Adonis inside.

"You remember what we discussed last week?" Lance asked Adonis.

Adonis looked from Lance to Arykah to Monique, then back to Lance again. What he and Lance had discussed was private just between the two of them. Lance told Adonis that he didn't want the ladies involved. "Yeah, I remember. But you said *they* weren't gonna play a part." Adonis put special emphasis on the word "they" and nodded his head in Arykah and Monique's direction.

"Things have changed," Lance said to Adonis. "Thelma and Louise are trying to go to jail. We gotta clue them in."

After an hour behind the closed door to Arykah's office, Lance, Arykah, Monique, and Adonis all left the church through the back entrance. They weren't seen by a single soul.

Chapter 8

Monday morning, Mother Gussie inserted the emergency key into Arykah's office door at the church and wasn't surprised to find that it didn't work.

Yesterday when Minister Weeks had announced to the congregation that the bishop and first lady had an emergency to tend to and they wouldn't be in attendance at morning service, Mother Gussie knew that the ink stain in Arykah's office chair had found its target.

It was known to all that Lance and Arykah arrived at the church every Sunday at approximately 9:30 A.M. Lance would kiss his wife's lips, then proceed to his office and meditate before morning service. Arykah and Monique always met in Arykah's office for girl talk before Lance knocked on her door at 10:00 to escort Arykah down to the sanctuary.

Yesterday, Mother Gussie had seen Lance and Arykah enter the church and greet the members lingering in the vestibule. She recalled four different women complimenting Lady Arykah on how cute her winter-white boots were. One of the women was plus size, and she approached Arykah. Mother Gussie was close enough to hear the woman confide in Arykah that she could never find stylish boots that fit her calves. Arykah opened her purse and searched for something. Mother Gussie saw Arykah pull a business card from her wallet and give it to the woman. Arykah pointed to the name on the card and said, "Buy your boots and take them to this guy. He's the best in making any boot fit big legs. All of my boots must be altered. He's the only one I trust. Make sure to tell him that I sent you, and he'll take good care of you."

The woman excitedly extended her arms toward Arykah and hugged her tightly. "Oh, thank you, Lady Arykah. You have no idea what you just did for me."

Mother Gussie was hot under her collar. Since Lance had first introduced Arykah to the congregation as his wife, Mother Gussie and Mother Pansie had successfully convinced the women in the church to alienate Arykah. But seeing the woman reach out and hug Arykah threatened Mother Gussie's plan to oust her altogether.

When the woman extended her arms, Mother Gussie saw that Arykah's first instinct was to step backward to prevent bodily contact. Because the women at Freedom Temple didn't hide their true feelings from Arykah, thanks to the mothers, Mother Gussie assumed that Arykah may have thought the woman was going to strangle her. But seeing the excitement in the woman's face and hearing how grateful she was to receive the hookup, Arykah returned the love and wrapped her arms around the woman. When they let go of the embrace, Arykah asked the woman what her name was.

"I'm Chelsea Childs," Mother Gussie heard the woman say.

Arykah smiled. "It's a pleasure to meet you, Chelsea."

Mother Gussie noticed Lance standing next to Arykah the entire time watching the exchange between the two women. Besides Monique, Arykah hadn't any friends in the church. Mother Gussie saw the expression on Lance's face and knew that he was happy to see at least one lady reach out to his wife, but he was even happier that Arykah had let her guard down.

"Let me know how your boots turn out, Chelsea," Arykah said. "When I had my first pair of boots altered to fit my calves, it really was an overwhelming experience for me when I pulled them up my leg and they actually fit." Arykah recalled the moment when she strutted in front of a mirror the first time she wore tailor-made boots. Elastic had been sown inside the boots and extra leather material was added to hide the elastic. No one could have ever guessed that all of Arykah's boots were altered.

Mother Gussie couldn't care less about Arykah or her boots.

"Yes, I will certainly let you know," Chelsea promised.

Arykah gave Chelsea one last smile; then she and Lance turned toward the stairs. But before Arykah could climb one step, Mother Gussie saw Chelsea grab her by the elbow.

Arykah turned to look at her. Chelsea wanted to say something to Arykah, but she didn't know how to say it. Words were forming in Chelsea's mind, and her lips moved, but no words came forth.

Mother Gussie didn't know why Chelsea had prevented Arykah from going up the steps, but she sensed an uneasiness about the situation.

Chelsea stepped closer to Arykah and Lance. "I want to apologize to you, Lady Arykah."

Mother Gussie frowned at Chelsea's words. She hadn't a clue what Chelsea was apologizing for. She and Arykah had only known each other for five minutes.

"I'm embarrassed to say that I let all the negative talk about you influence me from getting to know my pastor's wife. I played into what the elderly women were saying about you," Chelsea confessed.

Elderly women? Mother Gussie knew that Chelsea was speaking of herself and Mother Pansie.

"And I'm sorry that I didn't embrace you when you first got to Freedom Temple," Chelsea continued. "I knew you were having a tough time here. I saw how the women went out of their way to shun you and shut you out completely. We were told that you were unapproachable, cold, and shady, but I know better now, and I'm gonna make sure that everyone else knows it too."

If Mother Gussie could've screamed, she certainly would have. Did that really just happen?

She saw that tears had welled up in Arykah's lower eye ducts. Up until that moment, Arykah had built a wall to convince herself that she didn't need to be accepted by the folks at Freedom Temple. She behaved as if she didn't need any friends at the church. Arykah had let it be known that as long as she had her husband, she was all good. And that was just fine with the mothers. But looking into Arykah's eyes as she and Chelsea shared a moment, Mother Gussie knew that was untrue. Arykah *did* need friends. She needed an alliance, and she needed someone besides Monique looking out for her. Arykah needed Chelsea Childs.

"Thanks for sharing that with me, Chelsea. It means a lot," Arykah said emotionally.

Mother Gussie saw Arykah blink her eyes continuously to prevent a single tear from falling. *I can't stand that hussy,* Mother Gussie thought to herself as she watched Arykah turn from Chelsea and sashay up the steps ahead of Lance in her winter-white dress and her winter-white boots. Mother Gussie also caught the bishop admiring his wife's thick calves as he followed. But Lance's lustful eyes were the least of Mother Gussie's problems.

Arykah had just made a friend, and that, to Mother Gussie, was something that wasn't going to be tolerated.

At Sunday morning worship service yesterday, as praise and worship was well under way, Mother Gussie and Mother Pansie witnessed Minister Weeks approach Adonis sitting behind the organ and whisper in his ear. Adonis had waited until the choir had finished the second and final selection of the morning before excusing himself from the organ and exiting the sanctuary.

Adonis's early departure accompanied with Minister Week's announcement that Lance and Arykah would not attend morning service confirmed to Mother Gussie that drama was taking place upstairs. And it was drama that she and Mother Pansie had caused.

So, Mother Gussie didn't find it strange that the emergency key no longer opened the door to Arykah's office. Apparently between morning service until the moment Mother Gussie tried to enter Arykah's office, the lock had been changed. But a changed lock wouldn't deter Mother Gussie and Mother Pansie's plan to get rid of the pastor's wife.

Mother Gussie knew very little about Arykah, but the one thing she did know for sure was that Arykah was a stick of dynamite, or more like an M-80 waiting to detonate. She didn't have the pleasure of being a fly on the wall in Arykah's office yesterday, but Mother Gussie would bet a year's salary that the scene behind closed doors was anything but serene.

Mother Gussie walked across the hall and returned to her desk outside of Lance's office and called her friend. "Pansie, I couldn't get into Lady Arykah's office. The lock has been changed already."

"That fast?" Mother Pansie asked. "We need access to her computer."

"Don't worry about the lock being changed. If that fat broad thinks she's got one up on us, she's got another think coming."

"So what now, Gussie? We really need her computer for Plan B."

"Well, I can't get into her office." Mother Gussie sighed into the telephone. "So, we'll move on to Plan C."

A half hour later, Mother Gussie sat at her desk waiting for Lance to appear. It was almost 9:00 A.M. He was due any minute. If Lance decided to go to his construction company and not come to the church, as he often did, he'd always call Mother Gussie before 8:00 A.M. to inform her of his plans. Lance hadn't called that morning, so Mother Gussie anticipated his arrival. She was anxious to ask him about his and Arykah's whereabouts yesterday.

She wondered if Lance would tell the truth and say that Arykah had sat in red ink and needed to return home or if he would fabricate an excuse for missing morning service.

Mother Gussie heard the front door of the church open and close. Then she heard footsteps climbing the stairs. Lance was right on time. Mother Gussie would prepare his coffee just the way he liked it before she grilled him about yesterday.

Only moments stood between Mother Gussie finding out why the bishop and his wife were absent from morning service. Now the footsteps were just around the corner of her desk.

"Good morning, Bish—" Mother Gussie's words were cut off when she saw who stood before her.

"Good morning, Mother," Arykah said smiling. Her presence had startled Mother Gussie, and that's exactly what Arykah wanted. She wanted to scare the h . . . e . . . double hockey sticks out of the old hag.

There was no doubt in Arykah's mind that Mother Gussie was the mastermind behind the red ink finding its way onto her $600 Diane Von Fürstenberg wrap dress that she had purchased when she and Monique visited New York City during fashion week last spring.

Arykah knew that she was the last person Mother Gussie would ever expect to see at the church bright and early on a Monday morning. Mother Gussie's eyes resembled a deer's that had been caught in headlights, and in Arykah's mind, it was proof that she was guilty.

Arykah had to chuckle at the older woman's uneasiness. "I bet you weren't expecting to see *me* today, huh?"

Arykah's question could have been perceived two ways. An innocent person probably would have responded, "Yes, you're the last person I had expected to see, but it's a pleasure."

To Mother Gussie, however, Arykah's question was an understatement, and she perceived it the way Arykah delivered it. Without actually saying the words, "I know you did it," Arykah's question told Mother Gussie that her secret wasn't a secret. She had been found out.

Seeing Arykah come around the corner had almost caused Mother Gussie to pee in her panties. Arykah had just told Mother Gussie, in no uncertain terms, that she knew what she had done.

Mother Gussie presented a phony smile. "This is a surprise."

I bet it is. Arykah returned the bogus smile, but didn't offer a response. She stood on the opposite side of Mother Gussie's desk and glared at her.

Mother Gussie didn't know what to think of Arykah's stance. What do you say to someone who glares at you with a fake smile when they know that you've wronged them?

Arykah didn't move a muscle. She became a statue with a fixed stare on her face.

Mother Gussie felt a hot flash coming on. She knew Arykah was from the streets.

Arykah's position intimidated her, and it made her very uncomfortable. They were the only souls in the church. What would Mother Gussie do if Arykah became physical? Arykah's stare burned through Mother Gussie and it was at that moment that she knew that she had crossed the wrong woman, but still she couldn't admit to anything. "Is the Bishop with you this morning?"

"No. It's just you and me. No witnesses," Arykah responded without moving from her spot. She kept the phony smile and continued to glare at Mother Gussie.

Mother Gussie frowned. *What did she say?* "Excuse me?"

Arykah laughed at her expression. "I said, 'It's just you and me.'"

If there was ever a time when Mother Gussie wanted to run, it was then. She heard Arykah say there were no witnesses, and that meant that there was gonna be trouble. Mother Gussie knew that she had to remove herself from Arykah's presence, and she had to do it quickly. She stood and grabbed her coat from the coatrack that stood behind her desk.

"Um, I just remembered that I have an errand to run."

Arykah watched her put her coat on and reach for her purse that sat on the floor next to her desk. Without another word, Mother Gussie rushed past Arykah and practically ran down the stairs and left the church.

Arykah laughed out loud. "You better recognize who you're fooling with, old woman."

Mother Gussie wasn't around to hear Arykah's words, but by the swift exit she made to get away from Arykah, one would say that Mother Gussie definitely recognized.

Arykah unlocked the door to her office and searched for her date planner, which was another reason she had stopped by the church that morning before heading to the realtor's office. Putting fear in Mother's Gussie's heart was an added bonus.

Arykah located her date planner in the center drawer of her desk. As she was leaving her office, her cellular phone rang. She retrieved it from her purse and saw Loving Lance on the caller identification.

"Hello, husband," Arykah sang.

"What did you do to Mother Gussie?"

I diced her up like bell pepper and onion. "What do you mean?" Arykah had a mischievous smirk on her face. She understood Lance's question perfectly. How typical of Mother Gussie to call him. She probably told Lance that Arykah threatened to put her fist down her throat. Arykah's smile got wider at the thought of that actually happening.

"Are you at the church?" Lance asked.

"Yes."

"Why?"

"I stopped by to get my date planner. I left it in my desk drawer."

"You didn't mention that you were going to the church."

"What am I, six years old? I didn't mention that I was going to buy some weave today either. And I didn't mention that I have a colonic scheduled this afternoon. Since when do I have to mention my every move?"

"Don't get flipped with me, Arykah. I know what you're doing."

"Because I just told you what I was doing. I came to the church for my date planner."

"Mother Gussie said that you made her uncomfortable. So uncomfortable that she felt that she had to leave the church. What did you say to her?"

Arykah exhaled. "I have no idea what Mother Gussie's problem is. I wasn't here five minutes before she got her coat and left. She told me that she had errands to run."

Lance knew his wife, and he knew she was hiding something. "But what did you *say* to her, Arykah?"

"I didn't say anything other than 'good morning.' Mother Gussie said she was surprised to see me and asked if you were with me. I told her that she and I were alone. That's all."

Bingo. That was the information that Lance needed. "You told her that the two of you were alone and you were gonna do what to her?"

Arykah laughed out loud. "Did Mother Gussie tell you that I threatened her?"

"No. She didn't say that you threatened her. But I know you, Arykah. You're still hot from what happened yesterday. You may not have verbally threatened Mother Gussie, but I believe that you did something to make her leave the church and call me."

You do know your wife, don't you? Arykah glanced at her wristwatch. She had an appointment in an hour to show a home. And she had to stop by the realtor's office before then. "Lance, I don't have the time to go back and forth with you about your batty secretary. I have an appointment to get to."

"Okay, but we're not done talking about this," Lance said.

Arykah disconnected the call with Lance and locked her office door. She exited the church, then got in her car and called Monique at the radio station.

"How did it go?" Monique asked.

"I did exactly what you told me to do, and it worked. That old biddie couldn't get away from me fast enough."

Monique laughed. "Good."

Chapter 9

When Myrtle opened her front door, Monique hugged her tightly and kissed her cheek.

She had stopped by Myrtle's house on her way home from the radio station, and Monique was glad she did. She and Myrtle had been very close when she was engaged to Boris, Adonis's cousin. Even after Monique married Adonis, the relationship she had with Myrtle hadn't changed. She was still Myrtle's "baby girl," and Myrtle was still Monique's "Gravy."

"It's good to see you, Gravy," Monique said as she took off her coat and sat on the sofa in Myrtle's living room.

Myrtle closed the front door behind Monique and joined her on the sofa. "I'm glad you stopped by. I thought I was gonna have to put out an APB on you."

Even though Myrtle had told Monique over and over again that she was so happy that she had married Adonis, Boris was still Myrtle's son. She had birthed him and raised him.

And when Monique jilted Boris at the altar and ran into Adonis's arms, she couldn't face Myrtle for a month.

It was Myrtle who reached out after four weeks of Monique ignoring her telephone calls. Myrtle assured Monique that no love had been lost between the two of them, and Myrtle was as happy for her and Adonis just as she would have been if Monique had married Boris.

Adonis was her nephew, but after his parents had died in a car accident when he was just ten years old, Myrtle had raised him as her son. She told Monique to get over whatever guilt feelings she had for marrying Adonis because Myrtle still considered her as a daughter-in-law.

"I'm sorry that I haven't called or stopped by in a while. Things at the radio station are crazy. Theresa, my secretary, is on maternity leave, so I've been working ten to twelve hours a day just to stay on top of everything. I'll be glad when she drops that baby because I'm about to lose my mind trying to keep up with all of my appointments and meetings.

"And it seems like my phone rings more now than it rang when Theresa was there. I must say, 'WGOD radio station, Monique speaking' at least one hundred times a day."

Monique exhaled a sigh of exhaustion. "It's true when they say, 'You don't miss your water 'til your well runs dry.' Theresa was my water, Gravy."

Myrtle chuckled. "Well, at least you know what you have in Theresa. A good right-hand woman is hard to come by."

"You're right about that. So, what's been going on with you, Gravy? What's new?"

Myrtle extended her legs forward and crossed her swollen ankles. "Chile, ain't nothing new around here. I went to the church to play bingo this morning. But the highlight of my day was when I saw the ruckus across the street."

"What kind of ruckus?" Monique asked.

"Everyone on the block knows that the lady across the street, Lorraine Mungo, is messing around with the mailman."

"Why do you say that, Gravy?"

"Because he drops our mail in our boxes and keeps pushing that mail cart down the street. But when he gets to Lorraine's house, he lifts the cart onto the porch and goes inside and stays for about forty-five minutes to an hour."

"So, what are you doing, Gravy, looking out of your living-room window watching with binoculars held up to your face? You keep time on how long the mailman stays in your neighbor's house?"

"That's exactly what I do," Myrtle said with no shame at all. "Once Oprah goes off, I ain't got nothing to keep me occupied until *The Young & The Restless* comes on. But today, the mailman was in there for only about a half hour when I saw Mr. Mungo's car pull into the driveway. He came home real early. I've never seen him come home in the middle of the day. I think he must've suspected something."

Monique's eyes grew wide. "Uh-oh."

"Uh-oh, is right. I got on my telephone and called next door and told Bessie to look out her window because the crap was getting ready to hit the fan; then I hurried back to my window. Next thing I knew, the scene from that movie *Friday* was played out. The mailman came running out of the front door and down those steps so fast, you would've thought the devil himself was chasing after him. All he had on was his boxer shorts and one sock. I laughed 'til I just about wet my own underwear. That fool ran all the way down the street and around the corner in this cold weather, darn near stark naked."

Monique laughed along with Myrtle. "Ooh, wee. This is too good. What happened next, Gravy?"

"Mr. Mungo came on the front porch and pushed that mail cart down his steps and put it on the sidewalk with the mailman's uniform on top of it, then went back inside. I called the post office and reported an abandoned mail cart on my street. Fifteen minutes later, I saw a United States Postal Service van drive up. Two mailmen got out and put the cart and uniform in the back of the van and drove off. Me and Bessie were on the phone laughing about it for an hour."

"I bet you won't be seeing that same mailman come around here anymore, Gravy."

Myrtle laughed. "No, I probably won't."

Monique shifted on the sofa. "So, how is Boris doing these days?"

Myrtle shook her head from side to side. "Not good. Not good at all, baby girl. You know he was fired from the electric company, don't you?"

"Yeah. Adonis told me. What is he doing now?"

Myrtle shrugged her shoulders. "The heck if I know. Boris doesn't come around anymore. I haven't seen him since he got fired almost two months ago. He stopped coming to church. Morning Glory had to hire another organist. Whenever I call Boris's cell phone, he answers, then tells me that he'll call me back, but he never does. He's on that stuff heavy. That's why he lost his job. He was going to work high on a daily basis."

Monique felt horrible and responsible for Boris's predicament. Boris was on drugs throughout their relationship, but he always got himself together to report to work. The fact that he lost a good-paying job proved to Monique that Boris was worse off than she ever imagined. "Wow. That's too bad, Gravy. Maybe if I hadn't married—"

Myrtle cut Monique's words off. "Don't you dare blame yourself. Boris is a grown man, and he made his own choices. He chose to inhale that crack pipe, and he chose to stick that needle in his arm. And don't forget the way he treated you when you were together.

You remember all that suffering and crying you did? You made the right decision, baby girl. Don't you ever second-guess that. Had you stayed with Boris, you would've been a miserable soul."

"Boris is your son, Gravy."

Myrtle turned her entire upper torso toward Monique and cocked her head to the side. She slightly raised her voice an octave higher. "And your point is what? I'm not one of those mothers who defends her child when he's doing wrong. How many times in the past have I told you to pack your bags and leave Boris's trifling butt? I knew he was no good for you. Humph, you gave Boris way too many chances, if you ask me. You certainly gave him more chances than I gave his father."

That was what Monique loved most about Myrtle. She was always straightforward and fair. "I know you're right, Gravy. I just can't help but wonder that if I had not married Adonis, maybe Boris wouldn't have gone so far off the deep end. Marrying his first cousin, the cousin who was raised in the same house as his brother, had to have hurt him."

"Well, you can stop wondering," Myrtle snapped. "I know for a fact that Boris would not have made a good husband for you. And why are you so concerned about him anyway?" Myrtle pointed her finger at Monique. "See, that was your problem when the two of you were together. You always cared more for him than he cared for you."

Monique didn't respond. When Myrtle was right, she was right.

"Let's talk about you and Adonis. Y'all got a bun in that oven yet?"

"We ain't even been married for six months, Gravy. We have plenty of time for a baby."

"Maybe you and Adonis got plenty of time, but I ain't got all that time to be waiting on a grandnephew or grandniece. I'm getting old quick. My knees hurt, my back aches, and my right shoulder is acting up real bad. Y'all better bring a baby around here before the Lord calls me home, because it won't be too much longer."

Monique waved her hand to dismiss Gravy's comment. "Gravy, please. You're too honory to die. You'll probably outlive me, Adonis, and our children too."

"Just don't make me wait too long, baby girl. Maybe Adonis needs some of them Viagra pills."

Monique's dark skin turned crimson red. "Gravy, what in the world do you know about Viagra? And Adonis doesn't need any help in that department, thank you very much."

"Is he shooting blanks?"

Monique's mouth dropped wide open. "Oh my God. Gravy, I am *not* talking about our sex life with you. And no, Adonis is *not* shooting blanks. When we're ready to hear the pitter-patter of little feet, we'll make it happen."

"Well, what about Arykah and Lance? Are they trying to make a baby?"

"Gravy, Arykah got other things to worry about than making a baby."

"Such as what?" Myrtle asked.

Monique exhaled. "Arykah's got problems, Gravy. The mothers over at Freedom Temple are giving her the flux."

"What are they doing to my Sugar Plum? Do I gotta go over to that church and kick some butt? Does some order need to be set?"

Monique laughed at Myrtle. "You're always trying to come to somebody else's defense, Gravy. But Arykah can hold her own."

"Just tell me what's going on and I'll decide if I need to pay a visit to Freedom Temple."

"They did what?" Myrtle was flabbergasted.

Monique shared what the mothers of the church had done to Arykah. "And neither you nor Arykah thought to pick up the phone and call me about this?"

Monique saw blood vessels protruding on Myrtle's forehead. "Will you please calm down, Gravy. I told you that Arykah can handle her own."

"But she shouldn't have to handle her own," Myrtle said. "Who else besides you is watching her back? And what did y'all do about that red-ink situation?"

"We couldn't do anything. Lance wouldn't let us. But the mothers won't get away with what they did." Monique thought about the private meeting that was held in Arykah's office at church yesterday. "Eventually, they'll get what's coming to them."

"Y'all got a plan?" Myrtle asked.

Monique smirked.

Chapter 10

At noontime Tuesday afternoon, while seated with a client at Gibson's Steak House, Arykah inserted a forkful of well-done prime rib into her mouth. "Okay, Jeremy. This morning was the third time that I've shown you the estate in Belfor. A month ago you contacted me and stated that you wanted me to find you a five-bedroom, four-bath home with a walk-out basement. I've found the perfect home for you, and it has a chef's kitchen. Are you ready to make an offer?" Arykah worked with a strategy. Every time she showed a home to a client, she offered to buy them lunch or dinner afterward to discuss the details of the home to try to persuade them to buy. "And remember how lovely that first-floor study was? The built-in bookshelves and brand-new Berber carpet sets the tone for a bestselling author such as yourself to get lost in time while creating masterpieces."

Jeremy Montahue, a four-time *New York Times* bestselling author of horror fiction, had outgrown his two-bedroom, one-bath condominium in downtown Chicago. He was willing to give up his view of Lake Michigan and his five-minute walk to Navy Pier for a more luxurious single-family home. "Arykah, I must say that the home office in the Belfor estate was the highlight of the home for me. My home office is where I spend most of my time, but the office at the estate isn't manly enough for me. I'm not fond of the light colored carpeting or the standard egg-shell paint on the walls. There aren't any window treatments, which bring in way too much light for my liking."

Arykah laughed. "I can understand that coming from an author who writes about ghosts and goblins. So, let me ask you this, Jeremy. If the home office in the Belfor estate had dark wood paneling on the walls and dark wood flooring and thick, custom Italian drapes on the windows, you'd buy the house?"

Jeremy drank from a glass of pink lemonade, swallowed two gulps, then set the glass on the table. "If you can make that happen for me, Arykah, then you've got yourself a deal."

Arykah smiled. "I have the perfect interior designer for this project, Jeremy. Shall we make an appointment this afternoon and get started on making your vision come true?"

"Arykah, I have a manuscript to complete, and I'm working against a deadline. My editor will have my hide if I don't turn it in on time. My schedule doesn't allow me the luxury to shop and choose paint, drapes, and flooring. You know what my vision is for my home office. I trust that you can handle that for me." Jeremy's words weren't a question; they were a statement bordering on command.

Arykah knew that if she wanted the sale, she'd have to work harder for it. "Of course, I can, Jeremy." She picked up her glass of iced tea and held it across the table.

Jeremy picked up his glass of lemonade and connected it with Arykah's glass.

"To handling it," Arykah said.

Jeremy smiled. "To handling it."

Arykah paid the bill; then she and Jeremy headed to the realtor's office. She was excited to write up the paperwork for Jeremy to sign and present his offer of $760,999 for the Belfor estate to the seller.

An hour before Bible class began, Mother Gussie walked into Lance's office wearing her winter coat and holding a large envelope in her hand.

"I'm heading home, Bishop," Mother Gussie said. She extended the envelope across Lance's desk for him to take. "A courier left this for you."

Lance sat behind his desk studying the lesson he was going to teach that evening. He looked up and saw Mother Gussie extending the envelope his way. He took the envelope from her hand. "Thank you, Mother. You're not staying for Bible class?"

"My arthritis is singing. I'm going home to soak in Epsom salt."

Lance glanced at the envelope and didn't see a return address in the upper left corner.

He flipped the extremely thin envelope over and didn't find a return address on the back.

Then he looked up at Mother Gussie standing on the opposite side of his desk. "There's no return address on this envelope. Do you know who sent it?" he asked while reaching for his letter opener.

"No, Bishop. I have no idea," she lied effortlessly.

Lance slid the letter opener beneath the sealed flap of the envelope and tore it open.

He looked inside and frowned. The envelope contained an eight-by-ten colored photograph.

He pulled the photograph from the envelope and studied the picture.

Mother Gussie stood holding her breath.

"Wow," Lance said as he looked at the photograph.

"Something wrong, Bishop?"

For the longest moment Lance didn't say a word.

"Bishop?"

Lance placed his hand over his mouth and shook his head from side to side as if he was looking at something horrific, and then said, "You know, Mother, if I hadn't realized it before, I certainly realize it now."

That your wife is a tramp? "What's that, Bishop?"

Lance turned the photograph around to show Mother Gussie what he was looking at.

"That I have the most beautiful wife in this world."

The photograph revealed Arykah and a Caucasian man seated at a restaurant, having dinner and holding up drinking glasses across the table. They were smiling and seemed to be making a toast.

"Look at how pretty Arykah's hair is in this picture," Lance said. "And her blouse is pretty. I love when Arykah wears the color red. It accentuates her light complexion. And that smile she's wearing. Wow," Lance said again. "Isn't she lovely?"

That was not the reaction Mother Gussie expected from him. He didn't even acknowledge the man in the picture. She had hoped that seeing his wife out on what appeared to be a date with another man would send Lance over the edge. But all he saw was the fat cow in a red blouse.

"Isn't she lovely, Mother?" Lance repeated his question. "I mean, have you ever seen a more elegant first lady?"

Lance put Mother Gussie on the spot. *Heck, no, she ain't elegant. How can anyone consider a loud-mouthed, trailer-trash tramp to be elegant?* Mother Gussie looked at the photograph again and realized that her and Mother Pansie's Plan C had failed. "Yes, Bishop, Lady Arykah is quite lovely." Mother Gussie swallowed the words like she was swallowing thumbtacks.

Lance spun around in his chair and picked up an eight-by-ten frame from his credenza.

The frame held a picture of him standing on a golf course, wearing golf attire, swinging a golf club. He removed the photograph from the frame and replaced it with the photograph of Arykah and the strange man having dinner. Then he set the frame back on the credenza. "I think that's my new favorite photo of Arykah."

Mother Gussie looked at Lance, then at the photograph, then back at Lance.

"Good night, Bishop." With that being said, she pursed her lips, then turned and left Lance's office.

When Lance turned the knob on the master bedroom door, he saw candles burning on his and Arykah's nightstands. The smell of a country garden filled the room. The fresh flowers that sat in a vase on the dresser were doing their job. Jazz music flowed through the built-in speakers in the walls.

Suddenly, Arykah appeared from the master bathroom wearing a long, black, sheer duster. "Welcome home, Bishop," she smiled seductively.

Lance studied Arykah's nude body through the duster she was wearing. "I could get used to coming home to a greeting like this."

Arykah slowly strutted over to the bed and lay on it, all the while keeping her eyes on Lance's eyes. "I sold the Belfor estate today."

"Congratulations."

"And I couldn't think of a better way to celebrate than to make wild passionate love to my husband. So, you wanna join the party?"

"You know I do," Lance said mischievously. Arykah was turning him on big time.

She ran her hand along the length of the duster. "Well, come on over here and unwrap your gift."

"A gift you are, baby." Lance undressed and joined his wife on the bed.

On Sunday morning, Arykah appeared from the master closet dressed in a dark violet suit. It was the fifth outfit she modeled for Lance that morning. The jacket had an asymmetrical effect with pearls decorating the wrists at the end of the sleeves. The short skirt stopped just above Arykah's knees. She wore a matching dark violet hat with a five-inch wide brim. On her feet were black Jessica Simpson six-and-a-half platform stilettos.

Lance lay in bed. He had gotten used to Arykah's fashion shows every Sunday morning, and he looked forward to them. "Very nice, Cheeks. That's the perfect look for the perfect first lady."

Arykah brought Lance's attention to her feet. "But what about the stilettos? These are extremely high. Do they look hookerish?"

Lance laughed. "Hookerish? No, not at all. They look good on your feet. In fact, they look so good that I want you to come to bed in those tonight."

At Freedom Temple, Monique and Arykah were in Arykah's office chatting when there was a knock on the door.

"It's open," Arykah announced.

The door opened, and a woman poked her head inside. "Excuse me, Lady Arykah, may I have a word with you before morning service begins?"

Arykah stood from her desk and approached the woman at the door. "Absolutely. Come on in." Arykah opened the door wider and saw that the woman wasn't alone. With her was a young lady Arykah recognized as a choir member. "What's your name?"

Arykah asked the woman when she and the girl were inside the office.

The woman extended her hand to Arykah. "I'm Gladys Blackmon."

Arykah shook Gladys's hand and looked at the young girl. "I know your face. You sing in the choir, right?"

The young girl was afraid to speak to Arykah. Tears were on the borderline of her lower eye ducts.

"This is my daughter, Miranda," Gladys said.

Arykah looked into Miranda's eyes. "Are you okay?"

Now the tears fell onto Miranda's cheeks. She didn't answer.

"Miranda has gotten herself into some trouble," Gladys said.

Arykah's eyebrows rose. "Oh? You want to talk about it, Miranda?"

Still nothing from Miranda.

Monique stood from her chair. She knew when to give Arykah privacy. "Lady Arykah, I will meet you down in the sanctuary."

"Thanks, Monique," Arykah said.

When Monique closed the door behind her, Arykah invited Gladys and Miranda to sit in the chairs on the opposite side of her desk. Arykah sat behind her desk and looked at Miranda. "Okay, Miranda. Let's see if we can get you out this trouble you're in. Can you tell me what the problem is?"

No words came from the young girl's throat.

"Open your mouth, Miranda, when the first lady speaks to you," Gladys ordered.

Clearly, whatever the problem was, Arykah knew she wasn't going to get Miranda to confide in her. "Gladys, why don't *you* tell me what Miranda's problem is?"

Gladys sat back in her chair and crossed her left leg over her right knee. She exhaled loudly. "Miranda is fifteen years old and pregnant."

Not only was Miranda crying, but Arykah saw tears forming in Gladys's eyes as well.

Arykah looked into Miranda's eyes. "Is that true, Miranda? Are you pregnant?"

Miranda wiped tears from her face. "Yes."

"Tell her the rest," Gladys ordered her daughter.

Miranda hesitated. "I, um, I want to have an abortion."

Arykah focused on Gladys's eyes. "And how do you feel about Miranda's decision?"

Gladys tried to blink away her tears. When a single tear had fallen onto her cheek, she wiped it away. "I'm disappointed in Miranda. I'm a single mother, and I work two jobs just to keep the bills paid and food on our table. I'm not thrilled about her pregnancy, but I'm against her having an abortion. The last thing I wanted for my daughter was for her to become a teenage mother, but an abortion is something that I just can't approve of. But the decision isn't up to me. If Miranda wants to terminate her pregnancy, the laws in Illinois protect her right to do so. At fifteen years old, she doesn't need my consent."

Arykah felt Gladys's pain. She could only imagine having to work two jobs to make ends meet. Single mothers certainly have it hard. Arykah wondered if Miranda's father played a significant role in her life. But since Gladys didn't mention Miranda's father, Arykah didn't inquire about him.

"Miranda, I know you feel as though the weight of the world is on your shoulders right now. And I understand that, at fifteen years old, you don't want the responsibility of having to care for a baby. But have you considered adoption as an alternative? There are so many people who'd love to adopt your baby and give it a good life."

"We've talked about that," Gladys said. "But Miranda doesn't want to go through the embarrassment of carrying a baby to term at fifteen years old."

Arykah looked at Miranda. "Do you think of yourself as an embarrassment?"

"No."

"Then you shouldn't think of your baby as an embarrassment either. All babies are miracles, no matter how they get here."

Miranda wiped more tears from her face. "But folks will talk about me. What do I do when people walk up to me and say bad things?"

You tell them to kiss your—Arykah immediately apologized to the Lord for her thought. She leaned forward and placed her elbows on top of her desk and folded her hands. "Sweetheart, you can't control what folks will and will not say about you. But remember this one thing; you don't owe anything to anybody. I want you to repeat after me. Ain't nobody got a heaven or hell to put me in."

Miranda slowly said the words. "Ain't nobody got a heaven or hell to put me in."

"Say it louder," Arykah encouraged.

"Ain't nobody got a heaven or hell to put me in."

"Whatever decision you make, Miranda, I want you to make it because it's something that *you* want to do. Please don't base your decision on what other folks might say about you. I can't tell you what to do, but I do want to put something in your mind. In your womb may be a future president of our country. You really won't know what your child could be unless you afford it a chance at life. So, I want you to think about that and talk it over with your mom. She doesn't want you to have an abortion and, truth be told, I don't either, but the decision is yours."

"I don't want an abortion anymore," Miranda mumbled.

Gladys looked at her daughter. "What did you say?"

Miranda spoke with conviction in her voice. "I don't want to have an abortion. I wanna keep my baby."

Gladys reached over and hugged Miranda. "I'm so happy to hear that. We're gonna get through this."

Arykah was pleased with the outcome of the meeting, and she was happy that Gladys and Miranda came to her for help and guidance.

Miranda let go of the embrace from her mother and looked at Arykah. "Thank you, Lady Arykah. I'm so happy my mother made me talk to you."

Arykah smiled. "You're welcome. My door is always open to you. You have a long, difficult road ahead of you, but if you ever get discouraged, come see me. And don't forget to send me an invitation to the baby shower."

"Oh no. There won't be a baby shower," Gladys said.

Arykah frowned. "I don't understand."

"The mothers of the church don't condone unwed pregnant girls to have baby showers. They feel that throwing a baby shower for an unwed mother is an abomination against the Lord. Mother Pansie says that by giving Miranda a baby shower is approving of the sin she committed. She says that a baby shower is thrown to celebrate a new life that's conceived by married folks."

"Mother Pansie told me that my baby will be a bastard and bastards aren't to be recognized or celebrated," Miranda said.

Arykah sat behind her desk with her chin in her lap. Her mouth was open so wide, Miranda and Gladys could probably have seen what her last meal consisted of. "Never in all of my life have I heard such foolishness," Arykah chuckled. By no means did Arykah think what Mother Pansie said to Miranda was humorous.

The chuckle was a reaction to how much gall Mother Pansie had for uttering such evil and hateful words to a fifteen-year-old girl. It was quite sad at how low the mothers of the church would stoop to keep control over the women. "Miranda, listen to me. Being the pastor's wife, I have to step in and take action when I am made aware of wrongdoing in this church. I apologize for what Mother Pansie said to you about your baby, and I want you to let it roll off your back." Arykah turned her attention to Gladys. "Now about the baby shower. How do you feel about it?"

"To be quite honest with you, Lady Arykah, I want Miranda to have a shower because I'm already struggling to support just the two of us. I know that I can't afford to purchase a stroller, a crib, a high chair, a swing, and everything else a baby needs."

"Well, Gladys, if you feel that way, why would you let the mothers influence what you do for your own daughter and grandbaby?"

Gladys shrugged her shoulders. "I'm just trying to follow the wishes of the mothers of the church. They're full of wisdom."

"They're full of something, but it ain't wisdom." As soon as the words were out of Arykah's mouth, she regretted saying them. She had verbally expressed her private thoughts, which was something Lance had told her that she should never do when counseling people. "I'm sorry. I shouldn't have said that. But if you want to throw Miranda a baby shower, Gladys, then you should do it. She's *your* daughter, that's *your* grandbaby, and it'll be *your* finances that will suffer if you try to do this on your own. That's what baby showers are for. Miranda certainly can't sleep in a crib. She can't sit in a high chair nor can she fit in a bassinette. The gifts will be for your grandbaby, not Miranda."

"I hear you, Lady Arykah. And thanks so much. Now we got one more hurdle to jump over," Gladys said.

"What's that?"

"Mother Pansie told me that I have to stand before the church today and confess my sin. She said that I have to ask the church for forgiveness," Miranda said.

"That's Mother Pansie's rule," Gladys added. "Whenever a single woman or young girl becomes pregnant, Mother Pansie makes them stand before the church."

It took every ounce of self-control and every fiber of Arykah's being to remain calm.

She opened her mouth to speak, then closed it because the devil was writing on her tongue. The three of them sat in silence. Gladys and Miranda saw Arykah fighting with herself to force her own lips to stay sealed.

Finally, Arykah balled up her lips, opened her desk drawer, and withdrew a yellow sticky pad and a pen. On the pad she wrote, *I'm trying to stay saved right now. Give me a minute to collect myself.* She slid the note across the desk.

Gladys and Miranda read Arykah's note and laughed out loud.

"Okay," Arykah said after she was able to dismiss what the devil wanted her to say.

She gained control of her own tongue. She had almost lost the battle, but she was able to remain in first-lady mode. "First of all, Miranda. That ain't happening. Not on *my* watch. You don't have to stand before the church and confess anything. The only one you owe an apology to is God. And only *He* can forgive your sins, not Mother Pansie, not Bishop Lance, and not me."

Lance knocked on Arykah's door and looked inside. "It's time to make our way down to the sanctuary."

Arykah smiled at her husband. She couldn't wait to tell him how disrespectful and out of control the moth-

ers were. But right then wasn't the time to do so. She
would save that conversation for pillow talk. "Okay.
We're done here," Arykah responded to Lance.

She looked at Gladys. "Are we good?"

Gladys stood and walked around to Arykah and
hugged her. "Yep, we're good."

Arykah let go of the embrace and looked at Miranda.
"Are we good?"

Miranda stepped to Arykah and hugged her. "Yeah,
Lady Arykah. We're real good now. Thank you so
much. And I'll personally bring you an invitation to my
baby shower."

"Good. I already know what the Bishop and I will
buy."

Arykah was on her feet singing along with the choir
when an usher came to her pew and extended his hand
in Arykah's direction. Arykah looked down the center
aisle and saw Myrtle Cortland slowly coming her way.
Arykah smiled so brightly that it matched the sun. She
didn't wait for Myrtle to reach the front pew. Arykah
walked down the center aisle and met Myrtle halfway
with open arms.

Everyone in the sanctuary saw Arykah meet and
greet the elderly woman and wondered who she was.

Myrtle embraced Arykah and whispered, "It's all
right now, Sugar Plum. Your help is here."

Arykah allowed her emotions to take over, and she
wept in Myrtle's arms. Lance was seated in the pulpit
watching. He knew Myrtle was coming to visit Freedom Temple that morning. Monique called to inform
him shortly after she had left Myrtle's house on Monday evening. Myrtle didn't want Arykah to know about
her visit; she wanted to surprise her.

Arykah broke the embrace and looked in Myrtle's eyes. "I'm so happy you're here, Momma Cortland."

Being the best friend of Myrtle's daughter-in-law certainly had its privileges. Not only was Monique the apple of Myrtle's eye, but so was Arykah. As far as Myrtle was concerned, Arykah wasn't just Monique's best friend, but Myrtle considered Arykah her daughter as well. The two of them had captured Myrtle's heart the moment Boris had introduced them to her years ago.

Myrtle grabbed Arykah by the hand, and the two of them walked to the front pew and sat down next to Monique. Mother Gussie and Mother Pansie were seated behind Arykah, Myrtle, and Monique.

"Welcome to Freedom Temple, Gravy," Monique said.

Myrtle leaned into Monique. "Where are they?"

"Right behind us."

Myrtle turned all the way around to face Mother Gussie and Mother Pansie. She addressed them both. "The two of you can get ready to make room for me on that pew." She turned back around and patted Arykah on her knee. "It's gonna be all right now, Sugar Plum. Mother Cortland is here." Myrtle didn't see nor would she have cared about the mothers' raised eyebrows.

Mother Gussie and Mother Pansie didn't say a word, but they certainly wondered who Myrtle was and why they needed to make room on the pew for her. They got their answer when Lance opened the doors to the church. That was when Myrtle stood and went to the altar.

After the benediction, Arykah stood next to Lance at the sanctuary door. She told Lance that she would stand with him after church and greet the members, and she kept her word. They both shook hands with the members as they exited the church.

"Lady Arykah, I love those heels," Chelsea said.

"Thanks, Chelsea. I saw you strutting in those boots this morning. Those are too cute."

Chelsea lifted up her long skirt so that Arykah could get a better look at how the boots fit her calves. "I am so happy that you hooked me up. If there is anything that I can do for you, Lady Arykah, please let me know." Chelsea meant those words wholeheartedly.

"As a matter of fact, Chelsea, I'm putting something together that I want you to be a part of. How can I reach you?"

Chelsea reached in her purse for scratch paper and a pen. She jotted her cellular number down and gave the paper to Arykah.

Arykah took the piece of paper from Chelsea, folded it, and slid it in her bra. "Thanks, I'll be in touch."

Chelsea hugged Arykah, shook Lance's hand, and then left the church.

When Arykah and Lance shook the last hand, they ascended the stairs to their offices.

Arykah opened her door and saw Myrtle and Monique sitting on the sofa inside.

Besides Lance, Monique was the only other person with a key to the new lock on Arykah's office door.

"Momma Cortland, you don't know what it meant for me to see you walking down that aisle. And you joined the church. That was totally unexpected."

"That was the plan," Myrtle said.

Arykah took off her hat and stepped out of the stilettos. "What plan?"

Myrtle looked at Monique and smiled.

Arykah looked at Monique. "What is she talking about? Did you know Momma Cortland was coming to join the church?"

"I knew she was coming, but I assumed it was to just visit. I was shocked when she stood and joined the church. But what really made my eyes pop out of my head was when she told the mothers to make room on that pew. I had no idea what that meant. Now I do."

"Oh my goodness, I heard what you said to the mothers," Arykah said to Myrtle. "I wanted to turn around and look at the expressions on their faces so bad."

Before another word could be said, Arykah's office door opened and Mother Pansie stormed in and approached her. "Did you tell Miranda that she didn't have to stand before the church and ask for forgiveness for getting pregnant?"

Arykah stood in the middle of her office gaping at Mother Pansie. *I know this broad didn't just walk into my office without knocking and try to front me off.* "First of all, this is *my* office. When my door is shut, you knock, then wait to be invited in."

"To heck with knocking on a door." Mother Pansie was hot. "Did you tell Miranda not to stand before the church?"

Arykah placed her hands on her hips. "Yes, I did. Miranda's pregnancy is her personal business. She doesn't owe this church an apology."

Mother Pansie stepped closer to Arykah. "You can't come into this church and start changing the way thangs is done around here. That young girl needs to confess her sins."

"Yes, she does. But to God, not the church."

Mother Pansie had enough. She pointed her finger at Arykah. "You know what? I'm just about tired of you."

"Hold on now, sister," Myrtle interjected from the sofa. She sat quietly for as long as she could. Now she must rise. She stood on her feet and positioned herself next to Arykah.

"Lady Arykah is correct," she said in Arykah's defense. "It is not up to the church to judge."

Mother Pansie snapped her head back. "And who in the heck are *you?*"

"I'm Myrtle Cortland. I'll be joining the Mothers Board real soon."

"I don't *think* so," Mother Pansie countered.

Myrtle stared into Mother Pansie's eyes. "I *know* so. And I got your number six ways from Sunday." That was Myrtle's way of informing Mother Pansie that she knew all about her and the dirty deeds she had done against Arykah.

"Mother Pansie," Arykah said, "I know you're old school. You may not like me or some of the decisions that I make. But unwed mothers will no longer be made to stand before the church and ask for forgiveness. That's one of the changes that you and Mother Gussie will have to accept. And please do not walk into my office ever again without knocking. I'd hate for you to catch me and the Bishop in a compromising position. We're still newlyweds, you know."

Monique hollered and Myrtle chuckled.

Mother Pansie exited and slammed the door behind her. She left with the same storm that she brought into Arykah's office.

Myrtle looked at Arykah. "Sugar Plum, I'm so proud of you."

Chapter 11

Lance tried not to stir. But the motorcycle was working his last nerve. The alarm clock on the nightstand read 4:45 A.M. It was pitch-black outside. He looked up at the ceiling and saw the lines the streetlights made through the mini blinds. The noise from the motorcycle became louder. The idiot was coming down the street again. Lance glanced to his right and didn't see Arykah lying next to him. The motorcycle's engine revved. Angrily, he threw the covers from his body and rushed to the window to see what fool was on the side of his house making the noise so early in the morning. He didn't see anyone on a motorcycle. Then Lance realized the noise was coming from behind him on the opposite side of the master bedroom door.

He turned from the window and walked to the door and yanked it open. Once in the hallway on his way to the living room, he concluded the noise was coming from a vacuum.

Didn't Arykah know what time it was? What would possess her to want to vacuum before daybreak? His intentions were to pull the cord to the vacuum cleaner from the socket and grill his wife about her eagerness to clean house in the wee hours of the morning, but his vision stopped him in his tracks.

Hair pulled back into a tight twenty-inch long ponytail, and an *extremely* short red silk camisole revealing oversized breasts that gave a bowl of Jell-O a run for its money caused Lance to pause. But it was the thigh-high, five-inch cheetah-print boots that looked as though they had been painted on Arykah's legs that brought drool to Lance's lips. He swallowed. Then he swallowed again. Arykah literally made Lance's mouth water.

Arykah had seen the boots in a *Frederick's of Hollywood* magazine. The skinny chick that modeled the boots had to be a size double zero, and Arykah knew there wasn't a chance in heaven the boots would wrap around her legs and thighs the way they wrapped around the extremely thin model's legs and thighs. So, Arykah did what she did best. She purchased the boots, paid extra for overnight delivery, and took the boots to the tailor who had, on many other occasions, altered boots to fit her proportion. When she was told that a whole yard of material was needed to carry out the task, Arykah wasted no time heading to the nearest fabric store.

Truth be told, Arykah thought the boots were trashy. That's why she had to have them. She wouldn't be caught dead wearing the boots out in public. But in her mind, nothing was too trashy for the bedroom, her and Lance's playground.

If the congregation at Freedom Temple knew what kinds of toys and gadgets their pastor enjoyed playing with, they'd shame him and leave the church.

The boots were just another prop that would stay hidden from the outside world. When the fun was over, Arykah would be sure to lock the boots away in a treasure chest she kept hidden in her closet. The boots would be an addition to the handcuffs, whips, and feathers already stored there.

She knew Lance was there. Knew he was watching. Arykah didn't acknowledge his presence, but she decided to put on a show for him. With her right hand on the vacuum cleaner handle, Arykah pushed it forward. She also stepped forward seductively with her right foot. Then she stepped backward with her right foot and brought the vacuum cleaner back to its starting point. She repeated the motion over and over again.

Arykah seemed to be doing the cha-cha. Lance had never seen someone vacuum so sexily. She pushed the vacuum, then pulled it back; pushed it forward again, then pulled it back. She had a rhythm going, but all Lance could concentrate on were the thigh-high cheetah-print boots and the Jell-O.

Arykah looked at the grandfather clock next to the fireplace. It was time. She shut the power off on the vacuum, stood it upright, then turned toward the laundry room. Lance watched as she sashayed in the boots and followed her like an obedient puppy. Her hips swayed from side to side as she walked. *Swoosh, swoosh.* It was like she was wading in water.

He didn't know where Arykah was going, but Lance wanted to remain in her company. He trailed her through the kitchen to the laundry room.

Lance saw Arykah use a stepping stool to climb on top of the washing machine and sit down. He was intrigued. "What in the world are you doing?"

As soon as he asked the question, the spin cycle on the washing machine started.

Her body vibrated.

Oh my God. Lance couldn't believe his eyes. The Jell-O, the boots, the Jell-O, the boots.

Arykah was wiggling uncontrollably. "You have about three minutes," her voice was slightly above a whisper.

"To do what?"

"To shake with me."

Lance never knew that love so early in the morning could be so good.

Hours after the fun in the laundry room, Lance had left for church. Since Arykah didn't have any appointments the entire day, she decided to devote her time to searching the Internet for Italian drapes. Jeremy Montahue's offer for the estate in Belfor had been accepted, and Arykah was keeping up her end of the bargain to redecorate the home office.

In the master bedroom, she propped her pillows against the headboard, then sat on the bed and rested her back against them. She extended her legs forward, then set her notebook on her lap. She logged on to the Internet to Google Italian drapes when her cellular telephone rang. She grabbed the telephone from her nightstand and saw Monique's number on the caller ID.

"Hey, doll," Arykah greeted.

"Hey, yourself. Your voice mail at the realty office informed me that you wouldn't be in the office today."

"That would be true," Arykah stated.

"So, what's going on? Are you feeling all right?"

"Yeah, I'm fine. I don't have any appointments today, so I decided to stay home and work on designing the home office in the Belfor estate. I have to present Jeremy with wood flooring samples and paint samples. I'm searching the Web for Italian drapes right now."

"Oh, wow," Monique said. "You're at home, but you're just as busy as you'd be had you gone into the office."

"For the commission that I'll receive for selling the Belfor estate, I truly don't mind. The closing is in three weeks, and I promised Jeremy that the home office would be complete and to his satisfaction a week after closing." Arykah exhaled. "So, what's going on with you?"

Monique was driving on the Dan Ryan Expressway heading north to WGOD radio station where she worked as a senior executive producer. "I got a call from Amaryllis last night. She said that she and Bridgette can't make the fat girl party next Saturday night."

"Are you kidding me, Monique? What is their issue?"

"According to Amaryllis, her guy, Charles, bought tickets to see Steve Harvey and Nephew Tommy at the Arie Crown Theater for next Saturday. Charles didn't know that we had scheduled the party for that night."

"Okay. But why can't Bridgette come?"

"Bridgette will be out of town on business."

Arykah was disappointed. She looked forward to the monthly fat girl parties. They were when she could be herself, act a fool, and not worry about being judged or criticized for her behavior. "Well, I guess Bridgette's gotta do what she's gotta do for her job."

"And we can't expect Amaryllis to stand her man up," Monique added.

"So, it'll be just you and me, huh?"

"Unless you want to invite someone else."

Bringing someone else into the circle had never crossed Arykah's mind. Since the first fat girl party almost a year ago, the parties had only consisted of herself, Monique, Amaryllis, and Bridgette. "Someone like whom?"

Arykah couldn't see Monique shrug her shoulders. "I don't know. Is there anyone else you'd like to invite?"

Arykah thought about Monique's question. "You mean like women from the church?"

"Well, a handful of ladies have warmed up to you, right?"

"Just a few, but I don't feel comfortable bringing anyone from the church into my personal world. You know I likes ta drop it like it's hot, and I don't want, nor do I need, any witnesses."

Monique laughed. "I know that's right."

Suddenly, Arykah had an epiphany. "You know what, Monique? Inviting a few of the women from the church may not be such a bad idea after all. But not for the fat girl party. I'd rather keep that part of my life separate."

"What do you have in mind?"

"Yesterday, after church, I told Chelsea that I'd be in touch with her to be a part of something I wanted to do. Ever since Lance made me realize that it was partly my own fault that the women shunned me, I decided to do something about it. How do you feel about postponing the fat girl party until Amaryllis and Bridgette can come?"

"That's fine. What else do you have in mind?" Monique asked again.

"I thought it would be nice if I hosted a spa day and invited Chelsea, Gladys, and Darlita."

"Who is Darlita?" Monique asked.

"You know Darlita. She's the woman who came to me for counsel. The woman whose husband had been cheating and wouldn't stop."

"Oh yeah," Monique said. "How is she doing?"

"Darlita is doing great since she left that fool. I know she's having a hard time with the separation, but she knows it was for the best. I'm sure she can use a spa day. So can Gladys, because she has an unexpected grandbaby on the way. There's gonna be a lot of changes in her household. I want to invite Chelsea simply because she's the only woman who apologized for treating me so cold."

"I'm not sold on Chelsea," Monique stated.

"Why would you say that?"

"I mean, I think it's all good that she apologized for allowing the mothers to influence her as far as you are concerned. But I have to wonder if she would have apologized if you hadn't given her the hookup about the boots. She just seems kinda suspect to me."

"Well, I thought about that too," Arykah admitted. "When Chelsea reached out to hug me, I almost took a step back because I didn't know what she was doing. But I believe her apology was genuine."

Monique didn't comment. As the first lady of the church, Arykah had to be forgiving and openhearted. Monique would just have to watch Chelsea closely. She seemed like an opportunist. A coattail rider. Someone who lived to benefit from other people's accomplishments.

"A spa day sounds great, Arykah. I know the ladies would love it."

"I think so too. But I want to take it a step further. I want to give Chelsea, Darlita, and Gladys a gift."

"Arykah, don't overdo it. You're trying too hard. You shouldn't try to buy friendship. If the women like you, then they like you. If they don't, then they don't. Treating them to a spa is more than generous."

"I know, but I still wanna get them each a gift."

Monique rolled her eyes at no one in particular as she exited the expressway at Pershing Road. "Just don't spend too much money."

Arykah had already decided what gifts she wanted to buy the ladies. And she knew Monique would have a stroke when she told her. Arykah took a deep breath, then rushed the words, "I'm buying each of the ladies a pair of Christian Louboutins."

Monique slammed on the brakes and veered from the left lane she was in. She came within an inch of

crashing into the car ahead of her that had stopped at
a red light.

After a long half hour of listening to Monique moan
and gripe about her spending too much money on
women that she probably couldn't trust, Arykah ended
the conversation by telling Monique that she really
needed to focus on finding Italian drapes.

"I know you're rushing me off the phone, Arykah.
But we're not done talking about the Christian Louboutins."

"You made your point, Monique, and I'll take into
consideration everything you said."

Monique didn't believe her. She knew Arykah was
going to do what she wanted.

"Uh-huh. Okay. I'll give you a call later on."

Arykah was glad that conversation was over. Now
she could focus on the matter at hand, which was to
earn her commission check. She settled back against
the pillows and browsed the Internet. When she double
clicked on www.italiandrapery.com, her cellular telephone rang again. She hoped it wasn't Monique calling
back to discuss the Christian Louboutins.

Arykah didn't recognize the number on the caller ID,
but she answered anyway.

"Arykah speaking."

"Howa? Ees thee Howa house?" a man asked.

Arykah frowned. She pulled the telephone away from
her ear and glanced at the caller ID again. The number
was not a familiar one. She brought the telephone back
to her ear.

"Excuse me?"

"Ah call fra dri cleena. Ees thee Howa house?"

"Oh, the dry cleaners. Yes, this is the Howard home.
What can I do for you?"

"Ees Meester Howa theyah. I talk to 'em?"

Lance told Arykah that he was going to take a couple of his suits to the dry cleaners on his way to the church that morning. Arykah wondered if there was a problem. "Mr. Howard isn't home at the moment. This is Mrs. Howard. Is there a problem with the suits he brought in?"

"He lef sumthin' in jakit."

That wasn't the first time the dry cleaners had called to tell Lance that he'd forgotten items in his suit jacket pockets. Two weeks ago, Lance had misplaced an expensive Faber-Castell fountain pen. Arykah hoped the dry cleaners was calling to say that they've found it.

"Oh, I see," Arykah said. "Did you find a fountain pen?"

There was a pause. "Uh, no. No inka pen. In pockit I see pepamin, thwendy dolla, do condom, and do movie dikkit."

Arykah's back came away from the pillows like a dead woman rising in a casket. She was as stiff as a board. In fact, she stopped breathing. The clocks stopped. The refrigerator stopped humming. Everything stopped. *What the heck did he just say?*

"Hollow? Hollow?" The man thought Arykah had ended the call.

Arykah shook her head vigorously to clear out her brain. She needed to erase the words the man said to make room for new words. Correct words. Words that made sense. Any words besides the words he had spoken to her. Words that wouldn't get Lance killed. She needed clarity. "Um, yes, I'm here. What did you say was in the jacket?"

"Uh, I fine thwendy dolla, do movie dikkit, pepamin, and do condom."

He said it again. Arykah hoped the reason the man was talking crazy was because he couldn't speak good English. There was no way on God's green earth the man was saying what she thought he was saying. "Are you saying 'two condoms'?"

"Ye, ma'am. Do condom, thwendy dolla, pepa—"

"Forget the money and peppermint," Arykah snapped. "I really need to understand what you're saying to me." Arykah spoke very slowly. "You said you found two condoms in *my* husband's suit jacket pocket? *Lance Howell's* suit jacket?" By putting emphasis on her husband's name, Arykah prayed the man would realize that he had called the wrong number.

"Ye. Also, thwendy dolla—"

Arykah screamed, *"Forget the money! I don't wanna hear nothing about money!"* Arykah massaged her temple with her free hand. It was a mistake. It had to be. She thought about something. "Wait a minute, mister. There are two condoms, right?"

"Ye. Do condom, thwendy dolla, pepamin, and do movie dikkit."

"I don't care about anything else but the condoms. Don't condoms come three to a pack?"

"Wha u seh?"

Arykah asked the question in general. It was a thought that she had uttered out loud. She didn't expect for the man to respond.

Condoms are purchased three in a pack. She and Lance had never used any form of birth control, yet a condom was allegedly missing from his suit jacket. And if a condom was missing, it must've been used. And what was up with the movie tickets? She and Lance hadn't gone to see a movie. They preferred to watch DVDs at home.

Arykah had to calm herself down. Obviously the man had made a terrible mistake.

There was absolutely no chance that Lance had been untrue to her. But when Arykah thought about it, he was surrounded by beautiful women every Tuesday in Bible class and every Sunday at morning worship. Skinny chicks. Horny chicks. Chicks who loved to grin in his face. Chicks with oversized silicone injected boobs. Chicks that'll do just about anything to land themselves a pastor. And there was also the possibility of Lance encountering a woman in the office at the construction company.

But why would Lance stray? Arykah jumped his bones every chance she got. She made sure that he never had the energy to go outside of their marriage. She took care of business at home. Lance was never left unsatisfied, unfulfilled, or wanting more. She wore him out often. Arykah was on top of her game as far as Lance was concerned. In the kitchen she may not be able to boil an egg, but in the bedroom, Arykah's performance was Oscar worthy.

"Excuse me, mister, but I'm sure you called the wrong number."

"Wrong nubba? Thees nubba Howa toll me."

Arykah wondered why Lance gave the dry cleaners her cellular number. Two times before, when the dry cleaners called to inform Lance of items left behind in his suit jacket pocket, they had called the home number. Arykah had never taken their clothes to the dry cleaners. That was a chore for Lance. Common sense told Arykah that if anything, Lance would've left his own cellular number as an alternate source of contact, not hers.

"What address do you have for Lance Howell?" Arykah asked.

The address the dry cleaners had on file was the address where she and Lance resided.

That didn't strike Arykah as being odd. Of course they'd have the correct address. Lance was a weekly customer. What struck Arykah as being odd was the dry cleaners called her cellular number assuming they were calling Lance's home number.

"I'm coming to get the items you found in my husband's jacket."

"No. I gee only to Howa. Hees jakit. *He* get items."

To heck with what he was talking about. "Yeah, okay," was all Arykah said and disconnected the call.

Twelve minutes later Arykah stood at the counter at the dry cleaners.

"Hollow. Wehcum," an oriental man greeted her. "Ah hep you?"

Arykah recognized his voice. He was the man she had spoken with on the telephone.

"I'm here for the items my husband left in his suit jacket pocket. His name is Lance Howell. I'm his wife. We spoke on the phone. I wanna see the jacket and the items *in* the jacket." Arykah sized the man up. He looked thin and frail. If he didn't cooperate, she was prepared to get physical. But no matter what, she wasn't leaving the dry cleaners without what she came for.

"Ah toe u on fone. Ah gee item only to Howa. Where Howa?"

Arykah was on a mission. She needed answers, and she needed them like yesterday.

She refused to waste another second being nice. "Look, fool. I didn't come here to go back and forth with you about this. Give me my husband's suit jacket now before I jump over this counter. And if I have to jump over the counter, I'm jumping on *you*." Arykah leaned her upper torso over the counter and glared into the man's eyes and spaced her words apart very slowly.

"Give . . . me . . . the . . . jacket . . . and . . . everything . . . in . . . it . . . *now!*"

"Yom, yom, com, som, chom," the man quickly said to someone over his shoulder.

He chose his battles, and a battle with Arykah he didn't want to fight. Seconds later, an oriental lady appeared at the counter with a suit jacket. As soon as Arykah saw the jacket, she knew it didn't belong to Lance.

The woman laid the jacket on top of the counter and stepped backward. The man followed suit and stepped backward as well. Arykah picked up the oversized tweed jacket and examined it. It reeked of cigarette smoke. Lance didn't smoke. It was two sizes too small for Lance's frame. And furthermore, all of Lance's suits were tailor-made. The jacket Arykah held in her hand was cheap and looked as though it may have been bought off the rack.

Already satisfied that the jacket didn't belong to her husband, curiosity killed the cat.

Arykah wanted to see the items the man had called about. She searched the interior jacket first and pulled out a single piece of Brach's peppermint candy. She reached in the interior pocket again and pulled out a folded twenty-dollar bill. In the left lower pocket, Arykah found two single Trojan's brand lubricated condoms.

"Are you kidding me?" Arykah chuckled the words when she saw that the condoms were small in size. The size of the condoms was further proof the jacket didn't belong to Lance.

When Arykah chuckled, the woman spoke to the man. "Tha, ju, han, mo, kas."

"Neeyo, fas, mum, lom, chedo," he replied.

For all Arykah knew, they could be discussing her insanity for laughing at condoms.

From the right lower pocket, Arykah pulled out two movie stubs redeemed over four months ago. She laid the items on the counter and, without saying a word, left the dry cleaners with the jacket in her hand.

Arykah got behind the wheel of her car and pulled her cellular phone from her purse.

She dialed Lance's cellular number.

"Hi, baby," Lance answered on the first ring.

Arykah forced a smile. She wanted her voice to sound happy. "Hello, honey. I was on my way to get me a bite to eat when I realized that you didn't have breakfast before you left the house this morning. So, how about I swing by the church and pick you up? Can you join me for brunch?"

"Oh, wow, baby. I'd love to, but I'm not at the church. I'm at a construction site. As soon as I left the dry cleaners this morning, I got paged that a beam had fallen forty feet and one of my workers may have been injured. Sorry, I can't have brunch with you."

"Aw, it's okay. How is your employee?"

"He's fine," Lance said. "The beam missed him, but he's pretty shaken up though."

"Thank God he'll be okay. Hey, babe, did you tell Mother Gussie that you weren't coming to the church today?"

"Yes. I always let her know when my plans change so that she won't be expecting me."

"Did you happen to mention that you had stopped by the dry cleaners?"

"Yes. I told Mother Gussie that I had stopped by the dry cleaners when I got paged. I told her that I was go-ing to the construction site straight from there."

Bingo. That's all the information that Arykah needed to hear. "Okay, babe, I'll let you get back to work. I'll see you at home this evening." She disconnected the call with Lance.

Arykah sat in her car. She was fit to be tied. Mother Gussie had set the whole thing up. Evidently she didn't take Arykah's last threat seriously. It was only a week ago when Arykah had nonverbally warned Mother Gussie to back off. But Arykah wasn't going to be bothered with words, spoken or unspoken, again.

She started her car and drove to Freedom Temple. Her marriage was not to be played with. Arykah could show Mother Gussie how serious she was better than she could tell her.

Mother Gussie was talking on the telephone when Arykah snatched it out of her hand and threw the receiver across the desk. She didn't know who Mother Gussie was talking to, but, at that moment, Arykah didn't give a darn.

Mother Gussie was startled. "What in the world?"

Arykah walked around the desk with the tweed suit jacket in her hand. Mother Gussie scooted backward in her chair. Arykah came and stood in front of her. They were so close that the tips of their shoes kissed.

Arykah leaned forward and touched Mother Gussie's nose with her own. "You think I'm playing with you?"

Mother Gussie scooted backward again. She had started to sweat. "I don't know what you're—"

"Shut up!" Arykah yelled. Her eyes were wide and blazing.

Mother Gussie flinched at Arykah's outburst.

Arykah held up the suit jacket. "You think this was funny? You wanna play games? Well, let me tell you something." Arykah placed the jacket against Mother Gussie's mouth and applied pressure. The action had pushed Mother Gussie's head back three inches. "When you play with a bulldog, you get bit in the face," Arykah warned. "I will shove this jacket in your mouth and dry your throat with it."

Arykah threw the jacket on Mother Gussie's desk and stood upright. She looked down at Mother Gussie. "Don't mess with my marriage. That's what you *ain't* gonna do." Arykah turned on her heels and walked ten feet away from Mother Gussie, then stopped and turned back around. "Please, Mother Gussie. I'm begging you. I'm begging you to not make the mistake of thinking that I'm not at all serious. I suggest that you and your friend find another hobby."

Arykah walked away and left the church. Mother Gussie held her breath. She didn't move. She didn't blink. She didn't even fart. She waited until she heard the church door slam before she exhaled. Her chair felt warm. Mother Gussie stood and looked down at her seat. It was wet. Her bladder had betrayed her.

"You wait 'til I see that hussy," Myrtle said when Arykah shared the latest tactic that the mothers tried to pull off.

"Pouring the red ink in your chair was wrong but trying to destroy your marriage is a whole new ball game," Monique said.

"I was so mad that I really wanted to do bodily harm to Mother Gussie," Arykah added to the conversation. She, Monique, and Myrtle were on a three-way call. When Arykah returned home from the church, she had called Monique at the radio station and Myrtle's home number.

"Arykah, I really don't understand what their problem is. The mothers dislike for you is so strong," Monique said.

"The attack started on the Sunday Lance announced that he had gotten married. He asked me to stand, introduced me as his wife, and the crap hit the fan. The Wednesday after you left Boris standing at the altar, you called to tell me that Adonis had proposed to you in the limousine when the two of you exited the church. You told me that you wanted me to fly to Jamaica because you and Adonis was gonna get married on the beach at the crack of dawn. Do you remember that?"

"Yes, I do," Monique answered.

"Well," Arykah continued, "I called Lance and asked him to join me. I had no idea that he was gonna ask me to marry him when we got to Jamaica. All the folks at Freedom Temple were shocked at Lance's announcement. One Sunday their pastor was a single man, and then the next Sunday, he announced that he was a married man. I can understand how that bit of information would be unsettling for some folks."

"I can understand that too, Sugar Plum," Myrtle interjected. "But it still doesn't give those old hags the right to turn every lady in the church against the bishop's new wife, and it certainly doesn't give them the right to harass you. Lance had a right to marry whomever he wanted."

"I'm not saying that it gives them the right, Momma Cortland. I'm just saying that I understand their hostility and resentment."

"But Mother Gussie and Mother Pansie have never taken the time to get to know you, Arykah. You were hated from the very beginning of your marriage to Lance," Monique stated.

"And what really surprises me," Arykah started, "is how all of the women in the church were so easily influenced. It's like the mothers have them under a spell."

"But you know how it is when a pastor is single, Sugar Plum. Especially a good-looking pastor," Myrtle said.

"Yep," Monique offered. "Not only is Lance good looking, he owns a construction company, and he's living in a massive estate. Everyone knows he's a wealthy man. I ain't sayin' you're a gold digger, Arykah. But you ain't messin' with no broke—"

"Don't you call my husband that name," Arykah interrupted Monique before she could add the last word to the famous phrase from the rapper Kanye West's song "Gold Digger." "And my honey knows his way around the kitchen."

"So, those qualities alone made Lance a target for every single woman in the church to try to get him. Heck, that may have been the only reason most of the single women attended Freedom Temple."

"You're right, Gravy," Monique said. "So when Lance announced that Arykah was his wife, it pissed a lot of people off. And Arykah wasn't even a member of the church. I don't think the mothers had to work too hard at convincing the women that Arykah was the enemy. When Arykah showed up as lady elect, the single women were already drinking hatorade."

It was late evening when Mother Gussie was walking home from the convenient store carrying a bag of groceries. She saw two little girls across the street enjoying a game of hopscotch.

"Mother Gussie."

Mother Gussie looked over her shoulder to see who had whispered her name. She didn't see anyone nearby.

"Mother Gussie." The second whisper came from in front of her. Mother Gussie looked ahead but still didn't see anyone. She kept walking.

"Mother Gussie."

She glanced in the parked cars lined up along the street. They were all empty. Mother Gussie increased her pace. She gripped the bag of groceries tighter as she walked.

"Mother Gussie." The whisper was above her.

Mother Gussie cried out. She looked up at the trees that towered over her. No one was in the trees. Straight-ahead at the end of the block were tall bushes. Mother Gussie told herself that if she could just make it to the bushes and turn the corner, she'd be home.

"Mother Gussie." The whisper was on her left shoulder. Too close for comfort.

She hollered out, then dropped the groceries and ran to the corner. When she rounded the corner, she looked behind her one last time. When Mother Gussie turned back around she collided.

"Boo," Arykah said, smiling.

"Errrrrrrrrrrrraaaaaallllllll," Mother Gussie woke up screaming.

Her husband jolted awake. He sat up and turned on the lamp that sat on the nightstand.

"What is it, Gussie?"

All of the color had drained from Mother Gussie's face. It was as if she had seen a ghost. "She gon' get me, she gon' get me," she cried while clutching the covers to her chest. "She gon' get me."

"Who's gonna get you?" Her husband was in a daze. He wasn't fully awake. He had no idea why she was screaming. "Who are you talking about?"

Mother Gussie's eyes danced from the ceiling to the window to the closet door. She rocked back and forth.

Chills were running throughout her body. "She gon' get me," she moaned.

"Who's gonna get you? Me?"

Mother Gussie looked to her left. It wasn't her husband in bed with her; it was Arykah's face she saw. She screamed at the top of her lungs. Mother Gussie threw the covers from her body, hopped out of bed, and ran from the bedroom. "She gon' get me! Lawd Jesus, she gon' get me!"

Her husband ran after her.

Chapter 12

Arykah entered the church Tuesday evening and shook the snowflakes from her coat.

It was mid-March, and at least two inches of snow had fallen with no signs of letting up.

She had spent all morning and afternoon mixing paint samples and choosing wood flooring to ensure that her client would be completely satisfied when he moved into his new home.

Arykah took off her wet coat and had started to climb the stairs to her office when she overheard a conversation between two teenage girls. They were standing close to the entrance of the sanctuary.

"I heard that his wife is going to join the choir," one girl said to the other.

"Girl, I don't care. I can sit next to her in the choir stand and *still* screw her husband."

At the fifth step, Arykah's climb ceased. She turned around, descended the stairs, and approached the girls.

The two girls saw Arykah walking their way and greeted her.

"Praise the Lord, Lady Arykah."

"Hi, Lady Arykah."

Arykah ignored their greetings. "Which one of you is screwing a married man?"

Both of their eyes popped out of their heads. They had no clue that their conversation wasn't a private one.

Arykah's eyes danced from one girl to the other. They looked real young. Arykah guessed the girls to be around sixteen or seventeen years old. Much too young to be having such an inappropriate conversation.

"Which one of you is screwing a married man?" Arykah repeated herself. Maybe she could have chosen an alternate way of asking the question, but Arykah figured that if one of the girls was bold enough to admit to fornicating and had no problem doing it, Arykah would be just as bold and had no problem calling her on it.

"*I'm* not," the girl standing on Arykah's left responded.

Arykah spoke to the girl standing on her right. "What's your name?"

The girl hung her head and looked down. "Natasha."

"How old are you, Natasha?" Arykah asked her.

Natasha answered the floor. "Seventeen."

Arykah placed two fingers beneath Natasha's chin and slightly lifted her face. "Look at me."

When Natasha looked into Arykah's eyes, Arykah saw tears on the verge of falling.

"Are the two of you here for Bible class?"

"Yes," both girls answered.

"And what is *your* name?" Arykah asked Natasha's friend.

"I'm Destiny, and I ain't having sex with nobody."

Arykah almost chuckled. Destiny sold her friend out quick, fast, and in a hurry.

"Destiny, you go ahead into the sanctuary. Bishop Howell will be starting Bible class soon," Arykah instructed.

Destiny looked at Natasha with pity in her eyes, then walked into the sanctuary.

"Is your mother here, Natasha?" Arykah asked.

"No."

"Come on up to my office. We're gonna have a little chat."

When Arykah and Natasha ascended the stairs, Arykah saw that Mother Gussie's chair was empty. It was unusual for Mother Gussie to be away from her desk on a Tuesday evening. On Tuesdays, Mother Gussie started her shift later than her normal start time.

She'd work from 11:00 A.M. until 7:00 P.M. And when Lance left his office to begin Bible class, Mother Gussie would shut down her computer and follow him down to the sanctuary.

"Come with me," Arykah said to Natasha as she walked past Mother Gussie's desk toward Lance's office.

Natasha became nervous. *She's gonna tell the bishop on me*, she thought.

Lance was sitting behind his desk going over his notes for Bible class when he looked up and saw Arykah entering his office. "There's my favorite girl," he said.

"Hello, my love," Arykah greeted him.

Lance saw that Arykah wasn't alone. "Natasha. Wow, what a special treat I got this evening. My favorite girl, and my favorite choir member both in my office. This turned out to be a great day."

"Hi, Bishop," Natasha said slightly smiling. She wondered if she'd still be Lance's favorite choir member when Lady Arykah told him her sin.

Arykah walked around to Lance's side of the desk and sat on the end, then crossed her left leg over her right knee. She'd always liked when Fran Fine from the television sitcom, *The Nanny,* sat on her boss's desk that way. Arykah thought it was a cute pose. "Where is Mother Gussie?"

"She didn't come to work today," Lance answered. "Deacon Hughes called and said she wasn't feeling well."

"Humph," Arykah commented. No doubt her confrontation with Mother Gussie yesterday had played a part in her absenteeism.

Lance saw that Natasha hadn't entered his office. She stood at the door with an uneasiness about her. "What are you ladies up to?" Lance posed the question in general. He didn't care who answered.

Natasha glanced at Arykah with a forced smile. It was Arykah who answered Lance's question. "Natasha and I are gonna have a chat before Bible class."

"Is that right?" Lance said. He looked at Natasha and knew that something was up. If Arykah was chatting with a young girl, then something was *definitely* up.

Arykah noticed the picture of herself and Jeremy Montahue on Lance's credenza.

"Where did you get that picture of me and Jeremy? He's the one who bought the Belfor estate."

Lance turned around and grabbed the frame. "Mother Gussie gave it to me. She said a courier brought it to the church."

Arykah frowned. "What courier? And who took the picture?"

Lance shrugged his shoulders. "My guess is that there was no courier, but I gotta get ready to go downstairs." That was Lance's way of dismissing the conversation with Natasha being present.

Arykah followed Lance's lead. "Okay, Natasha and I will be down shortly." She glanced at the photo again. Mother Gussie had her followed. Someone had taken that photo and somehow it ended up in Lance's hands. Arykah wondered why Lance never mentioned that he received the photo. She and Jeremy looked like they were on a date. She would be sure and ask Lance about it when they got home.

Arykah and Natasha left Lance alone and walked across the hall to Arykah's office. Arykah unlocked the door and turned on the light. "Come on in, Natasha, and have a seat."

Natasha followed Arykah inside and sat in one of the chairs opposite of Arykah's desk.

"Uh-uh." Arykah pointed to the sofa. "There."

Natasha obeyed and sat on the sofa. She watched Arykah hang her coat on a coat hanger just inside the door. Then Arykah stepped out of her Ugg boots and slipped into a pair of pink plush slippers that she kept beneath her desk.

"You hungry?" Arykah asked Natasha as she opened a cabinet next to her desk and pulled out a bag of nacho cheese-flavored Doritos and a bottle of Louisiana brand hot sauce.

"No, thank you." Natasha wished Lady Arykah would just say what she had to say and send her on her way. She knew she was in trouble; there was no doubt about that. But it seemed that Lady Arykah was prolonging the lashing.

Arykah opened the bag of Doritos, then opened the bottle of hot sauce and poured it in the bag of chips. She shook the bag to make sure the hot sauce reached the bottom.

Natasha watched Arykah place the hot sauce back in the cabinet, then open the door to a small compact refrigerator she kept against the wall behind her desk.

"You thirsty?"

When Arykah pulled out a sixteen-ounce bottle of Pepsi, Natasha's mouth watered.

She was very thirsty but was too nervous to eat or drink anything. "No, thank you."

Arykah looked at her. "You're very polite, Natasha. But don't you know that sleeping with a married man isn't polite?"

Natasha looked at the floor in front of her. "Yes, ma'am."

"Don't look at the floor," Arykah said. "Look at me. Cowards look at the floor."

Natasha connected her eyes with Arykah.

With her chips and drink in her hand, Arykah came and sat on the sofa. Natasha couldn't believe her eyes when Arykah brought the bag to her mouth, threw her head back, and gulped the chips.

Arykah took her time and chewed the chips before she swallowed. "You're seventeen years old, so that makes you a senior in high school, right?"

"Yes," Natasha answered.

Arykah opened the bottle of Pepsi and drank. After five swallows, she placed the cap back on the bottle. *Buuuuurrrpppp.* "How are your grades?"

Just like every other female in the church, Natasha had heard how ghetto, loud, and outspoken the bishop's wife was. But being up close and personal with Arykah, Natasha saw firsthand how true the rumors were. The first lady had just belched loudly and didn't ask to be excused.

"My grades are excellent. I'm on the honor roll," Natasha said proudly.

Arykah threw her head back again and took another gulp of chips. She chewed, swallowed, then looked into Natasha's eyes. "Then why are you so stupid?"

If Natasha had one wish that could be granted, it would be to disappear from Arykah's sight. She didn't respond. She couldn't respond. Arykah had shut her down.

"You do know that sleeping with a married man is a stupid thing to do, don't you?"

Natasha looked toward the floor.

"I told you to look at me. Why do you focus on the floor? We're having a conversation. If you're woman enough to screw another woman's husband, then be woman enough to face the consequences for doing so. I heard you tell your friend that you had no problem sitting next to the man's wife and still screw him. That's what tricks do. See, tricks don't have any self-respect. They're easily persuaded to cheapen themselves while thinking they're on top of the world. Tricks hide. They sneak around. They settle for sex in the backseats of cars. A trick can never be number one. She'll always be the dark little secret that no one can know about.

"A trick can't be seen on the arm of her man because she's not worthy. She's not even second best. She's told when to speak, when to sit, and when to breathe." Arykah swallowed more Pepsi, then asked, "How long have you been trickin'?"

Natasha wanted to crawl beneath a rock. Arykah had basically told her that she had no worth. She was wasting her life. She was nothing. She was useless. She was a cheap whore.

Arykah saw tears spilling from Natasha's eyes. "What do your tears mean?"

Natasha looked at Arykah as though she didn't understand.

Arykah rephrased the question. "Why are you crying?"

Natasha wiped her face with the back of her hand. "'Cause . . . I . . . I'm just . . . I don't know."

"You don't know what, that you're a trick? Because that's exactly what you are. You're a pretty girl, Natasha. You're on the honor roll, and you're graduating in a few months. You have too much going for you to be treated as though you're nothing."

Arykah noticed that Natasha was holding on tight to a Coach handbag. Arykah and Monique both owned that same bag. It wasn't cheap. It had cost them a pretty penny.

"He bought you that purse?"

Natasha nodded.

"I can only imagine what you had to do for it."

Natasha looked at the floor.

"Look at me, Natasha!"

Natasha looked at Arykah, and more tears spilled from her eyes. "I'm so sorry."

"For what?"

She wiped her tears away again. "For being stupid."

Arykah reached over and wiped a single tear that ran down Natasha's face. "You're a baby. You're not fully cooked yet. But you're old enough to know that what you're doing is wrong. You don't have to be nobody's fool. You deserve to be treated like a queen. Do you understand what I'm saying?"

"Yes."

"Don't settle for anything less than what you're worth. And remember, what goes around comes around. How would you feel if the man you vowed to love, honor, and cherish betrayed you?"

"It would hurt."

"Yes, it would. So, get yourself together and stop this reckless behavior."

"Are you gonna tell the bishop?" Natasha was worried. Lance adored her, and she adored her pastor. She knew that if Lance found out what she'd been up to, he'd be disappointed.

"This ain't his business. For now, this is between me and you. But your secrets, Natasha, aren't mine to keep. If I find out that you're still acting stupid, we're gonna have a problem. And I don't know who the man's wife is, and I don't wanna know, but if she's anything like me . . ."

Natasha reflected back to Arykah boldly approaching her and Destiny. She reflected back to Arykah calling her a trick and stupid. She recalled Arykah pouring the hot sauce on the Doritos, then turning the bag upside down and eating from it. She could still hear Arykah's loud belch. "I hope she ain't nothing like you, Lady Arykah."

Arykah ran her foot from Lance's waist up to his chest, then upward to tickle his neck with her toes. The candles along the edge of the Jacuzzi tub served as the perfect romantic setting. The water was steaming, and bubbles danced all around them. Lance gently grabbed her foot and inserted her big toe in his mouth, then withdrew it.

Arykah melted. The bathroom was foggy and hot. The candles provided just enough light for Arykah to see Lance's eyes drinking her in. His forehead was wet. Streams of sweat ran from his eyebrows down to his chin. His dark chocolate complexion glistened against the candlelight.

At that moment, just looking at him, Arykah fell in love with her husband all over again. "Oh my God, you're so handsome," she said.

Lance smiled. "You think so?"

"I absolutely do." She watched as Lance inserted each of her toes, one by one, in his mouth and withdrew them, giving her toes a personal bath.

With his eyes Lance invited Arykah closer to him. She knew he was ready. Knew what he wanted. He needed her, and, at that moment, she craved his touch. She scooted across the tub and placed both of her legs outside of Lance's legs. He grabbed Arykah by the back of her hair and yanked her head backward, exposing her neck and lengthening it, giving himself complete access to it. Arykah purred like a kitten when he leaned forward and placed his tongue on her chin and ran it down her neck to her cleavage.

Lance played with Arykah's cleavage with his tongue, then looked up at her. "I love the way you taste, Cheeks. You ready for me?"

"Always," she moaned.

He drained the tub and took his wife to bed.

Chapter 13

At 4:00 P.M. Saturday afternoon, Darlita, Gladys, and Chelsea were seated at Catch 35 Seafood Restaurant in Naperville, Ill. Earlier in the week, Arykah had called each of the ladies and extended an invitation to join her for an early dinner. On the telephone, Arykah revealed that she had some exciting news to share.

Their first lady was running late so the ladies decided to order drinks while they waited for her to arrive.

"Did Lady Arykah tell either of you why she wanted to meet today?" Gladys asked Darlita and Chelsea.

Darlita shook her head. "Nope. She just said that she wanted to have dinner and share some good news, but I have no idea what it is. She was acting kind of mysterious."

"Well, all I know is," Chelsea started, "that she told me on last Sunday that she was putting something together and she wanted me to be a part of it."

"I have absolutely no idea what she's up to. I was quite surprised that she called me," Gladys added. "We all know that Lady Arykah isn't too friendly." She drank from a glass of raspberry iced tea.

"I beg to differ," said Chelsea. "I think Lady Arykah has her guard up. Each of us knows that we were told that we *had* to hate her. From the moment she got to Freedom Temple, the entire church sent her bad vibes. When I approached her and complimented her on her boots, she spoke to me like we had been friends for years."

"One thing I can say about Lady Arykah is that she gives some great advice," Darlita stated, reflecting back to when she had confided in Arykah about her cheating husband.

After telling Arykah that she wanted to divorce her husband because he was a serial cheater and refused to honor his wedding vows, Darlita left Arykah's office assured that she was doing the right thing by freeing herself from an unhealthy and unhappy marriage.

"And she stands her ground," Gladys added. "If she believes in something, she supports it. She shut Mother Pansie down about making unwed mothers stand before the church and ask for forgiveness."

"Really?" Darlita asked. "I know Mother Pansie was hot."

"Yep," Gladys chuckled. "When I told her that Lady Arykah said that Miranda didn't have to stand before the church, Mother Pansie ran up those steps to Lady Arykah's office so fast, all I saw was dust in the air behind her."

Chelsea laughed. "And knowing Lady Arykah, I'll bet you fifty bucks that Mother Pansie left that office with her tail between her legs."

"I'm not gonna bet you anything because with a grandbaby on the way, I need *all* my money," Gladys laughed.

"Well, all I have to say is that I'm glad Lady Arykah has come along. She is shaking things up at Freedom Temple but in a good way," Darlita said.

Chelsea drank from a glass of strawberry lemonade. "Lady Arykah got that classy swag going on. She's conservative but at the same time, she's down to earth."

"And I'd give anything to see her closet," Darlita added. "Is it just me or have either of you noticed that Lady Arykah has been at Freedom Temple for almost five months and she has yet to wear a repeater? I mean, how big can her closet be?"

"And her shoes. How in the world can she walk in those high heels?" Gladys wondered out loud. "She may as well be walking on stilts."

Darlita looked toward the entrance door of the restaurant and saw a lady talking to a waitress. She resembled Arykah, but Darlita dismissed the thought of it being Arykah because the lady had blond hair. But the more Darlita stared at the woman, the more she looked like Arykah. "Is that Lady Arykah over there?"

Chelsea and Gladys both turned to see the woman Darlita was speaking of. The waitress pointed in their direction. All three of their mouths fell open when Arykah turned around and started walking toward them.

"Oh my God," Gladys said. "It *is* her."

Arykah approached their table. "Hey, ladies. I'm glad y'all made it."

They couldn't speak. Chelsea, Gladys, and Darlita stared at Arykah like they had no clue who she was.

Arykah stood before them with a blond Farrah Fawcett wig on her head and wearing a pink T-shirt that read *Fat Is The New Skinny* in gold letters across the front. She also wore black jeggings which were denim jeans that clung to her legs like leggings. Five-inch pink stilettos were on her feet.

She saw how the ladies gawked at her. "Yes, it's me. Y'all can close your mouths now." Arykah sat down at the table.

Chelsea was the first to speak. "I can't believe it. You look totally different."

She was referring to Arykah's blond wig.

"Has the bishop seen you with your new look?" Darlita asked.

"Let me tell you something, Darlita," Arykah said, placing the linen napkin across her lap. "I gotta keep my marriage hot. It's my job to keep my man focused only on *me*. So, every now and then, I change it up a little. I can't allow my husband to become bored. A bored man will eventually stray."

"Amen to that," Gladys said. "Where was your advice before my husband strayed? Heck, I would've come home with a green clown's wig and a big round red plastic nose if that's all it took."

All the ladies laughed at Gladys's comment.

"You know what, Gladys?" Arykah started. "Men like variety. That's why their heads are always turning when a woman walks by. Bishop Lance is no different. He likes pretty women. *All* men do. But because I know that my husband is a true man, and men never vary from the script, I have to always keep him interested in *me*.

"Shoot, Bishop Lance doesn't know who'll be at home when he walks through that front door. On a Monday night, I'll be a French maid, uniform and all. On a Tuesday night, I'll be an Asian lady with a short black bob cut wig, wearing a kimono, bowing down to him with his slippers in my hand. On a Wednesday night, Bishop Lance could walk in the front door and see BoonQueesha wearing a bustier and fishnet stockings twirling around a stripper pole in the living room."

All three ladies screamed. Everyone in the restaurant looked in their direction.

"Who is BoonQueesha?" Gladys asked, covering her gaping mouth.

Arykah looked at Gladys with raised eyebrows and a dancing neck. "*I'm* BoonQueesha."

Gladys couldn't close her mouth. "Oh my goodness. Lady Arykah, you are too much."

"Chile, please," Arykah said. "There's way too much temptation in this world. Married men don't stand a chance with all the floozies running around. I swear to y'all that role playing works. If a wife is serious about her marriage and keeping her man at home, she has to be smart. She has to find ways to keep him interested. By role playing, a woman can make her man believe that he has options. He'll have the fantasy of being with another woman without cheating on his wife because his wife *is* that other woman."

"I heard *that*, Lady Arykah," Chelsea said. "I ain't married yet, but thanks for the 411. I'll know exactly what to do."

"And start a wig collection," Arykah advised. She flipped her wig from her shoulders.

"Tonight, I'll be one of Charlie's angels coming to rescue the bishop from a hostage situation."

Darlita laughed. "I love it."

"One thing I can say for sure, Lady Arykah," Chelsea started. "Bishop Lance has certainly changed for the better since he's been married. He's much more laid-back, and he doesn't seem to take things so seriously anymore."

"And the bishop smiles more too," Darlita added. "After Gwen died, he—" Darlita caught herself.

Chelsea and Gladys looked from Darlita to Arykah.

"It's okay, Darlita. You can talk about her," Arykah encouraged. "Bishop Lance has shared with me about Gwendolyn. I know he was engaged to her, and I know how she died. He told me about the accident. He said it nearly killed him mentally."

"I am so sorry, Lady Arykah. I didn't mean to bring Gwen's name up. I was just saying how much happier the bishop is now that you're in his life. After Gwen died, he shut himself down. He was depressed all the time."

"Tell me about Gwen. What was she like?" Arykah asked the ladies.

"Well, she wasn't anything like you, that's for sure," Chelsea stated.

"Gwen was the quiet type," Gladys added.

Arykah chuckled. "You don't think of me as the quiet type?"

"*Heck, no,*" Darlita said laughing. "I definitely wouldn't list you in the 'quiet type' category."

"You are the total opposite of Gwen," Chelsea said.

"In what way?" Arykah asked.

"In *every* way," Gladys answered. "Gwen was shy, timid, submissive—"

"I'm submissive," Arykah interrupted Gladys.

"I meant that Gwen was submissive to the mothers," Gladys said. "Mother Pansie and Mother Gussie loved Gwendolyn because she did everything they wanted her to do. They thought that she was the ideal woman for our bishop, and they trained her to be the perfect first lady."

"So, that's why I can't catch a break with those two. I don't bow down to them," Arykah said.

"It's *that,* and the way you carry yourself," Darlita offered. "You wouldn't catch Gwen in heels higher than two inches. She didn't wear false eyelashes. She didn't own a lot of bling. All of her skirts were below the knees.

"I remember a time when Gwendolyn came to church with a low-cut blouse on. I thought she was cute, but Mother Pansie quickly threw a sweater around her shoulders and buttoned it up to her neck. She told Gwen to show some respect in the sanctuary and as the bishop's fiancée. Then she told Gwen that she had to be more careful of what she wore to church."

Arykah looked at Darlita. "Girl, are you serious?"

"Yep," Darlita answered. "That's why the mothers are gunning for you. You don't allow them to control you like they controlled Gwen, and they don't know how to deal with that."

"Forget the deacons. The mothers ran the church until you came along," Gladys said.

"So, they'll probably drop dead when they see my blond Farrah Fawcett wig come Sunday morning, huh?" Arykah asked.

Chelsea laughed. "I can't wait."

The waiter came to the table to take the ladies' orders.

"Okay, girls. Tonight is on me, so order whatever you like," Arykah said happily.

Gladys, Chelsea, and Darlita were impressed when they saw the cheapest entree on the menu cost fifty dollars.

When the waiter walked away with their orders, Arykah gave each of the ladies a three-by-five envelope she had pulled from her pink authentic Hermes Birkin bag. They opened the envelopes and saw an invitation inside.

Darlita was the first to pull her invitation from her envelope. She read it out loud.

"You're invited to spend an evening with Lady Arykah at The Massage Palace. Come and be pampered from your head to your toes. Saturday, March 19th, 2012, at seven P.M. This is a red-carpet event. Stilettos provided by Lady Arykah."

"What?" Chelsea and Gladys squealed at the same time.

"Is this for real?" Darlita asked, rereading the invitation. She grinned from ear to ear.

"Of course," Arykah answered. They had given her the exact reaction she was looking for. The ladies were excited, and so was she.

"Oh, Lady Arykah, this is so nice of you to do this. I've never been to a spa," Gladys said.

"I'm speechless," Chelsea said. "Thank you so much. This is so unexpected."

"You're giving us stilettos?" Darlita asked excitedly. "Like the kind *you* wear?"

Arykah smiled. She couldn't wait to tell them. "We will be walking the red carpet in Christian Louboutins."

Darlita, Chelsea, and Gladys screamed, drawing attention to their table again. Arykah was especially excited, even more excited than the ladies were. She was more than happy to treat them to an evening of elegance and relaxation.

"All of you must be at my house by five P.M.," Arykah said. "I've hired a limousine to drive us. But before we head to the spa, we're gonna have a stiletto party. We will put our heels on and dance. And I've convinced the bishop to make us hors d'oeuvres."

"What?" Gladys couldn't believe it.

"This is ridiculous," Chelsea said.

"I'm still stuck on the Christian Louboutins," Darlita added. "Wait!" She held up both of her palms and looked at Arykah. "The stilettos are ours to keep, right?"

Arykah laughed out loud.

The following Friday morning, Arykah and her client Jeremy Montahue closed on the Belfor estate. After Jeremy had received his keys and was on his way to his new home, Arykah called the church to share the good news with Lance.

"Thank you for calling Freedom Temple. How may I help you?"

Arykah frowned. It wasn't Mother's Gussie's voice that had answered. She didn't recognize the female's voice at all. But Arykah did take notice that it was a much younger voice than Mother Gussie's.

"Hi. This is Lady Arykah."

"Who?"

What do you mean 'Who?' Arykah couldn't imagine anyone answering the church's telephone not knowing her name. *"Lady Arykah,"* she emphasized.

"Oh, Lady Arykah," the female voice repeated.

"Who am I speaking with?"

"I'm Sharonda."

That's it? No last name? During the five months that Arykah had been at Freedom Temple, she'd met the majority of the women. But she didn't remember the name Sharonda. "Is Mother Gussie there?"

"No, she won't be back for a while. I'm filling in for her until she feels better."

Since the day Arykah nearly dried Mother Gussie's throat with the tweed jacket, Mother Gussie hadn't been to work. She told Lance that she needed to take a few days off, but apparently she decided to take an extended vacation.

"Oh, I see," Arykah said. "Is the bishop available?"

"Yes and no," Sharonda responded.

Arykah frowned again. *Who is this broad?* "Excuse me?"

"The bishop is in his office with his door shut. He told me to put your call through if you called."

"Okay, well, guess what, Sharonda? *I'm calling,*" Arykah said sarcastically. She could've kicked herself for not calling Lance's cellular telephone and bypassing the craziness.

Moments later Lance was on the line. "Hi, Cheeks."

"Hi, yourself, handsome. I'm calling with good news."

"You closed the deal?"

A huge grin was displayed on Arykah's face. "Yep. It's done. Jeremy is on his way to his new home, and I can expect a very nice commission check next month. I'm meeting with Jeremy at the estate this afternoon. I've scheduled an interior designer to come out and take measurements of the windows in the home office."

Lance always heard the passion in Arykah's voice whenever she spoke of her work.

He remembered the mothers trying to convince him to make Arykah quit her job. They told Lance that a pastor's wife shouldn't work outside the home because the Bible said that it's a man's job to be the breadwinner.

In fact, Lance did bring the bread *and* the bacon home. The church paid him a hefty salary and owning a construction company afforded Lance the 5,600 square foot home that he and Arykah dwelled in. He didn't hold Arykah responsible for any household bills and the late-model Mercedes Benz she drove was Lance's wedding gift to her. He took care of his wife in every way imaginable.

Lance knew more than anyone how much Arykah enjoyed selling high-priced homes, and she lived to spend the commission checks she earned from them. She enjoyed the finer things in life. It was a great help to Lance when Arykah purchased her expensive designer bags, shoes, and clothes herself. Not only was her own walk-in closet maxed out, but Arykah had also stolen one-fourth of Lance's walk-in closet. And the four guest bedroom closets were also filled with dresses, shoes, and bags that Arykah had snuck into the home after telling Lance that she would curb her appetite for shopping.

Arykah had no idea that Lance knew about the guest closets. She was her happiest whenever she shopped. Lance figured that as long as Arykah could afford her own expensive addiction, he didn't have a problem with her earning her own money.

And Lance too benefited from Arykah's hard work. Diamond Rolex watches, alligator shoes, and Taylor-Made golf clubs were just a few of the lavish gifts that Arykah spoiled her husband with. He and Arykah both paid their tithes and offerings faithfully.

So, as far as Lance was concerned, the mothers of the church needed to sweep around their front door before they swept around his. Lance was happy, and his wife was ecstatic.

That's all that mattered to him. Arykah's priorities were in order. Therefore, Lance would allow her to shop until she dropped.

"I'm so proud of you, ba—"

Arykah noticed Lance had cut his words short. "No, thanks, Sharonda," Arykah heard him say; then Lance brought his attention back to his wife. "Sorry about that, Cheeks."

"Honey, who is Sharonda, and why is she answering the phone at the church?"

"Sharonda is Mother Gussie's granddaughter. She just showed up at the church this morning. Apparently Mother Gussie doesn't plan to return to work anytime soon.

"Sharonda said Mother Gussie asked her to fill in for her. It's not even noon, and she's already asked me seven times if I needed anything. I shut my door to give her a hint that I didn't want to be bothered, but evidently a closed door means nothing."

"I don't think I met her. Is she a member of Freedom Temple?"

"Yes, she is a member. She was recently released from prison. I told you about Sharonda, remember?"

Arykah tried to jog her memory. She couldn't recall the name. "No."

"Think back to the day when you called the church to thank me for sending you flowers to the realty office. Mother Gussie answered and refused to put your call through to me. She interrogated you about why you were calling."

"*That* I remember," Arykah said.

"When you told me about it, I mentioned that Mother Gussie harassed every woman who looked my way because, in her mind, she was saving me for her granddaughter, Sharonda. Sharonda was in prison when you and I met. Mother Gussie had this crazy plan to hook me up with Sharonda when she got paroled."

The more Lance talked, Arykah began to recall that conversation. "Oh yes. Now I remember. Sharonda has three children, right?"

"Yep. Her third child was delivered while she was in prison."

"So, Sharonda has a crush on you, huh?"

"She's had a crush on me for as long as I can remember, but Sharonda knows that I'm happily married and there is absolutely no chance of her and I getting together."

"Humph, she *better* know it," Arykah stated. The last thing she needed was someone else creating problems and trying to come between her and Lance. But just like she got Mother Gussie under control, Arykah would have no problem putting the granddaughter in her place as well.

Lance chuckled. "Calm down, Cheeks."

"This *is* calm," Arykah responded. "But I think Mother Gussie sent Sharonda there to cause trouble."

"Be that as it may, it still takes two to tango. And you're my only dancing partner."

"Sho' you right, Bishop. And if Sharonda tries to cut in on my dance, I'm gonna dance on her *#@."

Lance couldn't do anything but laugh at his wife. Her promise to God to stop cursing was often forgotten. But Lance had to admit that some of the things Arykah said and the way she said them were hilarious. "Listen to you," Lance said. "Now you gotta repent."

"I have no problem with repenting," Arykah confessed while rolling her eyes at no one in particular. "And I'll make sure to repent if I have to put my foot in Sharonda's—"

"Okay, okay," Lance cut Arykah's words short. "What am I gonna do with you?"

"You can lay hands on me."

Lance chuckled. He knew Arykah was being mischievous. "Holy hands?"

"Nope. Freaky hands."

When Arykah pulled her car into the driveway later that evening, she saw a large brown box on the front porch. She exited her car and walked up the steps. As she got closer to the box, Arykah saw that it had been shipped via the United Parcel Service.

"Yea, our stilettos are here," she squealed. Arykah opened the front door and tried to drag the box inside the foyer but found it to be too heavy to move. "Lance!" she called out.

Moments later, Lance appeared from the master bedroom. "You bellowed?"

Arykah stood in the archway of the front door and pointed to the box on the porch.

"Babe, I can't get this box inside."

"How many purses were you trying to sneak in this time?"

"These aren't purses," Arykah said. "These are shoes, and they're not for me."

"Sure they aren't," Lance said, picking up the box and bringing it inside.

"Well, only one pair is for me," she admitted. "The others are for Monique, Chelsea, Darlita, and Gladys." Before Arykah parted ways with the ladies last Saturday evening, she'd gotten their shoe sizes. When she had returned home, she went straight to her notebook, got online, and ordered their stilettos. She paid extra for the stilettos to arrive in time for the stiletto party.

Lance set the box on the living-room floor. Arykah opened the large brown box and saw five Christian Louboutin shoe boxes inside. She squealed in delight, then clapped her hands together and sang, "Cakes and pies, cakes and pies." That was Arykah's favorite chant whenever things fell into place.

"That's a shame," Lance said. "Getting so excited over shoes. I don't get it."

Arykah looked for a size eight on the shoe boxes. "That's because you're not a woman, Lance. I don't expect you to understand." When she had found her size, she opened the box, looked inside, and squealed again.

For herself, Arykah purchased the style called the Pigalili, a boutique exclusive. The material on the stilettos was made of specchio leather and strauss. The entire length of the stilettos were beaded with silver authentic Swarovski crystals. Arykah thought the shoes were worth every bit of the $3,545 she had paid for them. She pulled one stiletto from the box and held it up to show Lance the signature red leather bottom sole. "See that, honey?"

Lance looked at the sole of the shoe but didn't see anything spectacular about it. He shrugged his shoulders. "Yeah, so?"

"What, are you blind? These are Christian Louboutins, Lance."

He just didn't get Arykah's excitement over the shoes. "Cheeks, if you like them, then I love them." Lance shrugged his shoulders again, then went back to the bedroom.

"Lord, forgive him. He doesn't know any better," Arykah murmured. She opened the other shoe boxes and was just as blown away at Monique's, Gladys's, Darlita's, and Chelsea's shoes, all different styles. Arykah couldn't wait until the ladies arrived the next evening. She thought that it wouldn't be a bad idea to have a paramedic on the premises because a heart attack or two may arise when they opened their gifts.

Arykah pulled the shipping receipt from the bottom of the large brown box. Five pairs of Christian Louboutins had cost her nearly $17,000. But Arykah didn't care about the cost. She was looking forward to having a fun evening with her new friends.

Arykah woke up Saturday morning to hammering and banging. When she saw that she was in the bedroom alone, she got out of bed in search of Lance. She put her robe on and left the master bedroom. The closer she got to the kitchen, the louder the hammering became. In the kitchen, Arykah saw men hard at work gluing tiles above the stove and installing a new hood.

Lance snuck behind Arykah and wrapped his arms around her. "Good morning, sleepyhead."

Arykah smiled when Lance pressed his face against the crook of her neck. "Good morning. What's all this?"

"This," Lance started, "is getting my beautiful kitchen back in working order. I'm feeding you and your guests this evening. I haven't prepared a meal in almost three weeks. I feel like a fish out of water."

"I know. And I probably lost a few pounds."

Lance wrapped his arms tighter around her waist. "Well, I can't let that happen. I love you just the way you are. Nice and fluffy."

After the men had left and Lance had his kitchen back, he prepared homemade waffles and deep fried chicken wings for himself and Arykah.

"Why is it that I'm the only one gaining weight from all of the cooking you do?" Arykah asked licking maple syrup from her lips. "I swear I'm a dress size larger than I was when we got married. You eat just as much as I do, Lance, if not more than me."

"I have a secret to keeping fit."

"What's the secret?"

"Exercising. A few hours after my food digests, I'll run a few miles. You wanna join me?"

Arykah slouched down in her chair and belched. "Uh-uh. You could've kept that secret."

Chapter 14

Arykah was running around the house like a chicken with its head cut off. Everything had to be perfect for when the ladies arrived that evening. Monique wasn't a stranger to the Howell house, but Chelsea, Gladys, and Darlita would be visiting for the very first time.

Arykah had heard the rumors that had been flowing around the church about how massive the bishop and Lady Arykah's home was. The associate ministers, the deacons, and the finance committee were the only church members that had stepped foot inside of their home when Lance held meetings and prepared a feast. Arykah knew that the ladies, aside from Monique, were coming to get an eye full, to see for themselves how she and Lance lived.

In the living room, Arykah looked all around. Everything was in its place. She glanced at the glass cocktail table. It was shining and smudge free. The mantle above the fireplace displayed a neat row of photos of Arykah and Lance from their wedding and honeymoon in Jamaica. The grandfather clock stood tall next to the fireplace, and the pendulum swung back and forth.

"Is the staircase to your liking, Mrs. Howell?"

Arykah looked toward the winding staircase. An elderly Polish woman stood at the base of the steps with a dust rag in one hand and a bottle of Murray's wood oil soap in the other. The wood flooring shined so bright that Arykah could see her reflection. She walked up the steps, then walked back down looking for any spot on the railing that hadn't been polished.

"Great job, Graciela." Arykah was well pleased.

The mahogany floors were shining and the winding staircase was sparkling. Arykah paid Graciela handsomely for her services, tipped her well, then sent her on her way. Next, Arykah went into the kitchen to check on Lance. She saw him standing at the stove with his white chef's hat on and a matching apron with the words *Chef Lancelot* embroidered on the upper left side.

"How's it going, Chef?" Arykah asked, sneaking a peek at what Lance was creating.

The aroma in the kitchen was delightful. Arykah saw milk chocolate melting in a sauce pan. "Ooh, chocolate. That's my favorite. What are you gonna do with it, honey?"

"That's for the chocolate-covered sliced apples."

Arykah frowned. She'd never heard of chocolate-covered apples. "Apples? Not strawberries?"

Lance went to the refrigerator and pulled out a tray of the first batch of sliced chocolate-covered apples he had already prepared. He took one from the tray and brought it to Arykah's lips. "Take a bite."

Arykah bit into the apple and could've sworn that she'd bitten into a piece of heaven. "Um, this is so good. I never thought of mixing apples with chocolate."

"The key," Lance said. "is the green Granny Smith apples. They are the same apples that are used for taffy apples."

"Oh, so that's the tang I taste?" Arykah asked.

"Yep, the sour taste of the apple blended with the sweet taste of the milk chocolate makes the whole thing pop."

"Very creative, babe. What else are you serving this evening?"

"I got a surprise for you," Lance said smiling.

Arykah returned the smile. "You know I like surprises."

Lance grabbed her by her hand and pulled her to the large center island. Arykah saw a white cardboard box sitting in the middle of the island. She had seen the box earlier that morning but thought nothing of it. It wasn't often, but whenever Lance was called upon to cater an event, he used white cardboard boxes to transport food. Arykah hadn't given the white box on the center island any thought.

Lance opened the box and told Arykah to look inside.

"Oh my God! Babe, when did you—? How did you—? Where did you get these?" Arykah couldn't believe what she saw inside the box.

Lance laughed out loud. "I think that's the first time that I've seen you at a loss for words."

Inside the white box were two dozen high-heeled-shaped cookies decorated in various colors of frosting. Arykah picked up a stiletto cookie with yellow frosting. "How cute is this." She picked up another stiletto cookie with red and white frosting. "These are fab, babe. Where did you get these?"

"From the cookie lady at church," Lance said.

"Sister Ethel Avery?"

"Yep. She sells cakes, cookies, and pies every Sunday after church."

"Honey, I know all about Ethel's sweet treats. I'm one of her biggest customers, but I didn't know she could get down like *this*," Arykah said biting into a cookie. "Oh, this is so good." She looked at Lance. "These are shortbread cookies. Did you know that?"

"Of course I did," he responded with a sure smile on

his face. "Isn't it my job to know that shortbread cookies are your favorite?"

"Honey, you are too much." Arykah kissed Lance's lips softly and looked inside the box again and was amazed at how detailed the stiletto cookies were designed. Some were decorated with edible crystals. Arykah saw a high-heeled shoe boot with edible shoestrings. "Ethel has outdone herself. I will definitely be sure to thank her personally at church tomorrow."

"Take a look at these," Lance said, pointing to a Chinese takeout container that sat on the counter. It was filled with what Arykah thought were lollipops wrapped in plastic.

"What are those?" she asked, already moving toward the container.

Lance pulled a treat from the container. "These are cakes on sticks. Ethel made these too. She put small bite-size balls of cake on sticks and decorated them with frosting and—"

"And put them in plastic, then placed them in a Chinese takeout container," Arykah completed Lance's statement. "I can't get over how creative Ethel is besides cakes and pies. I just had no idea. Did you pay her?"

"Of course, I paid her."

"How much?" Arykah asked Lance.

"Why?"

Arykah looked at how gorgeous the stiletto cookies and cakes on sticks were. "Because I'm going to double it. For this kind of creativity, Ethel deserves it."

Monique was the first of the ladies to arrive at Arykah's home.

"Hey, doll," Arykah greeted her with outstretched arms.

"Hey, blondie," Monique returned the greeting referring to Arykah's new blond wig.

She stepped in Arykah's foyer and embraced her best friend. "You are looking too cute."

For the evening, Arykah donned stonewashed skinny jeans and a lilac wrap top.

"Thank you. Come on in."

Monique followed Arykah into the living room and saw it empty of guests. "Am I the first to arrive?"

"Yep," Arykah said, plopping down on the sofa. "You just missed Lance."

"How is the bishop doing these days without a secretary?" Monique asked, sitting on the sofa opposite from Arykah.

"Humph! As of yesterday he has a new church secretary. A *young* church secretary."

Monique's eyebrows rose. "Really? Who?"

"Mother Gussie's granddaughter. Her name is Sharonda."

"Mother Gussie isn't coming back? Did she quit?"

"Girl, who knows what Mother Gussie is doing? I found out yesterday when I called the church and Sharonda answered. She didn't know who I was, and I surely didn't know who she was. But I do know that she has a crush on Lance and has had a crush on him for years."

"Who told you that?" Monique asked.

"Lance did. Sharonda was paroled recently."

"Paroled? What was she incarcerated for?"

"I don't know. Do you remember that time when I called to tell you how Mother Gussie disrespected me when I called the church to thank Lance for the flowers he sent me after our first date?"

"Yeah," Monique nodded.

"Well, Lance said that Mother Gussie had high hopes of him and Sharonda getting together when she got released from prison. She saw me as a threat."

Monique shook her head from side to side. "Arykah, please. Are you serious?"

"I finally got Mother Gussie to back off of me, and now her granddaughter appears out of the blue."

"You know what I think?" Monique said. "I think since you put fear in Mother Gussie's heart, she purposely sent Sharonda, who she knows has a crush on Lance, to start some crap."

"Yep," Arykah nodded. "I told Lance that. But, honey, I ain't gonna fret one bit, because if Sharonda tries to cross me, I'll snatch her."

Monique laughed out loud. "Would you snatch her, girl?"

Arykah lowered her head and glared at Monique as if she were a stranger. "Excuse me. Have we met? Don't act like you don't know me, Monique. I will snatch Sharonda so fast, she'll get a crook in the side of her neck." Arykah raised her hand in the air, closed her fist, then quickly brought her arm down, demonstrating just how she'll do it. "Chile, I'll snatch a broad in a hot second."

Monique laughed at her best friend again. "Girl, you are nuts."

The telephone rang. It was the guard at the gate again announcing to Arykah that she had more guests. Arykah told the guard to send them through. Five minutes later, Arykah greeted the ladies at the door. When she opened it, Chelsea, Gladys, and Darlita were standing on the porch.

"Hello, ladies. Welcome. Come on in." Arykah stepped aside to allow the ladies inside. "The three of you just happened to arrive at the same time?"

"We chose to carpool," Gladys answered while taking in the view of the marble floor in the foyer. A very large letter H, painted in black, was embedded on the floor just inside the entrance of the door.

"Give me your coats," Arykah said as the three women made their way inside.

"This is so beautiful," Chelsea complimented when she saw the winding staircase.

"And big," Darlita added, looking all around. "Extremely big."

"Thanks, ladies," Arykah said, and hung their coats in the front hall closet. "We have about two hours before the limo gets here." She waved her hand to the ladies indicating that they should follow her. "Come on. Monique is already here."

Arykah brought the ladies into the living room. "Everyone knows Monique, right?"

"Of course," Darlita responded, and made her way toward Monique. "Hi, it's good to see you."

Monique stood and embraced Darlita. "How are you doing?" When Monique saw Darlita, she remembered her as the woman who was having marital problems. Up until that moment, she couldn't place her face when Arykah mentioned her name last week on the telephone.

Gladys greeted Monique next with a hug and a smile. "Monique, you get prettier every time I see you."

Monique was surprised by Gladys's comment. The two had only acknowledged each other in passing. They had never been introduced to each other. Monique assumed she was guilty by association. Because the women at Freedom Temple hated Arykah, being her personal assistant and best friend, Monique was also on the receiving end of snarls and stares. "Thank you, Gladys. That's a nice thing to say."

"You're Adonis's girlfriend, right?"

Monique broke from Gladys's embrace and looked to her left where the question had come from. Chelsea stood about three feet from her. Monique held up her left hand to show Chelsea her three carat princess cut diamond platinum wedding ring. "Actually, I'm his wife."

Chelsea took a step backward. She seemed surprised by Monique's statement. *"His wife?* Really?"

Monique looked into Chelsea's eyes. "Really."

"Oh, wow. I never would've guessed Adonis was married."

What the heck is this tramp trying to imply? Monique knew there was a reason she didn't care for Chelsea. She told Arykah that she was trouble. "You don't have to guess anything. Adonis wears his wedding band every day."

"No, I don't think he does," Chelsea countered. "A wedding ring is the first thing I look for when I see a fine man like Adonis."

"Well, look again," Monique said sarcastically.

"Hey, guess what, ladies?" Arykah said before Chelsea could respond to Monique's last statement. She, Darlita, and Gladys were standing near Monique and Chelsea as they exchanged words. Clearly Chelsea implied that either she was interested in Adonis or Adonis gave off vibes that he wasn't a married man.

Arykah knew the latter was untrue. She knew Adonis very well. Arykah considered him as her brother. Arykah also knew what Adonis had to go through to get Monique.

He had sacrificed his relationship with his first cousin when he'd stolen Monique's heart from him. Even before Arykah knew that Adonis was in love with Monique, she, herself, was smitten with him. But Adonis only had eyes for Monique; therefore, Arykah had to back off. There was no way Adonis would jeopardize his marriage. Monique was his everything.

"Bishop Lance prepared some appetizers for us. Let's all go into the kitchen."

"Can you take us on a tour of the house first, Lady Arykah?" Darlita asked. She had been waiting all week long to see if the rumors about the bishop's house were true.

"Oh yes, take us on a tour," Chelsea said.

Monique sat down on the sofa. She sized Chelsea up from her feet to her face. She was built like a bitter grapefruit. Chelsea was yellow in complexion with freckles on her face and neck. She was also wide and round. *I'm gonna have to watch this chick*, Monique thought.

"Okay, sure," Arykah responded to both Chelsea and Darlita's request. "First, I'll take you ladies down to the lower level to see the bishop's gym and the home theater."

"Home theater?" Gladys asked. "This really *is* a mansion."

Monique opted to stay seated on the sofa in the living room. She was a regular at the Howell home, so she didn't feel the need to follow Arykah around on the tour. Monique didn't wanna be bothered with Chelsea anyway. Chelsea had motives. Her aura was suspect and questionable. Monique thought that it was only a matter of time before Arykah realized that Chelsea wanted more than just a hookup to get fitted boots. She had an agenda.

"Oh, my goodness. Would you look at the size of that screen?" Gladys said as soon as Arykah opened the door to the home theater. "I've never seen anything so big. What size is it?" she asked Arykah.

"That's a wall projector," Arykah answered. "But I have no clue what size it is. I'd have to ask the bishop."

Darlita sat down in one of the ten oversized plush La-Z-Boy recliners. "Oh, wow. I could get used to this."

"Do you and the bishop spend a lot of time in this room?"

"The bishop much more than me," Arykah answered Chelsea's question. "He and I try to do a movie night at least once a week, but this is definitely his hangout on Saturday and Sunday afternoons. Whenever you see the bishop rushing me out of the church doors after the benediction, he's usually trying to get home to some kind of game. Monique and I are often forgotten for hours while he and Adonis yell at that big screen."

"So, Adonis spends a lot of time here, huh?" Chelsea asked.

What's up with this broad and all the questions? Arykah wondered. "Well, he *and* his wife, Monique. You remember her, right? The woman upstairs in my living room. She's Adonis's wife." Arykah wanted to make it perfectly clear to Chelsea that whatever game she was playing or whatever plot she was brewing wasn't going to work. "Monique is my very best friend, and because she and I are close, the bishop and Adonis have become good friends as well."

"Amen," Gladys murmured. She knew exactly what Chelsea was doing and she understood where Arykah was coming from.

After the tour of the home theater and gym, Arykah took the ladies back up to the main level to the master bedroom. When Arykah opened the double doors she heard all three ladies gasp at the same time.

"All I gotta say, Lady Arykah, is that I wanna be just like you when I grow up."

Arykah laughed at Darlita. "Your king will come, Darlita."

"Yeah, but I gotta get rid of the frog first."

"I do believe that my entire two-bedroom apartment would fit inside this one room," Gladys said. "This is crazy huge."

"And look at how big this bed is," Chelsea said before sitting on the chocolate-colored silk comforter and lying down on it. "Is this a California king-sized bed?"

What the—??? No, this tramp ain't lying on my bed. "Get up from my bed, Chelsea," Arykah demanded.

"Chelsea, what is *wrong* with you?" Gladys asked her. "Why would you even think of lying on their bed?"

Chelsea stood from the bed. "So, this is where the action happens, huh, Lady Arykah? Can the bishop lay it down in the bedroom like he lays it down in the pulpit?"

Darlita gasped. "Oh my God."

"Girl, are you high?" Gladys couldn't believe Chelsea's gall. *How dare she come into their pastors' home and disrespect it? Chelsea's inappropriate behavior is exactly why black folks aren't invited to nice places,* Gladys thought. She was embarrassed. "I can't believe you just asked Lady Arykah that question. Where is the respect?"

Chelsea looked at Arykah. She really didn't mean to be disrespectful. "I'm sorry, Lady Arykah. I don't know what came over me. I was so excited to be here and be a part of your evening that I lost control. Please forgive me. I never intended to overstep my bounds with you, and I certainly didn't intend to disrespect you or your home in any way."

Had it only been she and Chelsea present, Arykah would have gone to war with her.

Arykah would have told Chelsea about herself and maybe even dismissed Chelsea from her home altogether.

It was obvious that Chelsea had a problem. Maybe she had an attention deficit disorder, or Chelsea could very well be bipolar. Arykah didn't know what her issue was at that moment, but it was clear to everyone that Chelsea was a little off balance. From the moment she entered Arykah's front door, her mood, tone, and behavior suggested that she lacked common sense.

Arykah didn't know why Chelsea was acting out. Maybe Chelsea felt comfortable misbehaving because Arykah had shared with the ladies how she role-played for Lance. From now on, Arykah would be very careful what she shared with anyone. "It's okay, Chelsea. You just need to calm down," Arykah said. "Lying on my bed wasn't a cool thing to do, though."

Gladys and Darlita stood in the middle of Arykah's bedroom wondering what Chelsea would do next. Both of them felt that Arykah would've been justified if she asked Chelsea to leave her home. But the three of them carpooled in Darlita's car. If Arykah put Chelsea out, she'd have to find her own transportation home because neither Darlita nor Gladys was going to miss out on what Lady Arykah promised to be an evening to remember.

"I apologize, Lady Arykah." Chelsea looked from Arykah to Darlita and Gladys. "I apologize to all of you."

"You should apologize to Monique too, Chelsea," Gladys advised. "She doesn't know you from a can of paint, but you came at her from a bad angle. You basically implied that her husband isn't acting like he's married."

"You're right, Gladys. I'll go and talk to Monique right now."

Arykah, Darlita, and Gladys all watched Chelsea leave the bedroom.

"Wow," Darlita said when she was sure that Chelsea was out of hearing range.

Gladys chuckled. "Lady Arykah, I wish you could've seen the look on your own face when Chelsea plopped down on your bed. Your mouth fell open."

"She almost got jumped on," Arykah laughed. "But I'm trying to stay in first-lady mode."

"Can we move on to your closet, Lady Arykah?"

Huh? Arykah panicked. She wanted to play dumb and ignore Darlita, but Arykah had clearly heard her question. Arykah's pleasure chest was in her closet. She knew the ladies would want to see the house but Arykah never thought Darlita would ask to see her closet. "My closet?"

"Yep, that's what I wanna see. Chelsea, Gladys, and I were talking last week at the restaurant and your wardrobe came up. We were saying that in the six months you've been at Freedom Temple, you haven't worn a repeater. I know your closet has to be gigantic." Darlita was honest about being nosy.

Being a pastor's wife put Arykah under a microscope. And it was no secret that she loved to dress nicely. Indeed, she was a shopaholic and had plenty of dresses, suits, and skirts for church. Arykah was exquisite and "vanity" was her middle name. But she had no idea that folks were watching her that closely to know that she hadn't worn a repeater in six months. She herself really hadn't paid that much attention and didn't do it intentionally.

Darlita noticed Arykah's hesitation. "Come on, Lady Arykah. We know you got some fly threads. Are you gonna show us your closet or what?"

"Uh, sure," Arykah said. She didn't mind Gladys and Darlita seeing her clothes, handbags, and shoes. Her pleasure chest was hidden in her closet beneath long dresses. Arykah didn't know what she would do if either Gladys or Darlita saw the chest and asked what was in it. Exposing the reality that she and Lance were total freaks was something that she would never do. Because of what just happened with Chelsea, Arykah didn't know what she'd do if the ladies found out about the props she and Lance entertained themselves with. Their toys and battery-operated gadgets had to remain their secret. She prayed the chest wouldn't be seen.

Arykah stepped to her walk-in closet door and pressed her left thumb against a black magnet that was mounted beneath the door handle. Gladys and Darlita saw a red light on the magnet turn to green, then they heard a click.

"You have *got* to be kidding me." Gladys was dumbfounded when Arykah turned the doorknob and pulled it open. "Only *your* thumbprint will open the door?"

"That's right, Gladys," Arykah answered. "A girl needs her private sanctuary."

"So, the bishop can't get in here?" Darlita asked.

"Nope. He has his office for his personal space, and I have my closet that I use for my private time with God. The bishop's closet is next to mine."

"He has a lock on his office door?" Gladys asked.

Arykah looked into Gladys's eyes. "Chile, please. He knows better. There's only one door in this house that locks, and it's *my* closet."

Darlita walked into Arykah's closet with her mouth open wide. Her eyes were the size of golf balls. She tried to see all of the contents of the closet in one glance but couldn't do it. Darlita looked all around as though she were a child entering Walt Disney World for the first time. The closet was the size of a large bedroom. Dresses, slacks, and blouses, some with tags dangling from sleeves, hung on wooden hangers. The same exact hangers that Darlita had seen on the racks at Saks Fifth Avenue and Nordstrom's.

In the middle of the closet was an island with rose-colored granite. Drawers were all around the island, and Darlita guessed they held Arykah's jewelry, belts, scarves, and undergarments. At the far end of the closet was a floor-to-ceiling mirror covering an entire wall.

All of Arykah's shoes, two hundred pairs, were in glass shoe boxes. Twenty shoe boxes were stacked on ten racks. Darlita saw that the highest rack was over eight feet tall, but she didn't see a ladder anywhere in the closet. "How on earth do you get to the shoes on the top rack?"

Arykah pressed a button on the wall just inside the closet. The racks started to rotate.

Gladys stood in disbelief as she watched the racks move. They put her in the mind of the big spinning wheel on *The Price Is Right*. When the highest rack had lowered to Darlita's waist level, Arykah pushed the button on the wall again. The racks stopped moving.

"That's how," she said to Darlita.

"I've never seen anything quite like this," Gladys said. "What gave you the idea of putting a revolving shoe rack in your closet?"

"I watch the HGTV Channel faithfully. I'm always amazed at the latest designs and gadgets they put in new homes. If I see something that I like, I get it. The revolving shoe rack was installed after I almost fell off a ladder while trying to reach a shoe box that was way too high."

Darlita looked at all of Arykah's shoes through the glass boxes and noticed something about them. "Lady Arykah, not one heel is lower than five inches."

"The taller the heel, the sexier I feel," Arykah stated.

"But how can you walk in them?"

"Every stiletto isn't made for walking, Gladys." Arykah opened a glass shoe box and pulled out a black stiletto. It had a six-and-a-half-inch heel with a two-inch platform. The stiletto was designed by Jessica Simpson. "For instance," she said, "this style is called the Beckery. This right here wasn't made for walking. The pair came with instructions. You're supposed to put them on when you get to your destination, then sit down, cross your legs, and look stunning. I may be able to walk in these to the ladies' room if it's close, but the the Beckery design is definitely a 'sit-down' type of stiletto."

"Is there a certain type of class you take for learning how to walk in heels that high?" Darlita asked. The heel Arykah held in her hand was longer than half of a ruler. She just couldn't imagine balancing herself on them.

"Girl, no," Arykah chuckled. "Practice makes perfect. You wanna know what I do to practice? I clean house in my stilettos."

Gladys's mouth dropped open for the third time that evening. Arykah was blowing her mind. "You do *what?*"

"I vacuum, I wash clothes, I mop the kitchen floor, and I dust in my stilettos. And there is nothing sexier than walking up steps in stilettos. That's what Bishop Lance told me."

Darlita sighed. "My, my, my. The things you learn when you come to the first lady's house."

Monique and Chelsea appeared at the closet door. "What's going on in here?" Monique asked.

Arykah glanced at them both. She was so busy entertaining Darlita and Gladys she had forgotten that Chelsea went to apologize to Monique. "Are y'all okay?" Arykah asked them both.

Chelsea looked at Monique and smiled. Then she looked at Arykah. "Yep, we're cool."

Arykah checked Monique's face for confirmation. When Monique smiled, Arykah spoke. "Okay, well, let us all go and enjoy the treats the bishop prepared for us."

Arykah knew her best friend well. Monique's smile was forced, but, at that moment, Arykah couldn't question her about the conversation between her and Chelsea. Arykah would have to wait until the evening ended.

"Lady Arykah, this is absolutely stunning," Chelsea said when she entered the kitchen.

The cherry wood cabinets complimented the gray-colored granite countertops extremely well. Floor-to-ceiling windows in the great room could be seen from the kitchen. Top-of-the-line stainless steel appliances and dark wood flooring was a sight to see for the ladies.

"I could've sworn that I've seen this kitchen in the *Home & Garden* magazine," Gladys stated. "Did you decorate this kitchen yourself, Lady Arykah?"

"No, I can't take the credit. This home was completely done when I sold it to Bishop Lance."

Gladys, Chelsea, and Darlita gasped.

Clearly Arykah's statement was news to them. "Y'all didn't know that?" Arykah asked.

"No, we didn't," Chelsea said. "At least I didn't know it."

"Neither did I," Gladys confirmed.

"Same here," Darlita chimed in.

"That's how we met. All of you do know that I'm in real estate, right?" The three ladies nodded their heads. "Yes, we know that, but we didn't know that you were the agent that sold the bishop his home. He had announced to the church that he was searching for a larger home than the one he was living in," Darlita stated.

"I was at church that Sunday when he made the announcement," Chelsea said.

"Bishop Lance also said that he felt that the Lord was getting ready to bless him with his Eve," Gladys added. "And he said that he had to get ready for her."

Arykah knew exactly what Gladys was talking about when she said that Lance had announced that he had to get ready for his Eve. Arykah remembered that night when she had driven, in the pouring rain, to Lance's home after Monique told her that she was going to marry Boris. Arykah got so upset at Monique that she stormed out of Monique's house and sped to Lance's new home, the same home she now resides in.

She was soaking wet when she arrived, and Arykah recalled Lance taking her to his master bedroom and showing her a closet full of ladies' clothes and shoes. Lance led Arykah to the master bath where she saw every toiletry that a woman could desire. Arykah asked Lance why he had clothes and toiletries for a woman when he wasn't married. It was then that Lance stated that he was preparing to receive his wife. Days later, Arykah learned that Lance had been preparing to receive her.

Arykah had a change of heart and decided to support Monique's marriage to Boris. But that marriage never happened.

Darlita nodded her head. "Uh-huh. And when he said that he felt that the Lord was getting ready to bless him with his Eve, all the single ladies at church sat straight up on the pews. Everyone knows that Bishop Lance is as fine as aged wine, and he had women coming at him from all directions."

Chelsea chuckled. "Oh my goodness, Lady Arykah. There was this one chick who wanted to sink her claws into Bishop Lance so bad that every Sunday, when it was offering time, she would take her tithes, always cash, and walk right past the basket the deacons held next to the altar. Instead of placing her money in the basket, she walked into the pulpit and put her money in the bishop's hands."

"Are you serious?" Monique asked.

"Yeah, that really happened," Gladys laughed. "And after about four or five Sundays of her doing this, the bishop told the finance committee to just pass the offering baskets up and down the pews."

"Wow, the lengths that women go to just to land themselves a preacher," Arykah stated. "It's so sad."

"No, what was really sad was how no one acknowledged you, Lady Arykah, when Bishop Lance came to church one Sunday morning and announced that he had gotten married in Jamaica the week before. You were sitting on the front pew, but no one knew who you were. And right after praise and worship, Bishop Lance stood and walked to the microphone in the pulpit. He opened up by saying how God allowed us second chances in life."

Listening to Gladys speak of her very first day at Freedom Temple as lady elect brought back the scene to Arykah's mind.

When she and Lance woke up that Sunday morning and were getting ready for church, Arykah was so nervous. She knew that Lance was going to announce to his congregation that he was no longer a single man.

"And what he meant by second chances," Chelsea started, "was that he had lost Gwen, the love of his life, in a terrible car accident. Bishop Lance told us how he had given up on finding a woman whom he could cherish forever because he thought that Gwen was God's chosen one for him. And after being single for years, he really didn't think that finding true love, getting married, and having a family would happen for him."

"And that's when he asked me to stand," Arykah said.

"Yep, and when you stood up, everybody was whispering, 'Who is she?'" Darlita remembered.

Thinking back on that day made Arykah nervous all over again. "My feet were shaking, and my hands were shaking. Everything was shaking. I didn't even want to turn around and look into the members' faces because I knew what was coming out of the bishop's mouth next."

"Then he said it," Gladys said. "As soon as you stood up, Bishop Lance said," she paused. The kitchen was quiet for about five seconds. "He said," Gladys started, then paused again and looked at everyone in the kitchen.

"This is my wife, Lady Arykah Miles," Arykah, Darlita, and Chelsea sang together.

Monique wasn't present at Freedom Temple that Sunday morning when Lance introduced Arykah as his wife. She and Adonis had decided to stay in Jamaica and enjoy their honeymoon another week after the wedding. They flew back to Chicago the Monday after Lance's announcement. "Wow, I could just imagine everyone's faces."

"I held my breath," Arykah said to Monique. "I thought I was gonna pass out."

Darlita laughed. "I think the mothers *did* faint."

Arykah rolled her eyes. "And they've been giving me grief ever since that day, but I don't wanna talk about the mothers right now. This is a stress-free evening."

"I know that's right," Chelsea said while at the same time admiring the stove. "Um, Lady Arykah, I know Bishop Lance is a skilled chef, but how many burners does he really need?"

All of the ladies chuckled.

"Seriously though," Chelsea chuckled with everyone else. "Does he ever have all six burners going at the same time?"

"Actually, he does have them all going at once," Monique answered. "I've witnessed Bishop Lance have collard greens simmering in one pot and sweet potatoes boiling in another pot. At the same time, he was frying chicken in a skillet and frying sweet corn in another skillet. On one of the rear burners, he had a wok going with vegetable stir-fry, and he used the other rear burner to steam rice."

Listening to Monique caused Darlita's stomach to growl. "My Lord, my Lord. I have heard that Bishop Lance was no joke when he was in the kitchen."

"Well, look what he made for us," Arykah said, directing the ladies' attention to the goodies on the center island.

Stuffed artichokes, twice-baked potatoes, chicken marsala, string bean casserole, Swedish meatballs, and Lance's secret recipe for sweet potato cream cheese pie was what he provided for the ladies.

"Oh, wow, look at this feast," Gladys said.

Darlita was famished. She eyeballed the stuffed artichokes. "I feel like royalty."

They oohed and aahed over the feminine treats. The stiletto shaped cookies were a huge hit.

"Sister Ethel Avery made the cookies and the cakes on sticks," Arykah revealed.

Monique knew Ethel. She had bought a few cakes from her. "No, really?"

"Can you believe it? Aren't they cute and dainty?" Arykah asked the ladies about the decorative cookies.

"Yes, they are," Darlita answered.

"Bishop Lance made his special chocolate sauce, and I want you all to try something."

Arykah went to the refrigerator, opened it, and pulled out two trays of chocolate-covered apples. She set the trays on the center island, next to the food, and told the ladies to try them.

"Simply delicious," Chelsea moaned when she bit into a chocolate covered apple.

Darlita enjoyed the sour taste of the apple blended with the sweet chocolate. "Lady Arykah, how do you do it? How do you stay away from the bishop's cooking? If I were you, I'd be as big as a house."

"I *am* as big as a house, Darlita, because I *don't* stay away from his cooking."

"No, you're not," Gladys said. "You're not big. Wait 'til we get to church tomorrow and I'll show you big."

Chelsea laughed. "You're talking about Barbara Brewer, Gladys?"

"Now *she's* a big broad," Darlita said. "Her nickname is 'Heavy.'"

Monique frowned. She weighed 265 lbs. and wore a size twenty-two W. She was extremely heavy, and Monique would be heartbroken if anyone called her that as a nickname. "That's cruel."

"Barbara gave herself that nickname," Chelsea replied.

Monique didn't understand. "What woman would do that?"

"A woman with low self-esteem who is embarrassed by her size and is quick to make fun of herself before someone else does it," Arykah answered. "It's called 'beating them to the punch.' It softens the blow. Been there, done that."

The ladies prepared their plates and drinks before heading into the formal dining room. Arykah had place cards in the shape of stilettos created with each of the ladies' names on them.

"These are cute," Gladys mumbled to herself when she had seen her name on a place card before she set her plate of food on the table. She screamed shortly afterward when she pulled her chair from beneath the table and saw a Christian Louboutin shoe box on the seat. *"Oh my God!"*

Monique, Chelsea, and Darlita came into the dining room from the kitchen with their plates of food to see what Gladys was carrying on about.

"Look in your chairs," Gladys told them excitedly.

Arykah came into the dining room with her camera to capture the moment when everyone saw their gifts in their chairs.

Darlita screamed out next when she saw the shoe box in her chair. Arykah was able to get a snapshot with Darlita's tonsils showing. Chelsea let out a shriek when she saw her shoe box in her chair. Arykah snapped Chelsea's face when her eyeballs popped out of her head.

"You did it anyway," Monique said to Arykah. She had tried to talk Arykah out of buying such expensive shoes for the ladies, but when Monique saw a Christian Louboutin shoe box in her chair as well, she was fine with it. Arykah snapped Monique's face when she opened her box and saw the stilettos inside.

Gladys pulled out her shoes and admired them. "Oh my goodness."

"Look at me, Gladys," Arykah said. When Gladys looked at her, she was still in shock and couldn't close her mouth. Arykah snapped her photo.

"These are gonna be good," Arykah said about the photos. "I got some good ones."

The ladies couldn't stop gawking at their shoes. "Lady Arykah, you are something else," Darlita said already replacing her shoes with her new ones.

Arykah looked around the dining room and saw that the ladies had completely forgotten about the food. They were all putting on their stilettos.

"I thought you were starved, Darlita," Arykah joked. "Aren't you gonna eat?"

Darlita waved her hand at her plate of food to dismiss it. "Uh-uh. I ain't hungry no more. You can wrap my plate to go." Darlita's focus was on her stilettos. At that moment food was the furthest thing from her mind.

"Wrap my plate too, Lady Arykah," Chelsea added.

"Your pastor made all of this food. No one wants to eat?" Arykah asked them knowing they could care less about Lance's labor in the kitchen at this moment.

The reaction the women gave when they saw their stilettos was exactly what Arykah had expected. She planned it that way. She had plenty of saran wrap and Styrofoam food containers for the ladies to take their food home with them. Once they had seen their shoes, Arykah knew that Gladys, Monique, Chelsea, and Darlita weren't going to eat a thing.

"We'll thank the bishop at church tomorrow," Monique said. She was the first to stand in her new heels. Arykah had given her a pair of scarlet red, 100 percent silk, six-inch heel platform stilettos that allowed Monique's toes to peep through the front. "Sexy, sexy, sexy," Monique said as she sashayed around the dining-room table.

"I'm afraid to stand up," Darlita said. On her feet were royal-blue leather stilettos with a five-and-half-inch heel. She had never worn a shoe that high.

Arykah went to Darlita and pulled her up from her chair. "It's like riding a bike for the first time. Take a few steps forward and you'll get the hang of it."

Darlita slowly put one foot ahead of the other while holding on to Arykah's hands.

After she took her tenth step, Arykah released Darlita's hands. "You got it. Keep going."

Darlita's legs were wobbly, but the more steps she took, the more confident she became. It wasn't long before she was strutting to the kitchen and back to the dining room on her own. "I love them, Lady Arykah."

"I'm glad you do, Darlita. When I saw those on the Web site, they had your name all over them."

"I love this color, Lady Arykah," Chelsea said as she modeled burgundy, six-inch heels covered in black lace.

Arykah looked at Chelsea's shoes. "Now *those*, Chelsea, are saying something. Black lace over any color makes a bold statement."

"And the statement that I want them to make," Chelsea said, "is 'Husband, come and get me.'"

The ladies laughed at her comment.

"Well, I think that if you wear those to the grocery store, you just might meet your husband in the freezer section," Arykah smiled.

"Just make sure to stop by the frozen dinner aisle. That's where all of the single men shop," Darlita added. "Trust me, I know."

"Well, Lady Arykah, I think you just unleashed the cat in me." Gladys modeled six-inch leopard print platform heels. The stilettos made her feel tall. They were the highest heels she had ever worn in her life, but she sashayed in them like a professional.

Arykah got a big kick out of watching her guests enjoy their gifts. "Is everyone happy?"

"Happy? Honey, we're ecstatic!" Chelsea answered for them all.

Arykah pulled her chair from beneath the dining-room table, opened her own box of Christian Louboutins, and showed the ladies her exclusive pair. They oohed and aahed over Arykah's shoes as they did when they saw the stiletto cookies. Arykah slipped into her Pigalili's and said, "Let's dance."

Darlita became nervous. *"Dance?"* She had just learned to take baby steps in her new stilettos. Dancing in them was out of the question.

"Yeah, let's dance. I'm ready," Chelsea stated.

"Come on, girls. Follow me." Arykah led the ladies into the great room. The forty-by-forty-foot space was enormous. The gas fireplace provided warmth, and the two oversized chocolate-colored leather sectionals gave the room a cozy feel.

"What in the world is that?" Gladys asked. "Is that a bear?" She stood next to one of the sectionals gawking at a bearskin rug on the floor in the center of the room.

"It sure is," Arykah confirmed. "It's a grizzly. I had it shipped here from Canada. It was hunted in the Canadian Rockies."

The grizzly bear rug spanned seven feet long and three feet wide. It was dark brown, and the long guard hairs were soft to the touch and had a light blond tip. The head was massive and round with a concave face. The thick black claws were three inches long.

"That is beautiful, Lady Arykah," Darlita said. She saw the bear's teeth and fangs. "But it looks ferocious."

Arykah chuckled. "I'm sure it was when it was alive and weighed over seven hundred pounds. This rug is one of those purchases that I made when I saw one like it on the HGTV Channel. I also had to purchase a wildlife permit so that it could be legally bought and shipped here."

"Lady Arykah, please forgive me if what I'm about to ask you is out of order, but I just have to know."

Arykah knew what Chelsea's question would be even before she asked it. She wouldn't have been the first guest to ask, and Arykah knew Chelsea wouldn't be the last.

The grizzly bear rug was a showpiece. When guests entered the Howell's great room, the sight of the grizzly bear always stopped them in their tracks.

"I paid $4,800 for it, Chelsea."

Chelsea shook her head from side to side. Not to imply that Arykah may have overspent on the bear rug, but Chelsea thought that Arykah was living the life. A great life. Chelsea wondered how it felt to be in the financial position to purchase anything you want. To have the husband of your dreams and the home of your dreams is what every woman prayed for. To Chelsea, Arykah was definitely blessed beyond measure. Chelsea could see her cup running over. It wasn't that Chelsea was jealous of Arykah's life; she actually admired her first lady. And being in Arykah's presence and seeing how real and down-to-earth she was caused Chelsea to gain a new respect for Arykah. "Go head on, Lady Arykah. Live life to the fullest. I really admire you."

That comment touched Arykah deeply. Folks always ask her the price of the grizzly bear rug. In the past when Arykah revealed the cost of the rug, noses would turn up, frowns would appear, and heads would shake. Oftentimes Arykah would pause when she was asked how much she had spent on an item. Whether it be her clothes, car, hairdo, or furniture, she really didn't care to share how much money was spent.

She loved the finer things in life, and she didn't pinch any pennies. Arykah knew she was a blessed woman and most women didn't possess the things she had. Lance had told her that if folks were bold enough to ask how much something cost, make sure to tell the truth. And if anyone had a problem with what Arykah did with her money, in the gospel according to Lance, they need not ask. "Aw, thanks, Chelsea. And I admire you as well."

"Mush, mush, mush," Gladys joked. "Can we get this party started or what?"

"Let's do it." Arykah grabbed the grizzly bear rug by its left rear paw and dragged it across the room. She then went to the stereo set that was embedded in the wall next to the fireplace and searched through her library of CDs. When she had found what she was looking for, she inserted the disc into the CD player and pressed the play button.

She looked over her shoulder and said, "Y'all better get ready to move."

Moments later the ladies heard, *"This joint right here it makes me wanna—Whoo!"* Mary J. Blige's song "Just Fine" filled the great room. *"Feel free right now, go do what you want to do."*

Arykah was the first to dance to the fast-paced music. "Come on now, ain't no wallflowers in here."

Monique grabbed Chelsea by her hand and escorted her to the center of the great room. The two of them joined Arykah on the floor and danced.

Mary J. Blige's song set the tone for Arykah's stiletto party. The lyrics sent a message to anyone and everyone who had a problem with the way someone lived their life. In the song, Mary J. Blige said that her life was just fine and she wasn't going to change it to please no one. She let the world know that she wasn't worried about what anyone said about her or what anyone thought about her.

When Arykah looked up she saw Gladys and Darlita dancing too. What Arykah loved about that moment was that neither of them were doing any particular dance. They were all just taking in the lyrics and moving their bodies freely.

"Just fine, fine, fine, fine, fine, fine, ooooh," they all sang along with Mary J. Blige.

The song was nearing the end when the doorbell rang, through the intercom, and interrupted the ladies' flow.

Arykah looked at her wristwatch. She was having so much fun that she had lost track of time. "Our limo is here, ladies," she announced.

"Already?" Darlita asked. She wasn't complaining. She was looking forward to going to the spa, but she was mastering the stilettos and enjoyed dancing in them.

Arykah answered the door and told the limousine driver that she and the ladies would be out momentarily. The ladies wrapped their plates of food in the Styrofoam containers that Arykah had provided for them. They left the containers of food on the center island in the kitchen. They would get their food when they returned to Arykah's home, after the spa, to get their cars.

"Remember that we're walking the red carpet into the spa, ladies. So, keep your stilettos on," Arykah instructed.

In the front hall the ladies put their coats on and left Arykah's home. They climbed in the white Hummer limousine she hired for the evening.

"Looka here, looka here, looka here," Chelsea said. The Hummer was long, it was white, and it looked like it stretched for half a block.

"Lady Arykah, you went all out, didn't you?" Darlita asked.

"We're gonna have to start calling you Oprah. And we're your Gayles," Gladys commented. "Because this here is some Oprah and Gayle stuff you're doing."

"I'm just happy that my Gayles are having a good time. I really wanted this evening to be a memorable one," Arykah said getting comfortable on the leather seat.

"It already is," Monique stated, looking down at her new stilettos. "That's for sure."

The limousine pulled away from the curb, and the ladies were en route to their next destination. Darlita leaned back in the plush leather seat and extended her legs forward. "I feel like royalty."

"We all do," Chelsea added.

Arykah looked into the eyes of her guests. "The night is young. The best is yet to come."

For the next forty-five minutes, the ladies made small talk during the ride to the spa.

When the limousine came to a complete stop outside of The Massage Palace, the ladies could hardly keep still in their seats.

The driver exited the Hummer and walked around to the rear passenger door and opened it for the ladies. Gladys was the first to step out on the red carpet that had been rolled out from the door of the spa to the limousine. As soon as her foot touched the carpet, she was greeted with flashes of light. Arykah had hired three professional photographers to behave like the paparazzi.

Monique followed Gladys out of the limousine and posed for the cameramen. She pointed to her feet and said, "Don't forget the shoes. Make sure to get the shoes."

The cameras were in Darlita's face as soon as she exited the limousine. "Wow." She was a celebrity that night, and she loved every bit of it. She gave the famous beauty pageant wave with her hand and blew kisses at the cameras.

Chelsea climbed out of the limousine and immediately went into celebrity mode. She posed and smiled, then smiled and posed.

"What's your name?" one of the cameramen asked her.

Her grin got even wider. "Chelsea."

"Chelsea, over here," the cameraman on her left called out to her.

Chelsea looked into the lens of his camera and laughed. She was loving the moment.

"Chelsea, who are you wearing on your feet?" the cameraman on her right asked her.

Prior to the ladies arriving at the spa, all three cameramen had been briefed by Arykah to focus on the ladies' shoes.

"Christian Louboutins, dahling," Chelsea answered in her best Zsa Zsa Gabor voice.

Monique, Gladys, and Darlita were standing off to the side laughing at Chelsea. She was giving the paparazzi exactly what they wanted.

Arykah exited the limousine last. She immediately posed for the cameras. Arykah turned her back to one of the cameraman and lifted the bottom of her shoe. The cameraman took photos of the red sole. Arykah called Gladys, Monique, Chelsea, and Darlita over to where she was standing. She instructed all three cameramen to take many shots of the group. All five ladies worked the red carpet. No one could have convinced them that they were not the highest-paid celebrities in Chicago. They were causing a scene outside of The Massage Palace. Folks that were walking by had stopped to see who the famous ladies were.

"Who are they?" Arykah heard someone ask. She smiled in their direction.

When the cameraman told Arykah that they had all the shots they needed, she escorted the ladies into the spa where the owner, an elderly Caucasian lady, was waiting inside the door. Next to her was another woman, dressed in what looked like a nurse's uniform, holding a tray with flutes filled with champagne.

"Welcome back to The Massage Palace, Mrs. Howell," the owner greeted Arykah.

Arykah smiled. "Helga, it's good to see you again."

Arykah and Monique were not strangers to The Massage Palace. It's where they came often to unwind and get pampered. Arykah introduced the ladies to Helga. "These are my guests for the evening. Darlita, Chelsea, Gladys, and, of course, you know Monique."

Helga shook each of the ladies' hands. "I welcome all of you. My staff and I are delighted to have you here this evening. Your rooms are ready. Come this way, please."

Each of the ladies followed Helga and grabbed a glass of champagne from the tray on the way. They were assigned to private rooms where massage beds were set up for them.

When Arykah made the reservations with The Massage Palace, she specifically stated that she wanted each of her guests to have full-body massages, manicures, and pedicures.

Three hours later, the ladies met up together in the sauna.

"So, did everyone enjoy their pampering?" Arykah asked.

"Well, I can only speak for myself," Gladys said. "I enjoyed it tremendously."

Monique wiped her sweaty face with a small white towel. "I second that. This is exactly what I needed."

Darlita pulled the belt to her plush white terry cloth robe tighter. "I don't know how I could ever repay you, Lady Arykah. No one has ever done anything like this for me."

Because the room was steamy and cloudy, Arykah could barely make out Darlita's silhouette. "You don't have to repay me, Darlita. That is not what this evening is about. I wanted to treat all of you because I like you and I knew we'd have a great time together. I enjoy making people happy."

"And that's exactly why you're blessed the way you are," Chelsea said. "I've watched you from the first day you stepped foot into Freedom Temple. Everyone, me included, treated you so coldly. And for no real reason. We didn't know you, and we didn't wanna know you. I told you this two weeks ago, Lady Arykah, and I'll tell you again. I apologize for being the mothers' puppet. In some twisted way, I felt that I had to be loyal to them. I thought I owed them my allegiance."

"We all did," Darlita admitted sadly.

"But the moment I complimented you about your boots," Chelsea continued, "you spoke to me like we had been friends for years."

"And that's the true Arykah," Monique said to Chelsea. "She's open, approachable, warm, and very honest. When you befriend Arykah, you have a friend for life. She will have your back and fight the tallest giant for her friends."

"I know that to be true, Monique," Gladys said. She looked at Arykah through the steam. "And I am happy to have you as my friend. I thank you for coming to Miranda's defense." She knew Arykah had gone head-to-head with Mother Pansie for her daughter, Miranda.

"You're a superb first lady, but you're an even better friend," Chelsea said.

Because the sauna was so muggy and dark, the ladies couldn't see Arykah's tears streaming down her face. All she ever wanted was to be accepted by her new church family. Arykah was happy that she had reached out to Chelsea, Gladys, and Darlita. She was sure that the evening at the spa was just the beginning of many more fun times to come. "Thanks, Chelsea. That means a lot to me. And I am so happy that all of you accepted my invitation to come out and have a great time."

"Okay, group hug," Monique said.

Everyone surrounded Arykah and hugged her. "Thanks, Oprah. Thanks, Ms. Winfrey. Thanks O," the ladies joked.

Arykah laughed. "You're welcome, Gayles."

It was almost 10:00 P.M. when the ladies returned from the spa to Arykah's home for their food and shoes they had left behind. Chelsea, Darlita, and Gladys couldn't thank Arykah enough for what she did for them that evening. As they left her home, the ladies gave Arykah another hug and a kiss on her cheek. Arykah told the ladies that she was looking forward to seeing them at church the next morning.

Arykah walked into the living room and found Monique sitting on the sofa.

"Okay, why did you want me to stay behind?" Monique asked.

Arykah plopped down on the sofa next to Monique. "Because I wanna know what happened between you and Chelsea earlier this evening. Girl, I had to check her for lying on my bed and asking me about my sex life with Lance."

Monique's eyes bulged. "What?"

"Chelsea flat-out asked me if Lance could get down in the bed just as good as he got down in the pulpit."

"*What?*" Monique shrieked.

"She almost caught a left hook," Arykah chuckled.

Monique was too outdone. "That cow lay on your bed and asked you how good your man was?"

"Yep. But I didn't even have to put Chelsea in her place. Gladys beat me to it, and she sent her out here to the living room to apologize to you for acting like a stank broad."

"Well, Chelsea did apologize. She told me that she was out of line for implying that Adonis was living foul. I told her that I know my husband and I know he loves me. I also told Chelsea that Adonis wasn't going anywhere."

"You think she got the message?" Arykah asked.

"Oh, she got the message, all right. Because I also told her that if I caught her grinning in Adonis's face, there'll be consequences and repercussions."

Lance was asleep when Arykah crawled into bed and snuggled up behind him. She wrapped her arms around his waist and kissed the back of his neck.

He stirred and pressed the back of his body into Arykah's warmth. "Mmm, BoonQueesha is home."

Arykah sank into Lance's backside and tried to bury herself in his flesh. She smiled because she truly did have everything in life that she had prayed for.

And that's exactly why you're blessed the way you are. Chelsea's words danced in her head. She didn't want for nothing. Arykah loved the fact that she could be a lender and not a borrower. From her adoring husband, to her massive estate, to a job she loved, to her health and strength, Arykah was highly favored. "Father God, I thank you," she whispered. She lay her head on her pillow and held her husband in her arms all night long.

Chapter 15

At 8:35 A.M., the sun was high in the sky. Lance lay in bed with his hands stretched behind his head watching the Bobby Jones gospel celebration. Ricky Dillard and his choir, The New Generation Chorale, was putting on a show. Ricky directed the choir as if he were directing a twenty-piece orchestra. With his right hand, Ricky directed the soprano section to sing a high note. With his left hand, he ordered the alto section to sing a lower note. But when Ricky pointed his left foot at the tenor section and the men chimed in, Lance was outdone. "That dude is crazy."

Arykah stepped from her closet wearing a floor-length scarlet-red V-neck dress with an empire waist. A dressy but not too elegant beading lined the neckline and waistline. The price was still dangling from the sleeves. If Arykah wore the red dress to church that morning, it would be another Sunday that she wouldn't wear a repeater. On her feet were her brand-new Christian Louboutins. She came and stood in between Lance and the television. "How do I look, honey?"

Lance had only one word for his wife. "Magnificent." He loved the color red on Arykah. She lifted the front of the gown so that Lance could see her shoes.

"Are those the famous Christina Aguilera's?"

Arykah laughed out loud. "I do believe that you're mentally challenged, Lance. These are Christian Louboutins."

Lance frowned. "Who?"

Arykah waved her hand at him. "Oh, forget it." She rotated on her heels and modeled the outfit. "So, how's this for a Sunday morning?" Being a plus-sized woman, Arykah took extra precautions to always look her absolute best. She had come to terms long ago that vanity played a huge part in her everyday life. She was extremely vain, and she knew it.

"Absolutely stunning," Lance said. "I think I'll wear a black suit with a black shirt and my red silk tie."

"Perfect," Arykah said. Lance often tried to match her colors. She turned from him and started to head back to her closet.

"Mother Pansie called me last night when you were out with the ladies."

Arykah stopped walking and turned to look at Lance. Whenever Mother Pansie called Lance, it was always for some type of drama. "What did she want?"

"She informed me that she's gonna sit Miranda Blackmon down from the choir. She won't be singing with the young adult choir this morning. Miranda is pregnant at fifteen years old. The mothers feel strongly that the wrong message is sent when a young, unwed, pregnant girl participates in a church activity."

Arykah inhaled, then exhaled. She inhaled again, then exhaled. Her stomach and breasts rose and fell with each breath she took. Arykah was getting ready to snap, but before she went totally off, she would wait and get Lance's take on the situation. He only told Arykah what Mother Pansie said what she was going to do about Miranda. Lance hadn't yet shared with Arykah how he responded to her. Hopefully, Lance put the old woman in her place. Arykah wanted to know how Lance handled the witch. Before she spoke, Arykah prayed to the almighty, ever-loving, most high God in heaven, that she didn't have to show her behind on a Sunday morning. Arykah's behind was big, and it was wide. If need be, she would expose her entire backside.

Arykah folded arms beneath her breasts, sending them high into the air. "And how do you feel about Mother Pansie snatching Miranda from the choir?" Her neck danced along with her question.

Lance swallowed. Arykah's body language sent him vibes. Crossed arms, a dancing neck, and direct eye contact told him that she was a tad bit disturbed by what he had just told her. "Well, for one thing, Cheeks, I have to respect the mothers' opinions and—"

"Respect their opinions?" Arykah cut Lance's words off. *"Their stupid, ignorant opinions?* First of all, we're talking about a young, impressionable teenager who made a mistake, Lance. Gladys brought Miranda to my office, and the three of us discussed Miranda's pregnancy. They told me that Mother Pansie wanted Miranda to stand before the whole church family to apologize for getting pregnant and ask for forgiveness."

"That's usually how it goes, Cheeks."

Arykah stepped out of her stilettos, lifted her dress over her head, and threw it on the bed. She came and stood totally naked in front of her husband. "Why? Why do you make young girls stand before the church and put themselves on blast like that? That's humiliating, Lance. I know that pregnancy is something that can't be hidden. I know that eventually, when Miranda's belly gets bigger, everyone will know she's pregnant. But what I don't get is why someone has to be shamed for a sin they committed."

Under normal circumstances, Arykah's nude body would turn Lance on and he'd reach out and caress a body part. But the vibes she sent him that morning and her loud voice told him that sex was the last thing on her mind. She was ready for battle.

"Cheeks, when young girls are made to stand before the church, it isn't to shame them. It's to humble them and make them acknowledge what they've done."

Arykah looked at Lance like he was an alien. "Are you for real? That's the dumbest crap I have ever heard. Isn't a growing belly, morning sickness, and swollen ankles acknowledgment enough? Miranda doesn't owe the church anything. Freedom Temple isn't reserving her seat on the right hand of the Father. That's Jesus' job. And He's the *only* one Miranda owes an explanation to. *Not the freakin' church!"* she yelled.

Lance saw Arykah's nostrils flaring and her veins bulged from her neck. She was hot.

"Okay, Cheeks, you need to calm down."

"And *you* need to man up," she snapped. "Grow some cashews and man up." Arykah saw Lance's eyeballs pop out of his head. She knew she had just insulted her husband.

"Oh, you don't like what I'm sayin' to you? Well, let me tell you what *I* don't like, Lance. I don't like the fact that Mother Gussie and Mother Pansie are allowed to run through the church freely and bully people just because they feel they can. You give them way too much power."

"*I* give them power?"

Arykah put her hands on her naked waist. "Well, heck, aren't you the pastor of the church? Nothing gets done before *you* give the okay. No decision is made unless *you* sign off on it. *You* are the head shepherd, the bishop, the leader, and it's *your* head that'll roll when souls are lost. God has placed you in a position to win souls and to nourish His flock.

"Taking that girl out of the choir will be detrimental. Yes, Miranda has sinned, but so what? Just because she's pregnant she can't sing praises to God? How dumb is that? Miranda has admitted to falling down, and she admitted to making a mistake, but God forgives, Lance."

"You don't have to tell me that, Arykah."

"Apparently I do. Do you really believe that God doesn't want Miranda to sing to Him just because she's pregnant? You think He wants her to stop worshipping and adoring Him because she's pregnant? No, He doesn't. If anything, the choir is exactly where Miranda needs to be. She needs to keep singing and praising and clapping and loving God. He forgave her of her sin, and He still loves her. Miranda is still His child. God hasn't turned His back on her, so why are you trying to make her turn her back on Him? If you take that girl out of the choir and she leaves the church and gets into more trouble, that's gonna be on you. You'll have to answer for that. Now, you can mess around and let the mothers get you into trouble with God if you want to."

Arykah turned toward her closet, then turned back around. "What about the boy that got Miranda pregnant? Doesn't he sing in the young adult choir too? Was he told that he couldn't sing 'til after *his* baby comes? Was he instructed to stand before the church and confess that he'd gotten a girl pregnant?"

"Mother Pansie didn't mention anything about the boy."

"That's what I thought," Arykah said. "So, it's okay for Miranda to be yanked from the choir because her belly will grow and her sin will be exposed. But the young daddy can keep doing what he wants to do. You know that ain't right, Lance. If you take Miranda out of the choir, then you take her baby's daddy out of the choir as well. He doesn't get a free pass. They both laid down and made a baby. Miranda didn't do it by herself." Arykah turned to walk away but stopped and turned around a second time.

"And shame on you, as a pastor and as a man of God, for letting Mother Pansie throw you under the bus. If Miranda's soul gets lost, God will come after *you*, not Mother Pansie." Arykah was finished with the conversation. She left Lance to his thoughts. She walked into the master bath and started the water in the shower.

Lance lay on the bed, on his back, looking up at the ceiling. He thought about everything Arykah said. Clearly she was hot and bothered. He wanted to try to talk more about Miranda's situation with Arykah, but he knew she needed to cool off.

They showered separately, which was rare. Their shower stall was built for two, and Lance and Arykah looked forward to showering together every morning. Lance didn't follow Arykah into the shower that morning, nor did she invite him in. In fact, they dressed for church in complete silence.

Lance was the first, as always, to be ready. When he saw Arykah hook the clasp to her diamond tennis bracelet around her wrist, he knew she was ready. "Are we driving the Benz, the Lex, or the Jag today?" he asked her.

"You go ahead and drive whatever you want. I'll drive myself to church."

Lance frowned. "Why?" Since they'd been married, they rode to church together.

Arykah looked into Lance's eyes. "Because I said so." She walked by him and left the bedroom.

Lance followed after her. "Arykah, that's ridiculous. Why should we drive separate cars to the same church? What will folks think?"

Arykah stopped in her tracks and turned around. "Oh, now you're worried about what folks will think when they look at *you* sideways? Well, how do you think Miranda feels?"

Arykah walked through the kitchen to the garage door and opened it. She grabbed the keys to the Lexus off the key rack, just inside the kitchen door, and pressed the alarm button on the remote. Silently, she got in the driver's seat, shut the door, and pressed the button on the garage door opener above her head, on the sun visor. Then she started the Lexus and drove the car out of the garage and left Lance standing looking at her.

Lance was already seated in the pulpit when Arykah, Myrtle, and Monique walked down the center aisle to the front pew. That was the first time since they'd become man and wife that Lance and Arykah hadn't walked into the sanctuary together on a Sunday morning.

When Lance knocked on Arykah's office door at the church, then poked his head inside, he saw her sitting behind her desk. He announced that it was time for them to head downstairs to the sanctuary. Arykah told Lance that she wasn't ready to go downstairs and he should go ahead without her. He looked at Monique and Myrtle sitting in the chairs opposite of Arykah's desk. They wouldn't give him any eye contact. He closed Arykah's door and went down to the sanctuary alone.

Arykah purposely kept her focus away from the pulpit. Every Sunday, she and Lance flirted with each before he stood to preach his sermon. While praise and worship was going on, she would wink her eye at him or blow Lance a kiss, and he'd return the gesture with a wink and a smile. But right then, Arykah wasn't giving Lance any eye contact whatsoever. He tried to send her a telepathic message by staring at her. Maybe she'd feel his gaze and look his way, but she ignored him completely.

After praise and worship ended, the young adult choir marched into the sanctuary and took their place in the choir stand. Arykah didn't see Miranda, but she saw the young man who had fathered her baby. She had to restrain herself from going into the choir stand and pulling the young boy out by his ear. But Arykah knew that he wasn't the problem. Her battle was with her husband, the pastor of the church. Arykah leaned over to Myrtle and whispered, "I am so mad. I should've stayed at home."

Myrtle patted her arm. "It's all right, Sugar Plum." Arykah had shared with Monique and Myrtle the argument that she and Lance had that morning before church.

Both ladies understood her point and felt that Lance and Mother Pansie were wrong for sitting Miranda down from the choir. But Myrtle told Arykah that driving two separate cars to church didn't help the situation. Fighting with Lance at home was one thing, but Myrtle warned Arykah that driving separate cars and ignoring her husband at church would send up flares. She advised Arykah to be careful to not alert the vultures at church that she and Lance were fighting because they would pounce on him like a cat on a ball of yarn.

Listening to the choir, Arykah couldn't concentrate on what they were singing about.

She was so angry that she had begun to shake as if she had chills running through her body. The longer she sat there and watched the young boy who had gotten Miranda pregnant, the angrier she got.

She leaned into Myrtle again. "I'm going home. I can't be here like this. My spirit is jacked up, and I ain't gonna sit here and be fake."

Myrtle pressed her index finger down on Arykah's thigh to keep her seated. "That's *exactly* what you're gonna do," she said sternly. "When you get back home, you can rip Lance's head off, but right here and right now, you're gonna pretend to be the happily married first lady that everyone thinks you are."

Arykah got even angrier than she was five minutes ago. She sat straight up on the pew and pinched her lips together and looked forward, not gazing on anything in particular.

Lance saw the exchange between Myrtle and Arykah. He could tell by Arykah's body language that whatever Myrtle whispered in her ear was obviously something Arykah didn't want to hear.

His wife was upset, and Lance wondered what he could do to fix the situation.

Thinking back on everything Arykah had said that morning made him realize that she was absolutely right. Who was Mother Pansie to tell Miranda that she couldn't sing in the choir just because she was pregnant? Lance remembered Arykah's harsh words. *If anything, the choir is exactly where Miranda needs to be. She needs to keep singing and praising and clapping and loving God. He forgave her of her sin, and He still loves her. Miranda is still His child. If you take that girl out of the choir and she leaves the church and gets into more trouble, that's gonna be on you. You'll have to answer for that.*

Lance looked at the young boy who had fathered Miranda's baby. He was singing and clapping and praising God. His life hadn't changed. *Was he told that he couldn't sing 'til after his baby comes? Was he instructed to stand*

*before the church and confess that he'd gotten a girl
pregnant? So, it's okay for Miranda to be yanked from
the choir because her belly will grow and her sin will
be exposed. But the young daddy can keep doing what
he wants to do. You know that ain't right, Lance. Grow
some cashews and man up.*

Lance scanned the congregation until he spotted Miranda sitting next to Gladys in the rear of the church.
Without hesitation, he stood from his seat, left the
pulpit, and walked to the back of the church. Minister
Weeks was quickly on Lance's heels.

It wasn't uncommon for Lance to disrupt the service
and walk out of the pulpit to lay holy hands on the
people. It was Minister Week's job to move whenever
Lance moved.

When Lance got to the end of the pew that Miranda
sat on, everyone watched as he called for her to come
to him. Arykah saw Miranda stand and excuse herself
as she passed folks and stood before her pastor. The
young adult choir was still singing when Lance turned
to look at Arykah. In his eyes, Arykah knew Lance
needed her. She slowly stood and made her way down
the center aisle to where he and Miranda stood.

With Arykah by his side, Lance placed both of his
hands on top of Miranda's head and began praying
for her. Tears came to Arykah's eyes. After his prayer,
Lance held out his left hand for Minister Weeks to
pour holy oil in his palm. Lance then blessed the oil
and poured it from his palm to Arykah's palm. He instructed Arykah to place her hands on Miranda's belly.

With tears dripping down her face, Arykah did as
she was told. As soon as she touched Miranda's belly,
Arykah felt the fifteen-week-old fetus move. Immediately the Holy Spirit overpowered Arykah, and she
began speaking in an unknown tongue.

Gladys saw the power of God moving through Arykah. "Thank ya! Thank ya!" she shouted in her seat.

When Lance saw that Arykah had finished blessing Miranda, he hugged Arykah. "You had my back, baby," he whispered in her ear.

Arykah returned Lance's hug. "And I always will."

Lance kissed Arykah's cheek, and she walked back to the front pew and sat down.

Then Lance grabbed Miranda's hand and escorted her into the soprano section in the choir stand. Afterward, he returned to his own seat in the pulpit. Arykah turned around and looked into Mother Pansie's face and sent her a message with her eyes. *You ain't runnin' nothing.*

Mother Pansie glared at Arykah. She'd gotten Arykah's silent message clearly.

Mother Pansie crossed her arms over her chest and averted her eyes somewhere else.

Arykah turned back around and saw Lance looking at her. She winked her eye at him and Lance returned the wink, then smiled.

My wife is happy again, he thought.

Myrtle leaned into Arykah. "See what you would've missed had you left?"

"Thanks for making me stay, Momma Cortland." Arykah was pleased. Lance made her happy. She saw Miranda in the choir singing and praising God just as she should be. Arykah stood up and started clapping and singing along with the choir.

Mother Pansie sat behind Arykah wondering how she had gotten Lance to change his mind about Miranda. When she had spoken with Lance on the telephone the night before, he told Mother Pansie that she had his full support. Mother Pansie looked at Arykah's blond wig, her skintight scarlet-red dress, and her hooker heels. *That Jezebel seduced him.*

Mother Pansie was anxious for morning service to be over so that she could get started on the next plan to get Arykah out of Freedom Temple. But Mother Pansie was on her own now. Mother Gussie told Mother Pansie that she was done fooling with their pastor's wife. Arykah was constantly showing up in Mother Gussie's dreams in a bad way. The day Arykah came to the church and confronted her about the suit jacket fiasco when she tried to make Arykah believe that Lance had cheated on her, Mother Gussie had wet her pants. It was then that she realized that Arykah meant business. Mother Gussie believed Arykah to be the craziest woman she'd ever met. So crazy that Mother Gussie absolutely refused to come to church for work or morning service.

Lance hadn't spoken with Mother Gussie in weeks. He assumed she resigned from her position as the church secretary.

Sitting in church, angry, Mother Pansie knew she had been defeated again. Lance had stripped her of her position of counseling the women in the church and assigned Arykah to do it. Mother Pansie was overruled when she confronted Arykah about having Miranda stand in front of the church and confess her sin. And now Bishop Lance, himself, took the girl and put her back in the choir.

Three times Mother Pansie had been defeated, but she refused to give up. Having to look at Arykah's big behind, in a wig and dress that only a floozy would wear, Mother Pansie decided that she didn't need Mother Gussie on her team.

Mother Gussie was weak, but Mother Pansie refused to be intimidated by Arykah. The fat broad had to go, and Mother Pansie would see to it. Come hell or high water, Lady Elect Arykah would soon be gone. For Mother Pansie, it had become a personal matter.

Chapter 16

Monday morning, Arykah was in the shower when she heard the house phone ringing. Monday mornings were when new listings of homes on the market came across Arykah's desk at the realty office. It wasn't unusual for her boss to call Arykah at home when he got a hold of the listings before any other agent came into the office.

Arykah ran from the shower into the bedroom, soaking wet. She snatched up the receiver from her nightstand before the call went into the voice mail. "Hello?"

"Lady Arykah?"

Arykah frowned at the voice on the other end of the telephone. What could she possibly want on a Monday morning? Of course she was calling to speak with Lance to try to get him to put a leash on his wife.

"The bishop isn't here, Mother Pansie. Perhaps you should try him at the church."

Arykah heard the call disconnect, then the line went dead. Mother Pansie had hung up on her. *What the heck?* Arykah's first instinct was to call Mother Pansie back and ask what her problem was but decided against it. She had houses to sell. Arykah returned the cordless telephone to its base and was on her way back to the shower when she heard the doorbell ring. *Now what?* she thought.

She turned the water off in the shower, then grabbed her long quilted robe from the end of the bed and put it on. The doorbell rang again.

"Coming!" Arykah shouted as she left her bedroom and went to the front door.

"Who is it?" she asked, tying the belt to the robe in a knot around her waist.

"Delivery for Mrs. Howell," a man said.

With her spending habits, a delivery from the United Parcel Service was at Arykah's front door at least three times a week. She didn't think to look through the peephole to see Rafael, the driver assigned to Arykah's area. The same driver who always delivered her packages. Arykah had developed a trusting relationship with Rafael. Because her packages were often too heavy for her to lift, she would tip Rafael very handsomely to bring her boxes inside.

"You still married?" Rafael would ask Arykah in his Spanish accent every time he brought her packages. He flirted with her, and Arykah would assure him that as long as she lived in that big home, she would stay married.

"Okay, Rafael, I'm here," Arykah said after the doorbell rang a third time. She opened the door and one punch to her nose sent Arykah flying backward. The impact was so forceful that the back of Arykah's head slammed against the tile floor. She saw stars, and she saw a man's silhouette.

"Rafael?" she moaned trying to get up.

"No. Not Rafael, b*@+h," he muttered.

Arykah heard the front door slam. She tried to move but felt a kick to her ribs. She screamed out. The next thing Arykah knew, she was being dragged by her arms into the living room. She began kicking and screaming. She didn't know from which direction the next punch came, but Arykah felt a blow to her right eye.

"Shut up!" he yelled.

Dazed and confused, Arykah's vision was blurred. She felt her robe being snatched open.

"No!" she screamed. *"Nooooo!"*

The next punch knocked out two of Arykah's front teeth.

"I said shut the f*#k up!" He was on top of her. He positioned himself in between Arykah's thighs. She felt his fingers force themselves inside of her.

Arykah screamed again. *"Lance! Lance!"*

"The bishop can't save you now," he said.

His breath was foul; his body odor was offensive. Arykah fought, kicked, and scratched. She wasn't going down without a fight. But the more she fought and screamed, the harder his punches got. His fingers jammed in and out of her. Arykah felt his nails slice her inner flesh.

"Jesus! Jesus!" she screamed.

The next thing Arykah knew, he had traded his fingers for his manhood. He forced her body to accept his, to make room for him. She coughed up blood and had almost choked on her own teeth that had slipped to the back of her throat.

He had gotten a hold of both of Arykah's wrists and extended them over her head. Violently, he pressed them on the floor. He moved in and out of her over and over again. Thrusting, tearing, forcing her to take him in.

Arykah couldn't see his face. She couldn't make out his features. He was a stranger in her house.

His thrusts became faster and faster; then he yelled out and suddenly stopped. And just as quickly as he had barged into her home, he was gone.

Arykah lay on her back, staring up at the ceiling, unable to move. Her entire body ached. Her nude, violated body was exposed. Blood had run from her nose and mouth down the sides of her face and onto the white carpet beneath her. Her womanhood burned. Arykah reached between her legs and felt a warm liquid oozing out of her. "Oh my God," she cried. "Oh my God." She couldn't believe that she had just been violated in her own home. She had been raped.

With the little strength she had, Arykah turned over on her stomach and used her elbows to drag herself to the telephone on the cocktail table. Her thighs left a trail of blood behind her. It took Arykah four tries to get the number correct.

Lance saw his home number flashing on the caller ID on his cellular telephone. "You miss me already, don't you?" he joked.

She was crying. She was coughing and choking to get the words out. "He hurt me."

Lance frowned. "Cheeks?"

Arykah's sobbing became louder. "I was calling for you. Where were you?"

Still frowning, Lance didn't have a clue what she was saying to him. "What?"

Arykah screamed into the telephone. *"He raped me!"*

Lance jumped up from his desk at church. *"What?"* He was already running from his office. *"Baby, I'm on my way. I'm on my way, Cheeks!"* When Lance ran past Mother Gussie's desk he yelled, "Sharonda, call the police and send an ambulance to my house, now. *Right now!"*

Lance ran down the church steps, out the door, and got into his car at the speed of lightning. He had tears in his eyes. The thought of a man violating his wife infuriated him. "Baby, hold on. I'm coming home."

Arykah lay on the living-room floor moaning and crying. "Lance? Lance?" Her words were just above a whisper.

"Cheeks!" Lance yelled into the telephone. She didn't answer him. Lance was worried that Arykah had lost consciousness. "Arykah! Arykah!"

Still no response. He disconnected the call and dialed emergency.

"This is nine-one-one, what's your emergency?"

Lance could hardly get his words together as he fum-
bled with his keys. He had too many on the key ring.
He couldn't distinguish his car key from any other key.
"My wife . . . she . . . my wife . . . please—"

The operator couldn't understand him. "Sir, what's
your emergency?" she asked him again.

He found the key, slid it into the ignition, and turned
it. In the next ten seconds, Lance was speeding. "My
wife was raped. Please send an ambulance to my home.
Please!" he cried out. Lance was driving beyond the
speed limit and had already decided that if a cop tried
to pull him over for driving too fast, he wouldn't stop.
He would make the squad car chase him all the way
home. Nothing or no one would stop him from getting
to Arykah.

"Sir, what is your name?" the operator asked.

He sniffed and wiped his runny nose with the back of
his hand. "Lance Howell."

There was a pause before the operator asked Lance
to confirm his home address. "Sir, there's an ambulance already dispatched to your home and the police
are en route. They should be there momentarily. What
is your wife's name?"

"Arykah. Arykah Miles-Howell."

Another pause. "Okay, Mr. Howell, I have confirmation that the police have arrived at your residence. Is
there anything else I can do for you?"

"No, thank you," Lance answered.

"Well, good luck to you and your wife, sir."

"Thank you," Lance whispered.

Twenty-five minutes later, Lance drove on his lawn
like a madman. He was halfway to the living-room

window before the grass had slowed the car down. He put the gear in park, jumped out of the car, and left the engine running.

There were four police cars in the driveway and two were parked on the street. Lance saw a policeman standing next to the garage talking into a two-way radio. Three more policemen were huddled in a semicircle on the front porch. It was a real live crime scene.

Lance saw yellow tape that read, *"Police Line. Do Not Cross."* The tape spanned across the front porch and down the steps to the banisters.

"Hey. Hey, you," one of the policemen on the porch called after Lance as he ran past them into the foyer.

Lance walked in further and entered the living room, where he saw a crime-scene investigator and a female detective taking pictures of the blood-soaked white carpet.

"Arykah," he called out.

The policeman who had called after Lance followed him inside. "Who are you?" he asked Lance.

Lance couldn't take his eyes away from the massive amount of blood on the carpet. "This is my house. Where is my wife?"

"Can I see some identification, please?"

Lance didn't hear his question. He wanted to know where Arykah was. "Where's my wife?" he asked again.

"Identification, please." The policeman had to prevent Lance from taking another step further into the home. He could accidentally tamper with the evidence.

Lance pulled his wallet from his back pocket and opened it. He found his driver's license and gave it to the policeman. "Please tell me where my wife is. Is she okay?"

The policeman studied Lance's driver's license, then gave it back to him. "Mr. Howell, your wife was assaulted—"

"I know that," Lance yelled at him. He was losing patience. *"Where* is she?"

The female detective heard Lance yell and hurried over to where he and the policeman stood. "Sir, your wife has already been taken to the hospital, but I wanna ask you some quest—"

Lance looked at her. "Which hospital?"

"Mr. Howell, I need to ask—"

"Where did they take my wife?" He wasn't in the mood for answering questions. First things first. He needed to know Arykah's whereabouts.

The detective exhaled. She knew she wouldn't get anywhere with Lance until she told him where his wife was. "Dupage County Hospital, but please—"

Lance was already out the door and running to his car.

"Mr. Howell?" she called after him. When she and the policeman followed Lance outside, they saw that he had reversed the Jaguar backward on the lawn and was already heading down the street.

Monique's cellular telephone rang. She was sitting behind her desk at the radio station when she saw Lance's name on her caller ID. "Morning, Bishop."

"Arykah's been raped. I'm on my way to the Dupage County Hospital."

Monique's eyes bulged from her head. She stood up. "Oh my God. Lance?"

He started crying again. "Blood was everywhere."

Monique became frantic. "How . . . who . . . where . . .?"

"She was raped at home. That's all I know."

Monique started gathering her things. "Okay. Dupage County?"

"Yeah, Dupage County."

"I'm on my way." Monique disconnected the call from Lance and immediately called Adonis and told him what had happened to Arykah and which hospital she was in. An electrician, Adonis was out on an assignment. He told Monique that he'd leave work immediately and meet her and Lance at the hospital.

It took Lance half an hour to reach the nurses' desk in the emergency wing at the hospital. He was out of breath from running from the parking lot. "My name is Lance Howell. I was told that my wife, Arykah, was brought in."

The nurse keyed in information on the computer. "Yes, she was but—"

"Where is she? I wanna see her." Lance was sweating and panting.

"Mr. Howell, please have a seat in the waiting area. The doctor is with her now. I will let him know that you're here."

"Can you just tell me how she's doing? She lost consciousness while I was speaking with her on the telephone. Is she breathing? Is she alive?" Lance broke down and sobbed loudly at the nurses' station. "Why won't anyone tell me anything?"

The nurse pulled Kleenex tissue from a box on the desk and gave it to Lance. "Yes, Mr. Howell. She was conscious when the paramedics brought her in fifteen minutes ago. If you'll have a seat in the waiting area, the doctor will come out and talk with you as soon as he gets Mrs. Howell stable."

Arykah was alive. That was what Lance had been praying to hear. He had been pleading to God all the way to the hospital. Lance could calm down, but he couldn't relax.

He walked to the waiting room and sat down. He leaned forward and placed his elbows on his knees.

"My God," Lance said. "My God. Please let Cheeks be okay."

His cellular telephone rang, and he answered on the first ring. "Hello?"

"Bishop, this is Weeks. What happened?"

After Sharonda ordered an ambulance and the police to Lance's home, she had called Minister Weeks. She had been briefed by Mother Gussie where to find the bishop's personal information and to always contact Minister Carlton Weeks in an emergency. He was Lance's right-hand man.

"It's Arykah," Lance said. "Weeks, she was raped."

"Raped?" Carlton shrieked into the telephone. "What do you mean 'raped'?"

"She was raped at home this morning."

"Oh my God," Carlton said. "Is she gonna be all right?"

"I don't know. I haven't seen her yet. I'm at the hospital waiting for the doctor to come and talk to me."

"Which hospital?"

"Dupage County."

"I'm on my way."

When Lance looked up, Monique was running toward him.

"How is she?" she asked.

Lance stood to hug Monique, then sat down. "I don't know yet."

Monique sat in the chair next to Lance. "They won't let you see her?"

"I'm still waiting for the doctor to come and talk to me."

"Well, who told you that she had been raped?"

"Cheeks did. She called me at the church. She was crying. I heard her say, 'He hurt me.' Then she mumbled something else. I told her that I couldn't understand what she was saying, then she screamed that she had been raped."

Monique placed her hand over her mouth. "Oh my God."

"I should've been there. I wasn't there when she needed me," Lance cried.

Monique leaned over and wrapped her arms around Lance. She had to fight back her own tears. "Arykah is strong, Lance. She'll pull through this."

"Mr. Howell?"

Lance looked up and saw two men wearing scrubs standing before him and Monique.

He wiped his eyes, and the two men became one. He stood up. "Yes."

"Please sit down," the doctor said. He sat down in a chair directly across from Lance.

"Your wife is stable. She has a concussion. There was a blow to the back of her head. I've ordered a brain scan to see if any real damage has been done. We were able to stitch the gash in her head. I'm sorry to tell you that she was sexually assaulted."

Lance lowered his head. "Yes, I know."

"She was beaten badly," the doctor continued. "Her right eye is swollen. Over the next few hours it will close completely. The swelling will start to reduce in about two days. The bridge of her nose was fractured. She took a blow to her upper lip which knocked out two of her teeth."

"My God," Monique cried out. She couldn't imagine someone brutally beating Arykah that way. "Who would do such a thing?" she wondered out loud.

"Also," the doctor said, "she has a few broken ribs. I won't know exactly how many until I review the x-rays."

Lance started crying openly, and the doctor patted his knee. "If there's any consolation, Mr. Howell, your wife put up a darn good fight. She has plenty of the assailant's DNA beneath her fingernails. Whoever did this horrible thing has to look like a rake slashed his face. I've ordered a rape kit for Mrs. Howell. The DNA samples will be taken immediately."

"Good," Monique said.

The doctor pursed his lips. "I, uh, I'm sorry to say that we couldn't save the baby."

Both Lance and Monique sat straight up.

"Baby?"

Monique heard Lance but asked her own question anyway. "There was a baby?"

The doctor was confused. "You didn't know?" he asked Lance.

Lance shook his head from side to side. What was the doctor talking about? "Know what?"

"Mr. Howell, your wife was pregnant. She suffered a miscarriage because of the rape. She lost a lot of blood, but we were able to stop the hemorrhaging."

A baby. There was a baby, and now there isn't one. Lance laid his head on Monique's lap and cried.

Monique couldn't fight her tears any longer. She let them freely fall down her face.

She rocked back and forth and caressed Lance's shoulder as he lay on her lap. "A baby. This is going to kill Arykah."

"After the DNA samples are taken, I'll order a sedative to be given to Mrs. Howell intravenously. It'll make her rest comfortably for a few hours. I didn't tell her about the miscarriage. I'll leave that for you to do," the doctor said to Lance.

Lance sat up and wiped his eyes. "Thank you, Doctor. I'd rather she hear it from me."

The doctor stood up. "You can see your wife briefly."

"Thank you," Lance said again.

Monique wiped her tears. "I can't believe this is happening."

"I wonder why she didn't tell me that she was pregnant."

Monique thought back to the spa two nights ago. Arykah had a glass of champagne.

"She didn't know, Lance. Arykah never would've drunk champagne at the spa had she known she was pregnant. She didn't have a clue."

Lance stood up. "I'm going to see her. You can come with me if you like."

Monique was happy that Lance had invited her to see Arykah. She was more than willing to give Lance his privacy, but she was just as anxious as he was to kiss her best friend's cheek.

Arykah had been moved from the emergency room to the fifth floor of the hospital.

Lance and Monique walked into the private room and didn't recognize her at all.

Arykah's face was grotesque. Her right eye was almost swollen shut. Lance saw stitches going down the center of her top lip. Arykah's nose was no longer centered in the middle of her face; it had been tilted to the left side. Blue bruises, black bruises, and purple bruises colored her face. Dried blood was encrusted around Arykah's nostrils. There was a small clear tube running from her nose down the center of her hospital gown.

Lance couldn't stand to see her like that. He turned his back from Arykah and Monique saw his shoulders shaking. She knew he was crying. Monique stepped closer to Arykah's bed and looked down at her closely. If Monique hadn't been told that Arykah was lying in the hospital bed, Monique would never have believed that it was her.

She grabbed Arykah's hand and saw the IV needle taped to the back of it. Gently, she brought Arykah's hand to her lips and kissed it. "I'm here, sis."

Lance didn't touch Arykah. Instead, he sat down in the chair next to her bed.

More tears dripped from Monique's eyes. She looked at Lance and saw his eyes were closed. Monique knew he was praying.

A nurse came into the room and announced that Arykah had another visitor but only two people were allowed in her room at a time.

"It's probably Adonis," Monique said. "I'll leave so that he can come in."

"But only if it's Adonis," Lance stated. "Cheeks would kill me if I allowed anyone else to see her like this."

"Who else besides Adonis knows?"

"Minister Weeks knows what happened. He told me that he'd be here."

Monique left the room and found Minister Weeks sitting in the waiting area. "Minister Weeks."

He stood and greeted Monique. "Sister Cortland, how are you? How is Lady Arykah? How is the bishop doing?"

Monique hugged Minister Weeks and sat down in a chair. "Bishop Lance isn't doing too good. Arykah took a beating. I don't even recognize her. Her face is swollen, stitches are everywhere, and the bruises are beyond belief." Monique didn't tell Minister Weeks about Arykah's miscarriage. That was personal information that only she and Lance should reveal if they chose to. "And as for me and how I'm doing," Monique started, "I'm still in shock. I just don't understand how something like this could happen. I don't even understand *why* it happened."

"Bishop told me that she was raped at their home."

Monique nodded her head. "They live in a gated community. A security guard at the gate must call the residents and announce that a visitor has arrived. It's hard for me to believe that someone from their community did this to Arykah."

"And if she accepted a visitor, who could it have been?" Minister Weeks wondered.

"Babe?"

Monique looked up and saw Adonis walking toward her. She stood and ran to his open arms. "Oh, honey, thank God you're here."

Adonis held on to Monique for what seemed like forever. He thought about how he'd feel if it had been Monique that had been violated instead of Arykah. He kissed her cheek.

"How is she?"

"Not good," Monique answered. "But she's conscious and stable. Lance is with her now."

Adonis went to Carlton and extended his hand to him. "How you doing, Weeks?"

Carlton shook Adonis's hand. "Bless you, Brother Cortland."

Monique and Adonis sat down. "Did you call Aunt Myrtle?" Adonis asked Monique.

She shook her head from side to side. "Uh-uh. I didn't wanna call Gravy just yet. I wanna give her good news when I do. Arykah will be given a sedative through the IV soon. Her doctor said she'll sleep for a few hours. I'd rather wait 'til after that, then call Gravy."

Adonis felt Monique's hands shaking. "You all right?" he asked her.

More tears fell from her eyes. "No."

Adonis pulled her into his arms. "Arykah will be okay."

In Arykah's hospital room Lance pulled his chair closer to her bed and reached for her hand. He looked at her disfigured face and felt guilty that he wasn't home to protect Arykah when she was attacked.

Living in a gated community and paying three-quarters of a million dollars for his home, Lance assumed his neighborhood was a safe one. Doctors, lawyers, professional athletes, and retired entrepreneurs were his neighbors. Many of Lance's neighbors leave their homes in the winter and travel south or across the ocean to their million-dollar summer cottages.

He wondered what predator had abused his wife. Which neighbor? Was it the married heart surgeon that lived on the corner of the block? He and his wife had four kids. Lance wondered if a father and husband was capable of violating a woman. Could it have been the dentist across the street who wasn't married but took care of his elderly mother? Or was it the baker in the middle of the cul de sac on Lance's street? Arykah had told Lance that he always complimented her on her different hairdos. Lance had assumed that the baker had a little sugar in his tank. He wore his clothes tighter than Arykah did. And only men were ever seen coming to and leaving his home.

Lance wondered if the rapist had forced his way in the front door or if Arykah knew the person and had let him in. He didn't wait around to get answers or ask questions when he had sped away from home. His main priority at the time was to get to the hospital and see about Arykah.

"Baby, I'm so sorry this happened to you. I thought you'd be safe there. I really did. I thought you'd be safe at home."

Arykah squeezed Lance's hand lightly. He gasped and looked at her eyes. They were still closed, and she wasn't moving. Her steady breathing hadn't changed.

"Cheeks?"

She lay motionless on the bed. Lance looked closely for her eyelids to flutter. Maybe he had only imagined her squeezing his hand.

"Cheeks, baby, can you hear me? Please squeeze my hand again if you can hear me." Lance waited. He prayed out loud, "Oh, God, please make her squeeze my hand. Please, Jesus, please. Wake her up." More tears fell from Lance's eyes. He put his head down on Arykah's bed.

She squeezed his hand again. That time more firmly. Lance looked up and saw Arykah's left eye was open. He stood up. "Baby, I'm here. I'm here, my love." Lance kissed her forehead. "Can you see me? I'm right here."

Arykah slowly turned her head in Lance's direction. Her left eye looked at him. She didn't try to speak. Lance wasn't sure if she was looking at him or through him.

"Cheeks, can you see me?" he asked her again. She didn't blink or move. Lance became nervous. Does she have amnesia? Could she have forgotten him? "Do you know who I am?" Lance held his breath. He didn't know how he'd react if the doctor told him that Arykah couldn't remember him.

She squeezed his hand a third time. A single tear ran down Lance's face and snot was running from his nose. But he grew hopeful. "Do it again, baby. Squeeze my hand if you know who I am." He needed confirmation.

She did it. Arykah squeezed Lance's hand and held it tightly.

"Oh, thank God," he cried out. "Father, I thank you." Lance sat down in the chair and put his head down on Arykah's bed again. He sobbed loudly. "I'm so sorry, Cheeks."

Arykah released Lance's hand. She raised her arm and placed her open palm on the back of Lance's head. She couldn't console him, but she wanted Lance to know, through her touch, that he should stop crying. He shouldn't blame himself. What had happened to her wasn't his fault. She couldn't speak or move, but Arykah wanted her husband to know that she didn't hold him responsible for her pain and suffering. She could do nothing but lay still and listen to Lance cry.

A nurse came into the room and stood by Arykah's bed. She saw that she was awake.

"Well, hello there," she smiled at Arykah.

Lance looked up at the sound of the nurse's voice. He hadn't heard anyone enter the room.

The nurse patted Arykah's shoulder. "It's good to see that you're awake. I'm here to take your blood pressure. Is that okay?" The nurse knew Arykah couldn't consent or prevent her from taking her blood pressure. The question was merely a courtesy question. As she prepared to take Arykah's blood pressure, the nurse looked across the bed at Lance.

"And how are you, Mr. Howell?"

"Better now that she's awake."

"It was touch and go there for a while, but I knew she'd pull through. We're gonna take Mrs. Howell to another room and administer the rape kit her doctor ordered. It's only a fifteen-minute procedure. After that she'll be brought back here, and I'll give her a sedative through her IV."

"Um, what exactly do you do with a rape kit? Will it be painful for her?"

Arykah had been through enough trauma already. Lance didn't want her to experience more pain than she had to.

"I'm not gonna lie to you, Mr. Howell," the nurse said. "There's a lot of scraping and digging involved while administering a rape kit."

Lance frowned. "Scraping and digging? What are you scraping?"

"We're gonna scrape where she was raped. Front and back."

Lance knew exactly what the nurse meant. "Is that really necessary?"

"I'm afraid so. Semen samples, hairs, fingerprints, and skin cells are evidence that rapists leave behind. A rape kit must be used if you wanna catch the guy that violated your wife."

Lance looked at Arykah's battered face. "She's been through so much already."

"Yes, I know," the nurse agreed. "But afterward, Mrs. Howard will be given a sponge bath, and then the sedative will make her sleep."

"A sponge bath? Who'll give her a sponge bath?"

"Another nurse will do that."

"Uh-uh," Lance said. He didn't have a choice but to agree to the rape kit. He wanted Arykah's attacker caught, but knowing that another stranger would be bathing her while she's vulnerable and probably unresponsive, Lance wasn't having that. "I'll bathe my wife."

"Yes, sir," was all the nurse said.

Lance leaned over Arykah and kissed her forehead. "I'm gonna go and talk with our friends who are waiting outside." He kissed her forehead again. "I'll be right back, Cheeks."

Lance left the nurse alone to tend to Arykah, and he went to the waiting room and saw that Minister Weeks and Adonis had arrived at the hospital.

As soon as Monique saw Lance, she jumped up from her chair and hurried to him.

"How is she?"

Lance kissed Monique's cheek and hugged her tightly. "She's awake. She squeezed my hand. The nurse is with her now."

Lance put his hand on the small of Monique's back and escorted her back to where Carlton and Adonis were waiting. Both men stood when Lance got near.

Adonis was the first to embrace his friend. "I'm here for you, brother. Anything you need."

Lance was happy to have Adonis there. He knew he could count on him. "Thanks, Adonis."

Carlton stepped to Lance when he let go of the embrace from Adonis. "Bishop, is there anything the church can do for you or Lady Arykah?"

Lance shook Carlton's hand, then sat down in a chair. "No, not at the moment. As a matter of fact, Weeks, I don't want Arykah's accident to be made known to anyone other than the three of you." Lance looked at Carlton, Adonis, and Monique. "This must be kept under wraps. I'm sure Arykah wouldn't want to be the gossip of the church."

"Of course, Bishop," Carlton said.

"Absolutely," Adonis agreed.

Lance told Adonis and Carlton that Arykah was awake and the nurse was caring for her.

"That's good news," Adonis said. "Was she able to say exactly what happened at home this morning?"

Lance leaned back and crossed his left leg over his right knee, then exhaled. "No, not yet. Her top lip was busted. Her teeth had been knocked out. There are stitches. She can't speak. She can barely move."

Lance looked down the hall and saw the female detective heading his way. "Here comes that lady cop that was at the house."

When she had gotten close, Lance stood.

"Mr. Howell?"

"Detective? How are you?"

"I'm good, sir. But more important, I am wondering how Mrs. Howell is doing?"

"Well, she's awake. That's about all that I can tell you."

The detective pointed to a chair. "Please sit."

Lance sat and introduced the detective to Arykah's visitors.

She greeted Carlton, Monique, and Adonis, then turned her attention back to Lance. "Mr. Howell, does your wife have any enemies?"

That question threw Lance off. He looked up at the detective and frowned. "Enemies?"

"Enemies," she stressed the word. "People who hate your wife. Anyone who dislikes her for whatever reason. Can you think of someone who may have wanted to hurt her?"

"No," Lance said quickly.

"No one at all? Try to think if you overheard your wife arguing with anyone lately. Did she have any disagreements with anyone?"

Lance shook his head from side to side. "No."

"Well . . ." Monique chimed in.

The detective, Lance, Carlton, and Adonis all looked at Monique.

"Well, what?" the detective asked her.

Monique sat silent. She didn't know if she should reveal anything or not.

"What's your name again?" the detective asked when she saw that Monique had paused.

"Monique Cortland."

The detective wrote on a notepad she held in her hand. "Mr. Howell introduced you as his wife's best friend."

"Yes, that's right," Monique confirmed.

"Well, I trust that if you have any information that would help solve what happened to your *best friend*, you would tell it."

Monique got offended at the way the detective spoke to her. Of course she would do all she could to help bring Arykah's assailant to justice. And as Arykah's best friend, Monique didn't need to be told that. "Of course."

"Okay, well, what were you gonna say?"

Monique shifted in her chair. "When you asked Lance if Arykah had any enemies, my mind went to the members of our church."

"Really?" the detective asked with raised eyebrows.

"The church?" Carlton asked out loud.

"Not the entire church family, but I could name some folks that I think would want to see Arykah hurt."

"You're not suggesting the mothers did this to Arykah, are you?" Lance asked Monique. Yes, Mother Pansie and Mother Gussie had pulled some tricks, and they let it be known that they didn't care for Arykah. Lance would even go as far as to say that the mothers actually hated his wife, but they weren't capable of rape. They couldn't be that evil and relentless. He'd known the mothers his entire life. He refused to believe it.

"Not physically do it themselves. Of course not. But they could've gotten someone to do it," Monique stated as a matter of fact.

Carlton sat in disbelief at Monique's accusations. Just like Lance, he had grown up at Freedom Temple. Both Mother Gussie and Mother Pansie were like his own mothers. He remembered them pulling on his earlobe when he was caught misbehaving in Sunday School when he was a boy. He remembered them pinching his arm and twisting his skin whenever he acted out at church. Discipline, the mothers were capable of, but hiring a rapist was out of the question. It didn't happen. It could never happen.

The detective jotted down the mothers' names on her notepad. "Is there anyone else?"

"I can't think of anyone," Monique stated.

"Neither can I," Adonis said.

"No one at all," Carlton added. He wanted to tell the detective to scratch the mothers' names off her list.

The detective looked at Lance. "Anyone else, Mr. Howell?"

Lance leaned forward, rested his elbows on his knees, and exhaled. Monique had given him something to think about. The mothers' hatred for Arykah was evident. He thought about Mother Gussie setting Arykah up to fail with the Cartwright family. He remembered firing Mother Pansie and replacing her with Arykah. Mother Pansie was extremely angry at him for that. He recalled the red ink that was put in Arykah's office chair at church. Lance believed the mothers were responsible. And he believed they were responsible for sending him the photo of Arykah and her client having dinner. Arykah had never gotten around to asking Lance about the photo. And Lance didn't bother bringing the subject up because he knew that Mother Gussie was trying to set Arykah up. And when Arykah shared with Lance Mother Gussie's stunt with the dry cleaners, Lance was too outdone. He knew that the mothers didn't approve of his marriage to Arykah. From the moment he brought her to Freedom Temple, they had turned every female against his wife. Lance concluded that Monique was right in suspecting the mothers.

"I believe the mothers are responsible," Lance finally uttered.

"*Bishop?*" Carlton yelled out. "What are you saying?"

"There's a lot that you don't know, Weeks."

Carlton opened his mouth to speak, but then closed it. He had no words.

The detective stood to leave. "Thanks, everyone." She put the notepad inside her interior coat jacket. "I'll be in touch." She turned to leave, then stopped and turned around. She looked at Adonis. "Where were you at approximately nine this morning?"

Adonis cocked his head to the side, and so did everyone sitting. "I was at work," he answered sarcastically. How dare she treat him as a suspect? He loved Arykah and would never hurt her.

"And you, Mr. Weeks?"

"At work," he answered.

"If need be, I trust that both of you have alibis?"

"Detective, you're not suggesting that either of them had anything to do with—"

She cut Lance's words off. "And where were *you*, Mr. Howell?"

Lance stood up. "Excuse me?" First she questioned Adonis and Carlton's whereabouts, but now she had the gall to ask him his whereabouts as well.

"The next of kin is always a suspect in a crime such as this."

"So, what are you saying?" Lance asked. Was she accusing him of raping and brutally beating his own wife?

"I'm saying that I need to know your whereabouts at nine this morning."

"I was at church when Arykah called to tell me that she had been raped. Feel free to check our phone records."

"I absolutely will, Mr. Howell. My best to your wife." With that said, the detective walked away and left Lance and everyone else with their mouths hanging open.

Slowly, Lance sat down. He looked at Carlton. "Can you believe that?"

"Tell me what I don't know." Carlton needed to know why Monique and Lance believed the mothers were responsible for Arykah's rape.

Lance leaned back and exhaled. "I can't get into it right now, Weeks."

"Well, somebody is gonna tell me something. Bishop, you know that I've always had your back, and I've been rolling with you ever since you became the pastor of the church. But you gotta tell me why you think the mothers are responsible for this."

Lance knew he owed Carlton an explanation. He and Monique had just dropped a bomb. "You're right, Weeks. But I gotta get back to Arykah right now." Lance looked at Monique. "Tell him everything."

Monique nodded her head.

Lance stood and said to Carlton, "What she's gonna tell you has to stay here. Absolutely no one else can know. No one."

"You have my word. Give Lady Arykah my love," Carlton said.

Five hours later, on the south side of Chicago, she looked at him with fury in her eyes.

She couldn't believe what he had just told her. "You did *what?* I told you to rough her up. You were only supposed to scare her."

Streams of blood had dried along the lines of his jaws where Arykah's acrylic fingernails had raked his skin.

"Look at your face. How are you gonna hide those marks?" she fussed. She began pacing her kitchen floor. "Oh my, now what am I gonna do?" She wasn't remorseful that Arykah had gotten raped. She felt that Arykah really deserved everything that happened to her. Her worry was that she could possibly be found out.

"I couldn't help it," he said. "She was so pretty, and she was naked. I couldn't help it."

The woman stopped pacing and looked at him. "What the heck do you mean 'she was naked'? She opened the door with no clothes on?"

He sat in a chair next to the table and rocked back and forth. He was nervous. "I hit her, and she fell. Her dress came open. She was naked. I couldn't help it."

She rushed over to him and slapped his face. "Do you realize what you've done? You raped a woman. You're so stupid. Stupid, stupid, stupid. You can't do anything right. You're dumb and stupid."

He rocked back and forth again. "Stupid me, stupid me," he sang.

"Shut up!" she screamed. She began pacing the floor again.

"She wouldn't stop crying and screaming. I had to shut her up."

"I told you to rough her up. That's it. I didn't tell you to rape her."

He continued to rock back and forth. "She was so pretty. And she smelled pretty. I told her she was pretty."

She slapped his face again. "You're a stupid boy. Stop that rockin' and go take your crazy pills."

Chapter 17

It wasn't until two days after the rape that Arykah could move her lips and speak.

Lance had been by her side for the past forty-eight hours. He refused to leave her alone.

On the first night of Arykah's hospital stay, a nurse had come into her room and announced to Lance that visiting hours were over.

"I'm not leaving her."

"She's in good hands, Mr. Howell."

The only good hands that Lance felt comfortable leaving Arykah in were his own.

"My wife was raped and violently beaten. No one has called to tell me that the guy has been caught. She can't move, and she can't yell out, which means she's extremely helpless. I am not leaving her alone."

The nurse appreciated a faithful and loving husband. She didn't argue with Lance.

"I'll see to it that a cot, a blanket, and a pillow are brought in for you then."

"Honey?"

Lance was lying on the cot beneath a blanket when he stirred. He opened his eyes and saw Arykah sitting up in her hospital bed staring at him. He smiled. "Look at you sitting up. How are you feeling?"

The stitches in Arykah's top lip made it difficult for her to speak. The two front teeth that were missing caused her to have a lisp. "Better. Have I ever told you that you snore?"

Lance sat up on the cot. "Yes, you have. Many times."

"Well, you need to do something about that. I was dreaming about a lawnmower; then I woke up and realized that it was you cutting the grass."

"Oh, you got jokes." Lance was happy to see Arykah alert and in a good mood. Since she'd arrived at the hospital, she had been drugged and asleep for most of the time.

"I wanna talk to you about something, Bishop."

"Uh-oh. Whenever you call me 'Bishop,' it means that I'm in trouble." He swung his feet around and placed them on the floor. "What's up?"

Arykah exhaled. "I heard you crying the day I was brought here. I heard you saying to me that you blamed yourself that you weren't home to protect me."

"I do blame myself. I am your husband, your protector, your bodyguard."

"But we're not joined at the hip, honey."

"Well, maybe we should be."

Arykah exhaled again. Lance was showing signs. The kind of signs she didn't like. He was becoming overprotective. Arykah imagined him nailing all the windows and doors shut at their home. She imagined Lance going so far as to hiring her a personal bodyguard that would sleep in one of their guest bedrooms. Arykah imagined Lance demanding that she quit her job and stay at home where she could be watched twenty-four hours a day.

"Listen, you can't be with me every second of the day."

"But a personal bodyguard can."

Arykah shook her head from side to side. "I knew you were gonna go there. You're flipping out on me, but I'm gonna reel you back in. I don't want, nor do I need, to be treated as if I'm some sort of mental patient that can't be left alone. You're not gonna lock me in the house, Lance. I don't need a big, burly, scary-looking dude named 'The Crusher' living in my guest room. When I get released from this hospital, I'm going home and get my life back to normal. That's what's best for me."

"But what if that is not what's best for *me*?"

Arykah shrugged her shoulders. "How is me getting my life back to normal not what's best for you?"

Lance looked at Arykah's swollen right eye and the stitches on her top lip. Her nose was still disfigured. Yesterday the doctor told him that Arykah's ribs would heal on their own in time. But when Lance bathed Arykah, he saw purple bruises above her abdomen and on her side. And there was still the baby that Arykah had lost. He hadn't yet told her. "Babe, it kills me that I wasn't home to protect you on Monday. You're not a man, Arykah."

"Thanks for telling me that. I had no idea."

"I'm not kidding."

"You're not kidding that I'm not a man?"

"Cheeks, please. I'm so serious right now. You're not a man. You're not a husband. It's a man's job to protect his wife, his family, and his jewels. When a man fails to protect his jewels from harm, it puts him in a state of panic."

"And I understand that, honey. Really I do. But you can't hide me from the rest of the world. Life goes on." Arykah poked herself in the chest with her index finger. "*My* life will go on."

Lance hung his head. He sat on the cot in a somber mood. Of course he couldn't hold Arykah hostage in their home, but there had to be a way for him to better protect her. He'd have to figure something out.

"I know about the baby."

Lance's head jerked up. For the longest moment he didn't say a word. "You do?"

Arykah nodded her head. "I was conscious when the paramedics brought me here. I heard and felt everything. I feel like I'm sitting on a rolled up beach towel."

He wanted to chuckle about Arykah's reference to the super-sized Maxi pads the hospital provided their patients, but Lance felt the matter at hand was a serious one. He tried to read Arykah's mood. If she was sad she hid it very well. "Tell me how you're feeling about the miscarriage."

She shrugged her shoulders. "To tell you the truth, Lance, there's nothing *to* feel. I mean, had I known about the baby, I'd probably be in a different place. But I didn't even know I was pregnant. I never got the chance to become attached." She cocked her head to the side and looked at him. "Do you understand what I'm saying?"

"Yeah, I do." Lance was the one who had always brought up the subject of having kids. Arykah told Lance that she didn't have a strong desire to have any. If she and Lance conceived, she'd be fine with it. If they never conceived, she be fine with that as well.

Arykah heard voices outside her hospital room door. She looked down and saw shadows passing by. "Share with me your feelings about the baby. I know you want children. Are you sad?"

Lance opened his mouth to speak, then closed it.

"You can be honest with me," she encouraged him.

He gave her a slight smile. "I'm okay."

"You're not a good liar."

Of course he lied. Lance wanted children like he wanted his next breath. But Arykah had survived a traumatic experience. He wasn't going to lay his emotions on her. She needed to heal. If he confessed to Arykah that learning that she had miscarried really saddened him, Lance knew she'd feel guilty for her nonchalant attitude.

"No, really. I feel the same way that you do."

There was a knock on the door.

"Come in," Lance said. He was grateful for the interruption.

The female detective pushed the door ajar and peeked inside. "Good morning. May I come in?"

"Absolutely," Lance said. He stood from the cot and stretched. "Babe, this is Detective . . ." It dawned on him that he didn't know her name. He never gave her a chance to introduce herself on Monday when he sped home. He was too anxious to find out where Arykah was. And at the hospital later that day, when she had interrogated him, Adonis, and Carlton, he hadn't asked her what her name was there either.

"Rogers. Detective Cortney Rogers," she said, coming further into the room. She came and stood next to Arykah and smiled. Arykah's face hadn't healed much since Detective Rogers had first come on the scene in their home. There was so much blood coming from beneath Arykah's head at the time that Detective Rogers assumed she was deceased. But when she pressed her fingers against Arykah's neck, she felt a pulse. "How are you coming along, Mrs. Howell?"

Arykah placed her hand on her side. Her bruised and broken ribs were starting to hurt again. "I feel like I've been hit by a bus."

Lance saw that Arykah was becoming uncomfortable sitting up. "You want to lie down, Cheeks?"

"Perhaps you should," Detective Rogers encouraged.

"Yes, I do want to lie back," Arykah said, wincing at every move she made.

Detective Rogers stepped back and allowed Lance to adjust Arykah's bed; then she watched as he fluffed her pillows and made sure that she was as comfortable as she could be. Love poured from Lance. It was evident right then just as it was evident on Monday when Lance demanded to know where his wife was.

"Mrs. Howell, I'd like to ask you some questions about what happened at your home on Monday morning. Do you feel up to talking about it?"

Arykah moaned at the pain in her side.

"Maybe now isn't a good time, Detective," Lance stated.

"No, it's okay," Arykah countered. "Let's get it over with."

Detective Rogers pulled a notepad and a pen from her interior coat pocket. "What do you remember?"

Arykah exhaled. "Well, I was in the shower when I heard the telephone ring. It was Mother Pansie."

"What did she want?" Lance asked.

Detective Rogers jotted the name on her notepad. "Mother Pansie," she said out loud.

She turned back a few pages of the notebook and looked at her previous notes. "Mother Pansie," she said again. She looked at Lance. "That's the same name that Mrs. Howell's best friend gave to me. And you also stated that this woman should be considered as a person of interest."

"Yes, that's right," Lance confirmed. "Um, what did Mother Pansie want when she called?" he asked Arykah again.

Arykah looked from Lance to Detective Rogers, then back at Lance again. "Wait. You think Mother Pansie did this to me?"

"Well, Monique seems to think that the mothers may have had something to do with what happened to you. And I do too."

"Have you had any problems with the mothers of the church, Mrs. Howell?" Detective Rogers asked Arykah.

Arykah wanted to chuckle, but her ribs were singing a song. "Problems? Humph, that's really putting it mildly. They hate me. Both of them."

Detective Rogers looked over her notes again. "You're speaking of Mother Gussie as well, right?"

"Those old hags have been torturing me ever since the first day I came to the church."

"And when was that?"

"Almost six months ago," Lance answered. "But I wanna know what Mother Pansie wanted when she called."

"The same thing she always wants whenever she calls, Lance. I didn't even give her a chance to tell me what she wanted. I knew she was calling to speak with you. When I heard her voice, I told Mother Pansie that you weren't home and she should call you at the church."

"And then what happened?" Detective Rogers encouraged Arykah to keep talking.

"She hung up on me."

"Just like that?" Lance asked.

Arykah looked at Lance. "Does that surprise you?"

"Okay. So," Detective Rogers started as she was writing, "you were in the shower when the telephone rang. You answered the call, and Mother Pansie said what exactly?"

"She said my name," Arykah answered.

"So, Mother Pansie said, 'Arykah.'"

"She said, 'Lady Arykah?' It was a question; like she was verifying that it was me who had answered the telephone."

Detective Rogers was writing fast. "What happened next?"

"After Mother Pansie hung up on me, I headed back to the shower, but the doorbell rang. So, I shut the water in the shower off, then put my robe on, and went to answer the door."

"How much time had passed between Mother Pansie's call and the doorbell?"

Arykah thought about it. "Hmm, I'd say about ten or fifteen seconds. It wasn't long at all. As soon as I put the phone back on the base, I headed back to the shower, but the doorbell rang before I actually reached the shower."

"How many feet are there from your telephone to your shower?"

"I don't know." Arykah looked at Lance. "Honey, how many feet?"

"You answered the telephone on your nightstand, right?" Lance asked her.

Arykah nodded.

Lance looked at Detective Rogers. "It's probably about twenty to twenty-five feet from Arykah's nightstand to the shower."

Detective Rogers jotted down what Lance said. "Okay, so, Mrs. Howell—"

"Please call me Arykah."

Detective Rogers smiled. "Okay, then, Arykah, I want you to concentrate on what I'm going to ask you next. You can take your time to answer because I need you to be as precise as you possibly can. From the moment you put the telephone back on the base and headed back to the shower, how many steps had you taken before you heard the doorbell?"

Arykah looked up at the white ceiling above her. She closed her eyes and pictured her surroundings and where she was standing when the doorbell rang. "I'd say that I had gotten to my vanity table when I heard the doorbell."

"Her vanity is halfway between the nightstand and the shower," Lance offered.

"So, between ten and maybe fifteen feet?" Detective Rogers asked Arykah.

She nodded her head. "That sounds about right."

The detective jotted down more information on the notepad, then took her cellular phone from her interior pocket. "Let's try something." She gave Arykah her telephone. "Lay the phone down on the bed and I'm going to start walking toward the wall across the room. This is a small room, and it won't take me long to reach the wall. I want you to stop me when you think that enough time had passed from when I start to walk and time you think you heard your doorbell ring." She looked at Arykah. "Got it?"

"Yep. Got it."

"Whenever you're ready."

Arykah laid Detective Rogers cellular telephone on the bed next to her. The detective started walking toward the wall across the room while at the same time watching her wristwatch.

"Ding-dong," Arykah chimed when she felt that enough time had passed.

Detective Rogers stopped walking and turned around. "Thirteen steps. Two more and I would've gotten to the wall."

"What does all of this mean, Detective?" Lance was curious.

"It took nine seconds for Arykah to stop me. I'm wondering if nine seconds was enough time for Mother Pansie to have called whoever rang your doorbell to report that Arykah was home alone."

"If it happened that fast, then the guy was already waiting on the porch," Lance stated.

"And Arykah didn't give Mother Pansie a chance to ask if you were home. When she heard Mother Pansie's voice, Arykah immediately announced that you weren't home and that she should call you at the church."

"And that's when she hung up on me."

"And nine seconds later your doorbell rang. Coincidence? Maybe; maybe not."

"This is unbelievable," Lance said.

Detective Rogers began writing on her notepad again. "Okay, Arykah, you put your robe on and what happened next?"

"When I was a few feet away from the front door, the doorbell rang again. I asked who was at the door, and the guy said that he had a delivery for me. I thought it was Rafael, and I yelled to him that I was at the door."

Detective Rogers wrote the name down on the notepad. "Who is Rafael?"

"Her young Puerto Rican boyfriend that brings her secret packages that she thinks I don't know about."

Arykah's light complexion turned crimson red. She had been caught. "What are you talking about, Lance?"

"I'm talking about bags and boxes that are hidden in all of the closets throughout the house."

Arykah could do nothing but chuckle. She felt her stitches pull when she smiled.

"Rafael is the delivery guy that is assigned to my area. He drives the UPS truck."

Arykah looked at Lance. "I admit that I'm a shopaholic." Then she looked at Detective Rogers. "Rafael comes about two to three times a week."

"So, you didn't look through the peephole?" Lance asked.

"No," she was ashamed to admit. "I assumed it was Rafael because it was always Rafael."

"Except that time it wasn't him," Detective Rogers stated.

"Nope. It wasn't Rafael on the other side of the door, and I found that out when I opened it and got hit in my nose."

Detective Rogers could see Arykah tensing up. "What happened next?"

"I fell back on the floor. The guy came inside and kicked me in my left side. I heard the front door slam, and the next thing I knew I was being dragged by my arms into the living room. I was kicking and screaming and scratching. I remember getting hit in my right eye, and he told me to shut up. I'm not sure at what point my lip got busted. But the more I screamed, the angrier and stronger he got. He used his fingers on me at first—then he shoved himself inside me."

Lance twitched in his chair. That was the first time that he'd heard in detail what happened to Arykah. Listening to her describe the torture she suffered made him want to go out and buy a gun.

"Arykah," Detective Rogers started, "can you remember anything particular about him. What was he wearing? Did he have any visible tattoos? Was he light or dark skinned? Was he a short man or a tall man? Anything at all."

"I couldn't see his face," Arykah said.

"Did he wear a mask?"

"I don't think he wore a mask. I got hit in the nose as soon as I opened the door, and I fell down. He kicked me and ran around my head to drag me inside. At some point I got punched in the eye, and I just couldn't get a good view even when he was on top of me. But I do know that he was a bald man because I was scratching at his face and head and I didn't feel any hair."

"Was he wearing any cologne?"

"He was funky," Arykah remembered. "He smelled horribly, like he hadn't bathed in months, and his breath was foul."

"Did he say anything to you?"

"I remembered screaming for Lance, and the guy said that the bishop couldn't save me."

Lance stood and walked to the window and looked out of it. What Arykah had just said pierced his soul. The rapist was right. Lance wasn't there to save his wife.

Detective Rogers frowned at Arykah's last statement. "Do you generally call your husband 'Bishop'?"

"Huh?" Arykah didn't understand the question.

Lance turned around fast. He knew exactly where Detective Rogers was going with her question. "Oh my God," he said out loud.

Detective Rogers saw the look on Lance's face. She knew that he was reading her mind. "Mr. Howell, don't say anything." She concentrated on Arykah. "When you're talking to your husband, what do you call him?"

Arykah looked at Lance and wondered why Detective Rogers ordered him not to say anything. "What's going on?"

"Just answer her question, Cheeks," Lance said.

"What do you call him?" Detective Rogers asked a third time.

"I call him 'babe,' 'honey,' 'my love.' I have lots of pet names for him."

"Do you ever call him 'Bishop'?"

Lance came and stood at the foot of Arykah's bed. His blood was running hot through his veins. He and Detective Rogers were on the same page.

"Of course I call him 'Bishop' sometimes. Especially when we're at church. Or when I've asked him to do something and three hours later the task still isn't done, I may call him 'Bishop.' And sometimes I call him 'Bishop' when we're playing."

"Playing?"

Arykah tried to smile. "You know. Playing."

Detective Rogers knew what Arykah meant. "Oh, playing. Playing with each other. I get it," she smiled. "But what I wanna know is when you were calling out for your husband while you were being raped, what name did you call?"

"I was screaming his name."

Lance exhaled. "What name, Cheeks?" He was losing patience.

Detective Rogers looked at him. "Mr. Howell, please. Don't make me ask you to leave the room."

Lance nodded his head. He understood that he couldn't put words in Arykah's mouth.

He folded his arms across his chest and waited for her to say exactly what he and Detective Rogers needed her to say.

"Arykah, what name did you call out when you were screaming for your husband?"

"I was screaming 'Lance.' I was calling for Lance to come and save me."

Detective Rogers looked at Lance again. "Not a word."

He stood motionless.

"Arykah," Detective Rogers said. "You didn't scream 'babe,' or 'honey,' or 'my love'?"

Arykah looked at Detective Rogers like she was nuts. "What kind of question is that, Detective? Why would I call out any of those names? My husband wasn't making love to me. I was being raped by a stranger."

"I know that, Arykah. And the reason I asked you what name you called out is because you stated that when you called out Lance's name, the rapist told you that the bishop couldn't save you."

"Yes, that's right," Arykah said. She wasn't putting two and two together.

Lance could no longer keep quiet. "How did the rapist know that I was a bishop?" he blurted out to Arykah.

Detective Rogers scowled at Lance, but she didn't say anything to him. "Whoever raped you, Arykah, knows you personally. Or he has ties to someone else who knows you personally."

Chapter 18

When Arykah awakened from her nap on Thursday afternoon, she walked into her kitchen and found Myrtle standing at the stove making her famous homemade chicken noodle soup. Earlier that morning, Arykah's doctor had released her from the hospital with plenty of medication and strict instructions. She was not to overextend herself in any way, and she was ordered to get plenty of rest.

"Hey, Sugar Plum," Myrtle greeted Arykah by carefully giving her a hug and a kiss on the cheek. Myrtle knew that Arykah's ribs were broken, and she didn't want to squeeze her too tightly. "Are you hungry?"

With Myrtle's help, Arykah slowly walked to the kitchen table and sat down. "I didn't know you were here, Momma Cortland. Where's Lance? I remembered him lying down with me when we got home from the hospital this morning."

"Lance called me and said that you were sleeping. He asked if I could come and sit with you because he had some business to tend to. He sent a cab for me. He must've been in a hurry because as soon as my cab got here, the bishop was already backing out of the driveway."

"Really?" Arykah asked. She wondered what Lance was up to. That morning at the hospital, he told her that he would be taking a month off from the construction company. And he assigned Minister Weeks to conduct Bible class on Tuesday nights, but Lance would still take charge of his pulpit on Sunday mornings.

"He told me to reach him on his cellular telephone if I needed him, and he also told me to not let you out of my sight." Myrtle went back to the stove.

"He didn't say where he was going?" Arykah asked.

"Nope. And I didn't ask. It wasn't my place."

Arykah looked at the clock on the wall. It was almost two P.M. "And he's been gone since this morning?"

"Yep."

"Thanks for coming in, Mr. Howell. How's Arykah doing? She was released from the hospital this morning, right?" Detective Rogers shook Lance's hand and invited him to sit in a chair. They were in a small office at the rear of the Burr Ridge Police Department.

"Arykah's getting better by the day, Detective. Thanks for asking. Yes, she's home resting." Lance was curious why Detective Rogers had called and asked him to meet her at the police station.

"That's good," she stated. "Please let her know that I'm thinking of her."

"I certainly will," Lance responded.

Detective Rogers sat in a chair next to Lance with a remote control in her hand. "Well, I called you in to take a look at the surveillance tape that I confiscated from the security booth at the entrance gate of your complex." She pointed the remote control to a flat-screen high-definition television that was mounted on the wall in the office. As she pressed the play button, she said, "Check this out. This surveillance is from the morning of Arykah's attack. I think you'll find it quite interesting. Pay attention to the time of day it was on the bottom right-hand side."

Lance couldn't believe his eyes when he saw a bald black man walk right past the guard and into his complex at 8:27 A.M. Monday morning. "What the heck? Who is that guy, and where was the guard?"

"I interviewed a guy named Dwight Alexander, the guard that was on duty that morning."

"Yeah, I know Dwight."

"He said that someone in a car had driven up on the street, just outside the entrance of the complex, and asked him for directions. Dwight claimed that he left the booth, unattended, for about two minutes to give the person directions. I figured that was the moment this bald guy slipped passed Dwight without being noticed."

"Do you think the person that asked for directions was an accomplice?"

Detective Rogers shook her head from side to side. "No. Not at all. Dwight said the person asking for directions was an Asian lady with a screaming infant strapped in a car seat in the backseat of her vehicle. I believe the guy had been lurking around the security gate waiting for an opportunity to get past the guard's booth undetected. It was just perfect timing when the Asian lady drove up to distract Dwight." Detective Rogers pressed the rewind button on the remote control. "Take another look at this guy walking into your complex. After he passed the booth, he looked over his shoulder to make sure that he hadn't been seen. The camera mounted on the roof of the booth captured a good view of his face."

Lance leaned forward in his chair and looked closely at the man's face. He appeared to be about six foot two. He wore a short black leather jacket with dark pants and dark shoes. Both of his hands were in his jacket pockets, and his pace was quick.

"Do you recognize him at all?" Detective Rogers asked Lance.

"No. I've never seen him before."

"Are you sure? You've never seen him in your complex before? Maybe visiting a neighbor."

"Nope."

"What about church? Have you ever seen this guy at church?"

There were close to 500 members at Freedom Temple. While the women certainly outnumbered the men every Sunday, Lance couldn't place the man's face at church. "Not that I can recall."

Detective Rogers pressed the power button on the remote control and stood from her chair. "I'm expecting a call from the forensic scientist sometime today. Hopefully the fingerprints lifted from your doorbell will come back with a positive identification."

"And what if there are no matches? Then what?"

Detective Rogers saw the concern on Lance's face. "We'll get him, Mr. Howell. This is personal for me."

Lance cocked his head to the side. "Really? How so?"

The detective exhaled. "I'm a rape victim too. I was fourteen years old coming home from a friend's house trying to beat my curfew. I took a shortcut and walked through the alley behind my house. A guy jumped out from nowhere and grabbed me."

"My Lord," Lance said.

"He was never caught. That's why I'm making Arykah's case my priority. I'm determined to get justice for her and any other woman that predator may have attacked."

Lance was pleased to know that Detective Rogers was in his wife's corner. She wasn't just putting time in to receive a paycheck; she was passionate about the case. "I appreciate that, Detective."

"Please call me Cortney."

Lance smiled. "Okay, Cortney. And you can call me Lance."

"I'll be in touch as soon as I hear about the finger-prints."

As soon as Lance stepped outside of the police department, his cellular telephone rang. He saw his home number flashing on the caller identification. Immediately his heart started to race. "What's wrong, Mother Cortland?" he asked in a panic.

"Hi, babe. It's me."

"Cheeks, are you okay?"

Lance was riled up. Arykah feared that every time he left her presence he'd constantly worry about her. "Yes, I'm fine. Momma Cortland is here cooking up a storm. She's got a pot of chicken noodle soup on the stove. She found your Cornish hen in the freezer. It's in the oven with a pan of macaroni and cheese. Right now she's making her famous pineapple upside-down cake. Momma Cortland is giving you a run for your money, babe."

Lance chuckled. "Is that right?" Earlier that morning when he called and asked Myrtle to come and sit with Arykah, she told Lance that she'd be more than happy to help out in any way she could. Myrtle told Lance that she wanted to make chicken noodle soup for Arykah but hearing about the hen, macaroni and cheese, and cake was a pleasant surprise for him.

"Yep. You better get back here and claim our title."

"I'll be home shortly."

"Where are you? You slipped out on me."

"I'm at the police station. I just reviewed the surveil-lance tape from Monday morning. Detective Rogers and I saw a bald black guy walk right past Dwight at about eight-thirty in the morning."

268   Nikita Lynnette Nichols

"It could be him, Lance. The guy that raped me was a dark bald guy."

"The camera got a good picture of his face, but I didn't recognize him."

"I wanna see the tape." Arykah didn't get a good look of the guy during her attack, but she knew he was dark and bald.

"I definitely think you should review the tape. I didn't recognize him, but maybe you will. However, your doctor has you on lockdown for now. Maybe in a week or two; when you're stronger."

"So what happens now?"

"Hopefully the fingerprints lifted from the doorbell will find a match, but only if the guy has a criminal record."

"But what happens if he doesn't have a record? Will he just get away with what he did to me?" Arykah was worried that her attacker would never be caught.

"Cheeks, don't worry. We'll get him. I promise."

"But—"

"No 'buts.'" Lance refused to allow her to become discouraged. "Have I ever broken a promise to you?"

Arykah couldn't think of one. "No."

"And I won't start breaking any now. I'm on my way home. Can I bring you anything?"

"Yes, you can." Arykah perked up. "A pint of Chunky Monkey to go with Mother Cortland's pineapple up-side-down cake."

At 7:30 that evening, Lance opened the front door for Monique and Adonis.

"Welcome, folks. Come on in."

"What's happening, Bishop?" Monique stepped inside the foyer and kissed Lance on his cheek.

"All is well. All is well."

Adonis followed Monique inside. "Evening. I heard there was food here."

Lance chuckled. "Well, you came to the right place if you're hungry. Mother Cortland has been cooking all day." He noticed that Adonis was carrying a small black duffle bag on his shoulder. "That's the smallest duffle bag I've ever seen."

Monique brought her forefinger to her lips to quiet Lance. "Shh. It's a gift for Arykah."

"You bought her a miniature duffle bag? One pair of Arykah's earrings won't even fit in that thing."

"There's already something in the duffle bag," Adonis smiled.

Lance shut the front door, double bolted it, then looked outside through the glass. He was looking to see if anyone was lurking around in the shadows of the bushes. Until Arykah's attacker was caught and jailed, he wouldn't rest.

"What are you looking at?" Adonis asked.

"Nothing." Lance turned away from the door and led his friends into the living room where Arykah was sitting on the sofa.

"Hey, doll," Monique greeted her best friend. "Look at you sitting pretty." Monique sat next to Arykah, leaned over, and kissed her cheek.

"Not you too. Everyone is a liar these days."

"What are you talking about?"

"I'm talking about Lance telling me that I'm beautiful and gorgeous. And you coming in here saying that I'm pretty. You are all liars."

"No one is lying," Adonis said, sitting on the sofa opposite of Arykah and Monique. "You *are* beautiful and pretty and gorgeous." He set the small duffle bag on the floor next to his leg.

"Preach, brother, preach," Lance encouraged Adonis.

"Well, if that's the truth, Adonis, why does my mirror show that I look like the elephant woman?" Arykah was self-conscious of her still swollen right eye. Her nose was off center, and the stitches in her top lip hadn't yet dissolved. The black, purple, and blue bruises on her face were a constant reminder of her attack just three days before.

"You need to return that mirror from wherever you bought it and get a refund because it's lying to you."

Arykah looked from Adonis to Monique. "Please take your husband to an optometrist. Obviously, he needs glasses."

Monique chose to ignore Arykah's comment. Evidently Arykah was looking to have a pity party, but Monique was not going to indulge her friend. She and Adonis stopped by to cheer her up and take her mind away from the event that happened on Monday. "Um, we bought you a gift."

Adonis picked up the duffle bag and gave it to Monique. Monique set the bag on Arykah's lap.

Receiving gifts always cheered Arykah up. She slightly smiled. "Ooh, gifts. I like gifts." She unzipped the duffle bag and was surprised to see a little Yorkshire terrier pop its head out of the bag. "Oh, how cute," Arykah cooed.

"It's a Teacup Yorkiepoo," Adonis said.

"A Yorkshire terrier mixed with a poodle. And it's called a teacup because it's the size of a teacup. She won't get much bigger than that," Monique confirmed.

"We wanted to get you something to keep you company while you recuperated," Adonis said.

"I love it, Adonis," Arykah pulled the teeny puppy from the duffle bag. "Oh my God. She's adorable."

Lance shook his head from side to side. "That's all I need right now. Another diva in this house."

Arykah chuckled. "You got that right, honey. I'm big diva, and she's li'l diva."

Arykah gasped. "Lance, you just named her. We're gonna call her 'Diva.'"

Lance came to Arykah and scooped the puppy up in the palm of his hand. "Diva, huh? Knowing you, I thought you would've named her Gucci, or Prada, or after some type of designer."

"Well, she does need a middle name," Monique said.

"Don't encourage her," Adonis pleaded.

Lance gave the dark brown and black miniature fur ball back to Arykah.

"Hmm, let's see." Arykah thought of a middle name. "How about Diva Chanel Howell?"

"Arykah, can you get more snooty?" Lance asked.

"Oh, Bishop, you ain't seen snooty yet." Arykah brought the puppy to her face and kissed her teeny, black, wet nose. "Wait until me and Diva Chanel show up at church with matching dresses, hats, and bling." Arykah tickled Diva's belly. "You're my little diva. Yes, you are. Yes, you are."

"Thanks a lot guys. That was the perfect gift," Lance said sarcastically. Arykah was already a force to reckon with but with a mini-me in tow, Lance knew she was going to get out of control.

"Bishop, we gotta go shopping," Arykah stated.

"For what?"

"It's cold outside. Diva Chanel needs a fur coat."

Lance looked at Monique and Adonis. "See what y'all did?"

Arykah gave the puppy to Monique. "I can't bend over just yet. Can you put Diva on the floor?"

Monique gently set the puppy on the floor. "We bought food and puppy training pads too." She looked at Adonis. "Babe, can you please get the puppy's other bag from the car? I wanna put a few of the training pads down before Miss Diva has an accident on the new carpet."

Adonis rose from the sofa to honor Monique's request.

"By the way," Arykah said to Monique, "Lance told me that you took off from work yesterday to come here while the new carpet was being installed. I appreciate that. Lance said there was a lot of blood, and I don't know how I would've reacted had I walked in and saw it."

"It was no problem. Lance didn't wanna leave your side at the hospital, and neither of us wanted you to come home and see the stained carpet. That's what sisters do."

Adonis returned with the puppy's food and training pads. Monique placed four pads on the floor by the cocktail table. Diva wasted no time squatting on one.

"That's a good girl," Arykah said to her. "Now I'm supposed to give her a treat, right?"

"We got treats too," Adonis said, reaching in the bag he brought in from the car. He pulled out a small white chewable treat and gave it to Diva. "These are yogurt bites. The veterinarian said that puppies love them, and they train well with these."

"Well, now that Diva has her treat, can I have mine?" Monique asked Arykah. "I know Mother Cortland got down in your kitchen today. And where is Mother Cortland anyway?"

"She's upstairs resting," Lance answered.

Arykah struggled to rise from the sofa. She held her side and winced at every move she made. Lance was quick to assist her.

"Let's eat. I'm starved," Arykah said. "Hospital food is nasty."

Lance helped Arykah to the kitchen table and asked if she wanted a bowl of the chicken noodle soup Mother Cortland had made especially for her. Mother Cortland knew that Arykah was missing two teeth and her lip had been busted. She wanted to make Arykah a dish that would be easy on her mouth.

"Heck, no, I don't want any soup. I want the Cornish hen with mac and cheese."

"You can't chew that. But I'll be sure and let you know how good it is," Monique teased. She and Adonis were at the stove preparing their plates.

Arykah almost called Monique the "B" word. "You don't tell me what I can or can't chew. I'm not gonna sit here and slurp soup and watch the three of you chew like southern hillbillies."

"I'll have soup with you, Cheeks," Lance tried to comfort her.

Arykah didn't say a word. She slowly rose from the table and went to the cabinet next to the refrigerator, where she pulled out her blender and set it on the counter next to the stove.

"What are you going to do with that blender?" Monique asked her.

"Why are you in my business? You fix your plate, and I'm gonna fix mine."

Lance, Monique, and Adonis stopped what they were doing. They watched in amazement as Arykah cut three slices of the Cornish hen and put them in the blender. With a large silver spoon, she scooped three helpings of the macaroni and cheese and dropped them in the blender. They were absolutely stunned when Arykah went to the refrigerator and pulled out a gallon of milk and poured a fourth of a cup into the blender.

"I know you are not gonna do what I think you're gonna do," Lance said to her.

Without a response, Arykah placed the top on the blender and pressed the puree button.

"You are out of your mind," Monique said.

Adonis turned his nose up at Arykah's creation. "That ain't gonna taste good."

When her meal was turned into a liquid, Arykah removed the top from the blender and poured the mixture into a glass. She took the glass and placed it in the microwave and heated it for thirty seconds.

"You are nuts," Lance said to her.

Refusing to speak to any of them, Arykah removed the glass from the microwave and brought it up to her mouth. With one swallow she gagged. "Yuk. This is gross."

Adonis chuckled. "I told you. That's like blending a cheeseburger. It ain't gonna taste like a cheeseburger. It's gonna be nasty."

"What are you gonna do now?" Monique asked Arykah.

"I guess I'll have the soup."

Lance laughed. "Sit down, Cheeks. I'll get it for you."

Arykah sat at the kitchen table and saw Diva coming her way sniffing everything in sight. "There's my Diva." Arykah called for the puppy to come to her.

After Adonis put his plate of food on the table, he scooped Diva up and gave her to Arykah. "She's as light as a feather," he said.

Arykah brought Diva to her face. "You're so cute. And Mommy's gonna buy you so many cute clothes."

"Oh boy," Lance exhaled. He set Arykah's bowl of soup on the table in front of her. "How about a glass of sweet tea, Cheeks?"

"Tea would be great, babe. Thanks."

Lance returned Diva to the kitchen floor and was on his way to get Arykah's glass of tea when his cellular telephone rang. He pulled it from its holder that was attached to his belt loop. "It's Detective Rogers," he announced after he recognized the number.

Lance pressed the talk button and brought the telephone to his ear. "Hello, Detective Rogers."

Monique brought her plate of food to the table and sat next to Adonis.

Arykah filled them in on why the detective may be calling. "Detective Rogers said that she would call when she got the results from the fingerprints on the doorbell."

"You have a positive ID on the fingerprints?" Lance's voice rose. He looked at Arykah as he listened to the detective speak into his ear. "Arykah's rape kit?"

Arykah slowly stood holding her side.

"The semen sample matched whoever rang the doorbell," Lance told Arykah.

Arykah's heart started to race.

Lance told Detective Rogers that he was gonna put her on speaker. "Arykah is here, Detective. And so are our friends, Monique and Adonis. We can all hear you." Lance lay the telephone on the center island. "Go ahead, Detective."

"The semen collected from the rape kit, the skin cells that were scraped from beneath Arykah's nails, and the print from your doorbell all matched a guy who has a rap sheet a mile long."

Adonis and Monique stood from the table and came to the center island to hear Detective Rogers better.

"His name is Clyde Trumbull. He lives on the south side of Chicago."

"Clyde Trumbull," Lance repeated the name. "I don't know anyone with that name."

"How about you, Arykah?" Detective Rogers asked. "Does Clyde Trumbull sound familiar to you?"

Detective Rogers couldn't see Arykah shaking her head from side to side. "No. I don't know anyone by that name."

"Well, he certainly knows both of you. You should thank your best friend, Arykah. She hit the nail right on the head."

Arykah frowned, and so did Monique. "What do you mean?" Arykah asked Detective Rogers.

"Clyde Trumbull is the nephew of Ms. Pansie Bowak."

Arykah gasped so loudly that it caused her ribs to ache. She quickly consoled her aching side with her hand.

"I knew it!" Monique yelled out. "I *knew* it."

Lance and Adonis couldn't speak. They were in shock and remained silent.

"Ms. Bowak has been Clyde's legal guardian since he was sixteen years old. He's her late sister's only son. Clyde is thirty-nine years old but has been in and out jail since the age of twenty-three. You name it, Clyde has done it. Robbery, auto theft, breaking and entering, marijuana possession, and now sexual assault. He's bipolar and schizophrenic. I mean this guy is a real monster."

"Detective Rogers," Lance was finally able to speak.

"Please call me Cortney."

"Cortney, I am blown away at what you just laid on us. What happens now?"

"I have a warrant for Clyde's arrest. He'll be picked up tonight."

"What about Mother Pansie?" Monique asked. "We all know she's the mastermind behind Arykah's attack."

"Oh, I'm all over that, Monique. Don't you worry about Ms. Bowak. Once I get Clyde to sing—and I *will* make him sing—she'll be arrested too."

"My Lord, my Lord," Lance murmured.

"Seems like Clyde was Ms. Bowak's secret that she kept hidden from the outside world," Detective Rogers said. "According to a neighbor, Ms. Bowak didn't allow Clyde outside the home often. The few times she did expose him to the outside world was when he'd gotten into trouble."

"Well, that explains why she never brought him to church," Lance said. "This is so crazy. Mother Pansie darn near raised me in the church, and I never even knew she had a sister, let alone a nephew."

"Come on in . . . where the feast of the Lord is going on." The sanctuary choir at Freedom Temple was in high praise. "At the table. At the table . . . where the feast of the Lord is going on."

Lance sat in the pulpit. He was calm. He was cool. And he was collected. In his peripheral vision, he saw Minister Week's knees shaking.

Lance leaned over to him. "I shouldn't have told you anything, Weeks. You're a wreck."

Carlton took his handkerchief from his interior suit jacket and wiped sweat from his brow. "I can't believe it, Bishop. I just can't believe it."

Lance glanced at his wristwatch. It was all going down soon. He looked at Mother Pansie sitting on the second pew behind Monique and Myrtle. She was singing and rocking along with the choir, unaware that her world was about to crash. Lance wished that Arykah had been well enough to attend church and see justice get served.

He remembered Mother Gussie and Mother Pansie storming into his office after church. *"Bishop, she's not first-lady material."* Lance recalled the red ink they poured in Arykah's chair. He could still see the tears Arykah shed the night Mother Gussie lied about the time that Arykah was supposed to meet the Cartwright family for prayer. Lance had defended Mother Gussie. He thought back to the day when the photo of Arykah and her client having dinner had mysteriously shown up at church. And then there was the infamous suit jacket at the dry cleaner fiasco.

Lance realized that the mothers had spent a huge amount of energy in trying to oust his wife. They caused her grief and embarrassment. Therefore, he didn't feel the least bit guilty when he asked Detective Rogers to wait until Sunday morning, after Mother Pansie had left for church, to arrest Clyde Trumbull.

Lance's cellular telephone vibrated. He was expecting a text message. He nonchalantly read it.

We're coming in the church now.

Lance returned the telephone to the holder on his belt. He looked at Myrtle and Monique and winked his eye. Then he glanced at Adonis sitting behind the organ and winked his eye. Adonis had been instructed to continue to play throughout the chaos.

Lastly, Lance leaned over to Carlton again. "It's going down now."

Carlton's knees shook faster.

The doors of the church opened. Lance and Carlton saw Detective Rogers step to a female usher and flash her badge. The two women exchanged words; then the usher escorted Detective Rogers and two other policewomen down the center aisle. The usher brought them to Mother Pansie's row. Lance saw the usher point to Mother Pansie and say something to Detective Rogers.

The choir lost focus on what they were singing about. They stopped immediately, but Adonis kept playing. The entire church saw Detective Rogers gently grab Mother Pansie by her elbow and stand her up.

The look on Mother Pansie's face was horrifying when she realized what was happening. Detective Rogers read Mother Pansie her Miranda rights, then instructed the policewomen to place her in handcuffs. Mother Pansie's nephew, Clyde, was already at the police station. And although Detective Rogers hadn't question Mother Pansie yet, there was absolutely no doubt in her mind that Mother Pansie had sent her nephew to attack Arykah. He was incompetent and a nutcase.

Detective Rogers was sure that Clyde did not wake up the morning of Arykah's rape and choose her randomly to attack. He knew where she and Lance lived, knew to sneak past the guard on duty, and he knew that Lance was a bishop. Clyde had never been to Freedom Temple, and he'd never met Arykah. So Detective Rogers put two and two together and came to the conclusion that the only reason Clyde came to Arykah's house and assaulted her was because he had been told to do so. Told by someone who hated Arykah.

Mother Pansie looked toward the pulpit into Lance's eyes. She wasn't remorseful; she wasn't sorry. When her eyes locked on Lance's, he saw pure evil.

Mother Pansie didn't put up a fight. She held her head high as Detective Rogers escorted her out of Freedom Temple.

Lance stood from his chair and approached the podium. "At the table where the feast of the Lord is going on," he sang.

Adonis raised the volume on the organ. Slowly the choir began to sing along with their pastor. The mood at the church was a somber one. Everyone wanted to know why their beloved Mother Pansie had just been arrested. Lance didn't stop the service to give an explanation. He kept singing until the entire congregation joined in.

After praise and worship, he excused himself from the pulpit and left the church.

On cue, Minister Weeks stepped to the podium and took over the service.

When Lance arrived home, he found Arykah and Diva snuggled up on the sofa in the great room. Arykah was watching a movie on the Lifetime Movie Network Channel. He placed a large bouquet of roses on the table next to the sofa.

"Those are beautiful, babe."

"Yes, they are, but they're not from me. When I signed in at the gate, Dwight asked that I give the roses to you."

"You had to sign in?"

"Because of what happened to you, the home owners association has new rules. Residents must sign in and out of the complex, plus we gotta show our ID's. The guard on duty can never leave the post unattended for any reason. And visitors are required to show identification as well. They're only allowed past the gate if the resident they're visiting calls and gives permission to allow the visitor through."

"Wow. Talk about being on lockdown."

"What happened to you, Cheeks, could've been avoided. It shouldn't have taken a crime to happen for the new rules to be implemented. As much as we paid for our homes, you, me, and all of our neighbors should never have to worry about the safety of our families. Dwight sent the flowers because he knows he messed up. He wanted me to tell you that he is very sorry for what happened to you."

"Aw, Dwight is a good guy," Arykah said. "When I'm better, I'll go and speak with him." She repositioned herself on the sofa. "So, how did it go at church?"

Lance sat down on the sofa and laid his head on Arykah's lap. "Everything went according to plan."

"She didn't put up a fight?"

"Nope. Satan's sister is guilty."

"What about Mother Gussie?"

Lance sat up and looked at Arykah. "She called me when I left the church. Gossip travels fast. I left right after praise and worship was over. But just as I was getting into my car, Mother Gussie was blowing up my cell phone. First thing she said was, 'I didn't have anything to do with it, Bishop.'"

Arykah cocked her head to the side. "Oh really? Well, it's obvious that she knew what Mother Pansie was up to if she claimed she wasn't involved."

"Exactly. Someone had to have called Mother Gussie to tell her that her best friend was arrested at church. When she blurted out that she didn't have anything to do with it, I knew she was aware of Mother Pansie's plan. When I asked Mother Gussie what she was talking about, she paused."

"Uh-huh. She paused because she realized that neither of you had discussed Mother Pansie's arrest. And for her to call you and say that she was innocent, Mother Gussie inadvertently told on herself because she knew about my assault *before* it happened."

"She never answered my question when I asked her what she was talking about. But the fact that Mother Gussie knew what Mother Pansie had been planning and didn't tell me about it left a sour taste in my mouth. She knew what was going to happen to you, but she said absolutely nothing. I can't get past that, Cheeks. I told Mother Gussie that she was no longer welcomed at Freedom Temple."

Arykah's eyes grew large. "Wow. Was that a first for you? Dismissing someone from the church? It couldn't have been easy."

"It was very easy," Lance said. "When it comes to my wife, I don't play around. I have zero tolerance as far as you're concerned. Dismissing Mother Gussie from Freedom Temple was a first for me, but it won't be the last if I get wind of anyone else trying to harm you."

"You are the bestest husband on this side of heaven, Bishop. And you look kinda sexy when you put your foot down." Arykah ran her finger along Lance's goatee. "You're looking real sexy right about now."

"Don't start anything that you can't finish, Cheeks."

"Who says that I can't finish?"

"Your doctor, that's who. He told you to not overextend yourself. No strenuous exercises."

"My grandmother use to always say, 'Never let the weatherman stop your plans. So what if it rains?'"

Lance frowned. "What in the world does that mean?"

Arykah took her time to stand. She untied the knot of her robe, slipped it from her shoulders, and let it fall to the floor. She turned from Lance and started walking toward their bedroom. Seductively, she looked over her shoulder and said, "I can show you what it means better than I can tell you."

It had been awhile, and Lance was craving his wife. "What about the beach towel you're sitting on?"

"Don't concern yourself with the towel. There are ways around the towel. I'm a pro at what I do. You know that."

Arykah was telling the absolute truth. She was a master at loving Lance. She shined in the bedroom and was skilled beyond belief.

Lance rose from the sofa and followed Arykah to their bedroom.

Book Club Discussion Questions

1. After vacationing in Jamaica, Bishop Lance Howell returned to Freedom Temple with a wife in tow. What affect did Lance's actions have on the church?

2. Being a pastor's wife, do you think that Arykah should have toned down her dress code? Is it okay for a pastor's wife to wear skinny jeans, plenty of bling, and stilettos?

3. Was Mother Pansie right or wrong for taking Miranda from the choir because she was pregnant? Was Arykah right or wrong for fighting on Miranda's behalf to get her back in the choir? Lance was caught in the middle, but he ultimately sided with his wife. Did he make the right decision when he escorted Miranda to the choir?

4. Arykah didn't bite her tongue when she confronted the young lady who was having an affair with a married man. Arykah basically told the young girl that she was a whore. Was Arykah too tough, or should she have been more diplomatic?

5. Why do you think Mother Pansie and Mother Gussie had such a strong dislike for Arykah?

6. Was Arykah's character too bold, bossy, and outspoken? How would you have written her character differently?

7. When Arykah realized that Mother Gussie was behind the suit jacket at the dry cleaner fiasco, she drove to Freedom Temple and confronted her. Was it wrong for Arykah to have threatened Mother Gussie? If so, how should she have handled that situation differently?

8. At first, Lance didn't believe that Mother Gussie had set Arykah up to fail when she'd given Arykah the wrong time to be at Brother Cartwright's house. Was Lance wrong for not automatically supporting his wife?

9. At dinner, Arykah shared with Gladys, Darlita, and Chelsea that she role-played in the bedroom. As a pastor's wife, should she have revealed that information?

10. As a pastor, was it wrong for Lance to ask Detective Rogers to arrest Mother Pansie at church? Why do you think Lance wanted to embarrass her in front of the entire congregation?

Coming Soon

Damsels In Distress

by

Nikita Lynnette Nichols

Chapter 1

It was a late Saturday evening in April when twenty-seven-year-old Ginger Brown modeled a royal-blue, two-piece satin suit as her best friends, Portia Dunn and Celeste Harper, encouraged her to sashay and turn, then turn and sashay again. Ginger had recently bought the suit at Macy's to wear to church on Sunday. It was Women's Day and Ginger was looking forward to emceeing the afternoon service.

Portia and Celeste were seated on opposite ivory lounge chaise chairs in Ginger's immaculate living room in the city of Westchester, a small suburb just west of Chicago.

The thirty-two-inch space between the women that were seated served as a catwalk for Ginger to strut.

"All right, Ginger, girl, show us what you're working with," Celeste encouraged.

Ginger unbuttoned the jacket, slipped it off her arms, then swung it over her left shoulder to reveal the silver-gray satin camisole she wore underneath. Gracefully, she turned away from Portia and Celeste, then strutted back to her starting point just at the archway that separated the living room from the dining room.

As Ginger walked, Portia's smile quickly faded when she noticed black and blue bruises on Ginger's right shoulder next to the spaghetti strap of her camisole. She sat straight up in the chaise chair. "Ginger, what the heck is that on your shoulder?" Portia's outburst startled both Ginger and Celeste.

Ginger had no clue the boxing match from the previous night with her live-in boyfriend was evident. She was usually careful not to allow any bruises to show. Had she known the marks were visible, Ginger never would've taken off her jacket.

"Oh, girl, it's nothing," she said, quickly putting the jacket back on. "Ronald got a little high last night. Y'all know how he gets." Ginger's poor excuse for being a punching bag was for her own benefit. Truth be told, she was quite embarrassed. How could she have been so careless and allow anyone to see the bruises?

When Ronald came home the evening before with his eyes glazed, Ginger knew he had brought trouble home with him. She was in the kitchen, standing at the stove, frying pork chops.

He approached Ginger reeking of marijuana and lifted the lid of a pot that sat on the stove. "What is this?" he asked. His voice was almost a whisper.

Nothing infuriated Ginger more than when Ronald asked her a question that he already knew the answer to. Anyone in their right mind could see that the pot was half filled with white rice. Evidently smoking weed had taken Ronald's common sense away.

Ginger exhaled a loud sigh of frustration. She hated when he asked stupid questions.

"It's rice, Ron. I'm gonna make gravy to go with it."

Ronald placed the lid back on the pot, then turned to walk away. Ginger thought the conversation was over but was mistaken as Ronald spun back around. He slammed his open palm against Ginger's face and with all the strength he had, he pushed her backward. He sent her flying down, but on the way to the floor, Ginger's right shoulder connected with the edge of the marble-top kitchen table. She screamed out in pain.

"Who the *%#@ are you huffin' and puffin' at, huh?"
Ronald stood over Ginger glaring down at her. He
drew his leg back in preparation to kick Ginger in her
abdomen but stopped short. "I told you about catching
an attitude every time I ask you a question."

Ginger lay on the kitchen floor moaning and winc-
ing in pain. Her right shoulder was on fire.

"I don't want rice and gravy. Throw that crap out
and make me some corn." With that being said, Ron-
ald exited the kitchen.

Now Ginger stood in the living room having to defend the cause for the bruises to her friends. Celeste
stood, went to Ginger, and forcefully pulled the jacket
off her shoulders to get an up close and personal look at
the marks. Portia came and stood next to Celeste. The
bruises were blue, black, and purple.

It wasn't the first, second, or third time Celeste and
Portia witnessed bruises on Ginger. They've been
begging Ginger to end her abusive relationship with
Ronald ever since she moved him into her home three
years ago.

Last month, Ginger showed up at church with a
swollen busted lip that she tried to hide with lipstick.
Portia and Celeste were so angry that they wanted to
go to Ginger's house and confront Ronald, but just like
all the times before, Ginger had begged them not to
interfere. Now the three best friends stood in Ginger's
living room facing the issue again for what seemed like
the one-hundredth time.

"Is that fool still pounding on you, Ginger?" Celeste
asked.

Ginger's heart raced as tears began to run down her
chocolate-colored face. "Celeste, please understand,"
she pleaded.

Portia frowned. "Understand *what,* Ginger? That fool is out of control, and you need to get away from him."

"I'm calling the police." Celeste returned to her chair for her purse. Her cell phone was inside.

Ginger was quickly on Celeste's heels. As soon as Celeste pulled her phone from her purse, Ginger snatched it out of her hand. "No, Celeste."

Celeste placed her right hand on her hip and shifted all of her weight onto one leg.

"No? What the heck do you mean 'no'? Ronald needs to be locked up, and you need to be institutionalized for allowing him to beat on you."

By the expression on Ginger's face, Portia knew Celeste's words had hurt her.

Celeste had basically accused Ginger of being crazy.

Portia came and stood next to Ginger. "Celeste, I know you're upset but—"

"Upset?" Celeste had cut Portia's words off. "*Furious* is what I am, Portia. And why are *you* so doggone calm about this? We've been dealing with this crap for three years. Did you get a good look at her back?"

Ginger placed her face in her hands and cried. Not only was she embarrassed, but if a call was made to the police and Ronald found out about it, Ginger knew she'd be in even more trouble with him.

Portia wrapped her arms around Ginger. "It's okay, sweetie. We're gonna get through this. We'll work it out."

Celeste couldn't comprehend Portia's attitude about the situation Ginger was in.

"How do you suppose we 'work this out,' Portia? Huh?"

Portia guided Ginger to a chair and sat her down. "I don't know, Celeste. Let's talk about it."

In Celeste's mind, talking wasn't necessary. She hastily left the living room and walked toward Ginger's bedroom. "Yeah, okay. You and Ginger talk. I know what I'm gonna do."

In Ginger's bedroom, Celeste opened the closet door. She found a small suitcase and threw it on the bed. Next, she snatched blouses, dresses, and pants off of racks and threw them on top of the suitcase. Ginger and Portia came into the bedroom and saw Celeste on a rampage. Just as Celeste was headed for the dresser, Ginger ran and stood in between it and her friend.

"What are you doing, Celeste?" Ginger asked her.

"I'm helping you get through this. That's what I'm doing. Get out of my way."

More tears ran down Ginger's face. "Ron apologized. He promised to never hit me again."

"That's what he said the last time, and the time before that, Ginger," Portia interjected from the doorway. "When are you gonna learn that Ronald is sick?"

Ginger looked at her best friends through teary eyes. "Y'all just don't understand. He told me . . ." She couldn't finish her sentence as she choked back tears.

Celeste placed her hands on her hips again. "He told you what?"

Ginger knew that if she revealed what Ronald had told her years ago, all heck would break loose. She hesitated. She wondered how she could pacify this situation and calm Portia and Celeste down.

"He told you what?" Celeste's outburst startled Ginger.

Ginger opened her mouth and spoke softly. She looked into Portia's eyes because she didn't want to see the expression on Celeste's face. "Ron once told me that he'd kill me if I ever left him."

Both Celeste's and Portia's eyes grew wide. *"What?"* they screamed at the same time.

Celeste became enraged. She was even more eager to pack Ginger's clothes and get her out of that house. "Move out of my way, Ginger."

Ginger pleaded with Celeste to calm down. "Celeste, please understand."

"Why do you keep saying that, Ginger? What is it that you want us to understand? You ain't married to that fool. Ron won't even give you his last name. He's too darn lazy to get a job. All he does is smoke weed all day. He's living in *your* house while *you* go to work every day. *You* pay the mortgage, utilities, and *you* buy the groceries. Ron has you so twisted that he makes you ask his permission to go to church. Plus he's ugly. I don't see how you can stand to look at him let alone sleep with him. You deserve better, Ginger. So, since you don't have enough brains to pack your bags, I'm gonna do it for you." Celeste pushed Ginger aside and opened the top dresser drawer, then grabbed a handful of bras and panties and threw them on the bed.

Ginger grabbed her underwear from the bed and brought them back to the dresser.

"Stop it, Celeste."

Celeste ignored Ginger and proceeded to another drawer. She grabbed another handful of clothes and took them to the bed. On her second trip, she looked at Portia standing in the bedroom doorway. "What the heck are you just standing there for? You should be helping me."

Portia didn't move. She was torn. She knew Celeste was doing the right thing by packing Ginger's clothes, and of course she should be helping Celeste. But Ginger just said that Ronald would kill her if she left him.

Portia watched as Celeste transferred clothes from the dresser to the suitcase; then she watched Ginger transfer clothes from the suitcase back to the dresser. Portia knew Celeste was out of control, but then again, enough was enough.

Ginger was crying and begging Celeste to stop trying to pack her clothes.

Celeste forcefully took the clothes from her hand and looked at her. "Look, Ginger, I'm sick of this crap. Now, either we pack your clothes and you come home with me, or we pack Ron's clothes and put them out on the curb. One of you is getting the heck out of here tonight. Now, since this is your house, I'll let *you* decide. Because if he touches you again, I'm gonna pay somebody to touch *him*. So, who's leaving—you or Ron?"

Ginger didn't answer Celeste. She stood in the middle of her bedroom crying.

Celeste waited five seconds, then threw the clothes on top of the suitcase and walked to the dresser to grab more. Ginger reached out to try to stop Celeste but lost her balance and fell. She managed to grab a hold of Celeste's left leg. Celeste stumbled but was able to deliver the suitcase's deposit. Ginger begged and cried for Celeste to stop packing her clothes. "Celeste, please. Please, Celeste."

Celeste dragged Ginger from the dresser to the bed as she continued to pack her clothes. "Portia, get her off of me."

Portia had a decision to make. She could only pray that Ginger would eventually forgive her and Celeste for doing what had to be done. She went to Ginger and pulled her arms from around Celeste's legs. "Ginger, we gotta do this."

Ginger stopped fighting. She knew that her friends were relentless, and they were not going to let her stay in her home as long as Ronald resided there also. But Ginger also knew that she needed to come up with a plan to get Portia and Celeste to leave before Ronald got home. "Okay. Okay, I'll go to the police station." She told them what they wanted to hear.

Portia released Ginger's arms. "You will?"

"Now you're talking like you got some common sense," Celeste said.

"Get your big butt off of me, Portia."

Portia stood, and so did Ginger.

Celeste grabbed a suitcase by the handle and instructed Ginger and Portia to take one each. "Ginger, you're coming home with me after we leave the police station."

"Okay." Ginger didn't argue. She wanted them to leave. She had a plan.

Celeste, Ginger, and Portia rode in silence to the police station. It was when Celeste drove into a parking spot that Ginger said from the backseat, "I'm not doing it."

Both Portia and Celeste turned around and looked at her.

Celeste was furious. "What the heck you mean you're not doing it?"

Ginger turned away from her friends and looked out the window. "I changed my mind."

"Now what?" Portia asked Celeste.

Without a word, Celeste removed her key from the ignition. "I'll be right back." She opened the door and got out of the car. After she shut the door, she pressed a button on her remote. The feature that Celeste had on her car was the same feature that the police use as car bait. Once a button is pressed on the remote, the car can't be opened from the inside. Because the windows were raised, Celeste couldn't hear the foul names Ginger called her as she ran inside the police station.

Two minutes later, Celeste returned to her car with an African American woman, Officer Phyore Montgomery.

Celeste pressed the button on her remote again and opened the passenger door.

"Ginger is the one sitting in the backseat."

Officer Montgomery knelt and looked in the backseat. She asked Portia to get out of the car. With Portia out of the way, Officer Montgomery sat in the front passenger seat and faced Ginger. "Are you Ginger Brown?"

Ginger sat in the backseat with her mouth shut.

"I'm Officer Montgomery. I'm here to help you. Have you been abused?"

Not a word from Ginger. Celeste stuck her head inside the car. "Open your darn mouth, Ginger."

Officer Montgomery patted Celeste's arm. "Mrs. Harper, please calm down. Give her time."

Celeste rolled her eyes at Ginger and walked away.

Officer Montgomery saw tears streaming down Ginger's face. "Miss Brown, I've been on the force for twelve years. I've dealt with all kinds of abuse. Nine times out of ten, domestic abuse turns into murder because the victim is too afraid to report it. Your friends brought you here because they love you and want to help you."

Ginger looked through the glass and saw Portia and Celeste glaring at her. "They kidnapped me. Isn't that a crime? Can I file charges against them for bringing me here against my will?" Ginger had just lied to Officer Montgomery. Back at her house she had agreed to come to the police station just to get Portia and Celeste to leave before Ronald got home.

Officer Montgomery had already gotten the full story from Celeste why she and Portia had brought Ginger to the police station. "They brought you here to save your life."

Officer Montgomery didn't even entertain the thought of allowing Ginger to press charges against her best friends. "Have you been abused?" she asked Ginger again.

Ginger turned her head in the opposite direction. Tears ran down her face, but she refused to answer the question.

"Miss Brown, I can't help you if you don't talk to me," Officer Montgomery said.

"Mrs. Harper said that your boyfriend threatened to kill you if you told. Is that true? Because if it is, I will personally see to it that you're placed in protective custody. We can have him picked up tonight."

Nothing from Ginger.

Portia became frustrated. "Ginger, tell her about the time when you were five months pregnant and Ron kicked you in the stomach. That caused you to miscarry."

Officer Montgomery's mouth fell open. "Is that true?" she asked Ginger.

A tear dripped from Ginger's chin.

Officer Montgomery pled with her. "The only way to stop this is to press charges. If you don't press charges, it won't stop. He's not worth your life. I know you're afraid, but you have to admit to me that he put his hands on you."

Ginger focused on someone walking across the street. Officer Montgomery sat in silence for a few seconds. "You are a beautiful black woman. Learn to love yourself. It hurts me deeply to get called to a house because of domestic abuse and find one of my black sisters dead. And I'm gonna tell you something, Miss Brown. Eventually he *will* kill you. It happens like that all the time. So, get out while you can."

Officer Montgomery waited another few seconds for Ginger to confess that she was being abused, then got out of the car and looked at Portia and Celeste. "I can't do anything without a complaint from her."

That didn't please Portia. "This is bull crap. Look at her shoulder."

"I understand, but I can't make an arrest unless she files a formal complaint."

"So, what are we supposed to do?" Celeste asked.

Officer Montgomery shrugged her shoulders. "There's nothing anyone can do. Miss Brown has to help herself first."

"But what if we say that we actually saw her boyfriend hit her?" asked Portia.

Officer Montgomery sighed. She understood Portia and Celeste's frustration, but she couldn't take a false statement. Neither of them had actually seen Ronald put his hands on Ginger. They'd only seen the marks he left behind.

"If Miss Brown is not willing to file a complaint, according to the law, to heck with what anyone else says."

Celeste stormed around to the driver's door, got in, and slammed the door. Portia sat in the passenger seat. Officer Montgomery watched Celeste's tires burn rubber as she pulled away from the curb.

Celeste drove back to Ginger's house so that Portia could get her car. She pulled into the driveway and parked next to Ronald's car. "The fool is home. Hurry up and get out, Portia."

Ginger yelled from the backseat. "Let me out, Celeste." She knew Celeste was gonna try to take her home with her.

"No!"

Portia looked at her friend. "Celeste, Ginger is a grown woman. We can't make her do anything she doesn't want to do. Look what just happened at the police station."

"I don't care. If you hurry up and get out, I can drive off."

Ginger yelled again. "Celeste, I wanna get out of this car."

Celeste switched the gear to park, took her foot off the brake pedal, then turned her upper torso around to face Ginger. "You know that if you go in there with your bags, Ron's gonna go off."

"Well, then, keep the bags, Celeste. I'll get them from you tomorrow."

"If you live that long," Celeste commented.

Ginger couldn't believe what her friend had just said to her. "You know what, Celeste. Just because you live in a fairy-tale world with the perfect husband and the perfect job don't make you any better than anyone else."

"What the heck are you talking about, Ginger? I'm trying to keep this fool from killing you. You better wake up and realize who really loves you. I'm tired of begging you to save your own life. If you wanna let that fool knock your brains out, then that's on you 'cause I'm through with it." Celeste opened her door, got out, and then pressed the seat forward.

Ginger climbed out of the backseat. Portia exited the passenger seat and walked around to the driver's side where Ginger and Celeste stood.

Ginger looked at both of them. "I love y'all. I will see you at church in the morning."

Portia hugged Ginger. "I love you too, sis."

Ginger let go of Portia and looked at Celeste. "I'm sorry for yelling at you. I know you love me."

Celeste made no effort to hug Ginger. She was angry. "Yeah, whatever. I gotta go."

She got in the car and backed out of the driveway.

"You know Celeste is a hothead," Portia said to Ginger when they were left alone in Ginger's driveway. "But she only wants what's best for you. We both do."

"Portia, I love Ronald. And I know that he loves me too." Ginger made the statement as though she was simply telling Portia what time of day it was. It saddened Portia that Ginger may have actually convinced herself of that lie. "Ginger, is he loving you when he's bouncing you off the walls?"

Ginger lowered her head and didn't respond.

"Do me a favor, Ginger," Portia said. "When Ronald goes to sleep tonight, take a picture of his privates. I wanna see if it's been dipped in platinum. That's gotta be the reason you're tolerating this crap." With that being said, Portia proceeded to her car.

When Ginger entered the living room, she saw Ronald lying on the sofa watching a basketball game.

"What did I tell you about leaving this house with dirty dishes in the sink?"

Ginger closed the door behind her and stood with her back against it. "I'm sorry, baby, I forgot."

Ronald looked at the suit she was wearing. "Where have you been?"

Ginger nervously looked down at her suit. "I went to see a lady from the church. She's a seamstress. I needed to get my skirt hemmed for church tomorrow."

Ronald repositioned himself on the sofa. "You went to church last Sunday. You ain't going tomorrow."

Ginger started to panic. Her name was on the church program. She'd been looking forward to emceeing the Annual Women's Day program for the past three months. In preparation for the service, Ginger had been walking around the house pretending to hold a microphone in her hand, practicing her speech. What would happen if she didn't show up at church? Folks were depending on her to be there. Ginger had to be at church; she just had to.

She walked to Ronald and knelt down to kiss his lips softly before heading to the kitchen to wash the three glasses that she, Portia, and Celeste had drank tea from.

"Next time, I'm not gonna ask any questions about dirty dishes being left in the sink, Ginger. If you're gonna act like a two year old, then I'll treat you like one."

"It won't happen again," Ginger said over her shoulder.

"Make me a sandwich," he ordered.

Five minutes later, Ginger brought Ronald a bacon, lettuce, and tomato sandwich on a small wooden lap dinner tray. Next to the sandwich was a glass of grape Kool-Aid.

"Where's my napkin?" he asked. "And you know I like ice in my Kool-Aid."

Ginger quickly returned to the kitchen for a napkin and to put ice cubes in the glass of Kool-Aid. "Can I go to church tomorrow?" she asked as she gave Ronald the napkin and Kool-Aid.

Ronald looked at her. "Didn't we just come to the conclusion that you went last Sunday?"

"Yeah, but tomorrow is the annual Women's Day celebration. I've been asked to be the Mistress of Ceremony." Ginger stood in the middle of *her* living room, looking at this unemployed man who was *not* her husband lie on *her* sofa and watch the television *she* paid for, praying that he would *permit* her to go to church.

It dawned on Ginger that Celeste was right. Ronald was ugly.

Ronald drank from the glass and swallowed. "I should not let you go anywhere 'cause I'm tired of telling you about leaving dirty dishes in the sink."

With her suit still on, Ginger sat next to Ronald and pretended to be into the game he was watching. When he finished his meal and drank the last of his Kool-Aid, she took the plate and glass into the kitchen and washed them. Then she turned the kitchen light off, came back in the living room, and stood nervously by the sofa. "Honey, I know you're into the game, but I was wondering if you've decided to let me go to church."

Ronald made Ginger stand there for a long thirty seconds while he continued to watch the game before he asked, "What's in it for me?"

Ginger didn't say a word. She knew what to do next. Right there in the living room, she stripped naked, then knelt before Ronald. He grabbed Ginger by the back of her head and guided her face toward his lap.

Celeste walked in the door and slammed it shut behind her. Her husband, Anthony, was talking on the telephone with their pastor. He watched as Celeste threw her purse and keys on the sofa next to him and walked toward the rear of the house.

"It was good talking with you too, Pastor. We'll see you at church in the morning."

Anthony disconnected the call and went to find Celeste. He found her in the master bathroom sitting at her vanity removing makeup from her eyes with a cotton ball. In the mirror, Celeste saw Anthony leaning against the door frame watching her. She didn't acknowledge him, but by how far Celeste's lips were poked out, he sensed that she was upset.

Celeste tossed the cotton ball toward the trash can but missed. Anthony picked it up from the floor and threw it in the receptacle, then went and sat next to her. Celeste inched over to allow him more room.

Anthony faced his wife. "Let me guess. Ginger and Ron, right?"

"Yep, you guessed it."

Anthony extended his legs and crossed his ankles. He leaned backward and placed his elbows on Celeste's vanity. "What did that punk do this time?"

"He hit her again, Tony. You should see her shoulder. Bruises are every-darn-where."

"She showed them to you?" Anthony asked.

"No. Evidently Ginger didn't know the marks were there. Portia and I saw the bruises while she was modeling the suit she's wearing to church tomorrow; that is, if Ron even allows her to go to church. You know how he is."

Anthony could only imagine how Celeste behaved when she saw Ginger's bruises.

"You didn't freak out did you, Celeste?"

Celeste was applying moisturizer to her face when she stopped and looked at her husband. "Heck, yeah, I freaked as I should have. What would you do if your best friend was getting his butt whipped all the time?"

That wasn't the first time that Anthony had to remind Celeste to stay out of Ginger's business. "Look, baby, you and Portia have to come to the conclusion that Ginger is an adult. You can't live her life or make decisions for her, nor can the two of you fight her battles. Yeah, Ron is a punk. But until Ginger decides that she's had enough of his crap, there's nothing you, Portia, or anyone else can do.

"*My* concern is you. You're *my* wife, and I don't want you to have a stroke or develop ulcers over Ginger and Ron's issues. The only thing you can do for Ginger is pray for her and be there when she needs you."

Tears ran down Celeste's face. "Portia and I took her to the police station, but she wouldn't even get out of the car. I went inside and got a female cop, a sister, and brought her to Ginger, but she sat in the backseat and wouldn't open her mouth. Portia and I looked like two fools."

Anthony grabbed Celeste's hand and kissed her open palm. "You and Portia have been going through this with Ginger for years. Nothing will change until she faces reality and realize that it's up to her, and *only* her, to get away from him, so let's change the subject. How did your doctor's appointment go this morning?"

Celeste wiped the tears from her eyes. "And that's another thing that's getting on my nerves, Tony. I'm sick of being disappointed every month. We've gone to see three specialists, and none of them can tell us why we can't get pregnant. Today, Dr. Bindu took my temperature and gave me an ovulation predictor. He said that our best chances of becoming pregnant is between now and next Friday."

Anthony stood behind Celeste and massaged her shoulders. What he didn't know was that his loving wife, the wife he cherished, the wife he desperately wanted to have a baby with, had just lied to him. "So, what are we waiting on?"

Celeste dismissed Anthony's question and asked one of her own. "What am I gonna do about Ginger?" She was not in a rush to make a baby because a baby would never be made, not if it meant her body had to be involved.

Anthony let out a loud sigh. "Celeste, I want you to let Ginger take care of Ginger. And I want you to come to bed so I can take care of you."

In her bedroom, Portia pressed the play button on her answering machine. She listened to her messages as she undressed.

"Hey, beautiful. What's up with you? It's me, David. I've been calling you all day. Hit me on my cell when you get in." (Beep)

David insisted that Portia call him on his cellular phone. She wasn't worthy of his home number. Besides, his wife could answer.

"Hi, Portia. This is Greg. I've been trying to hook up with you for two weeks. What's up? Are you missing in action or what?" (Beep)

Every two weeks, like clockwork, when Gregory's wife gets a headache, he always wound up in Portia's bed.

"Portia, this is Richard. Why are you avoiding me? You think a brotha ain't got nothin' else better to do than track you down?" (Beep)

Three days ago, Portia received a dozen red roses at the car dealership where she works as an administrative assistant. The inside card read, *My dearest Tamara, I love you always, Richard.*

Portia did a little detective work and found out that Tamara was Mrs. Richard Clark.

"Hello, Portia. This is Gary. I'm in town for a few days. Let's get together. Give me a call at my mother's house. 555-3743. I would love to see you." (Beep)

Gary Stokes was stupid fine. He'd always been Portia's weakness.

***

Forty-five minutes later, Portia was standing at her stove unwrapping a king-sized milk chocolate Hershey's candy bar. She placed it into a small saucepan, then added two pats of butter. She heated the saucepan on low, then stirred the chocolate and butter until they blended well. On the sink next to the stove was a bowl of fresh, ripe, juicy sweet strawberries. Portia removed the melted chocolate from the heat, then dipped the strawberries, one by one, in the chocolate and laid them on a plate. She placed the plate in the freezer, then showered while the chocolate hardened. Fifteen minutes later, Portia removed the plate of strawberries from the freezer and set it on the sink next to an open bottle of Moscato. She filled a syringe with the wine and carefully inserted the needle into each strawberry and emptied the syringe. As she finished, she heard a soft knock on the front door and smiled.

She carried the plate of chocolate-covered strawberries into the living room with her.

Portia greeted Gary wearing a white sheer teddy and a smile. "Hi, there."

Gary stood in the doorway looking as fine as he wanted to look. Six foot five inches of solid muscle walked past Portia and left a whiff of Pleasures in the wind. She shut the door and leaned against it, admiring Gary's short, wavy hair. His goatee blended nicely with his mustache. His caramel-colored skin was as smooth as silk.

"Umph, umph, umph. It's a shame your wife lets you travel alone."

Gary's mischievous smiled melted Portia. "Why is that?"

"Because you don't know how to behave yourself."

"That's not true. I'm always on my best behavior when I'm away on business. It's only when I come to Chicago that I get into trouble."

Portia walked to Gary and wrapped her left arm around his neck while holding the plate of chocolate-covered strawberries in her right hand. "Is that what I am, 'trouble'?"

He pulled Portia's body closer to his. "With a capitol 'T.' But you're the kind of trouble I don't mind getting *into*, if you know what I mean."

Portia picked up a chocolate strawberry from the plate and inserted it into Gary's mouth. He bit into it, and when he tasted the wine, he smiled. "Um, yummy."

Portia returned the smile. "You like?"

"I love." Gary answered sinfully.

She set the plate of strawberries on the cocktail table and stood on her tippy toes to kiss Gary's forehead, his left cheek, and his right cheek. Portia took her time and ran her tongue along his mustache from left to right. Gary picked her up, and she wrapped her thighs around his waist. The married man carried Portia to her bedroom, and there wasn't any shame in their game.

UC HIS GLORY BOOK CLUB!

www.uchisglorybookclub.net

UC His Glory Book Club is the spirit-inspired brain-child of Joylynn Jossel, Author and Acquisitions Editor of Urban Christian, and Kendra Norman-Bellamy, Author for Urban Christian. This is an online book club that hosts authors of Urban Christian. We welcome as members all men and women who have a passion for reading Christian-based fiction.

UC His Glory Book Club pledges our commitment to provide support, positive feedback, encouragement, and a forum whereby members can openly discuss and review the literary works of Urban Christian authors.

There is no membership fee associated with UC His Glory Book Club; however, we do ask that you support the authors through purchasing, encouraging, providing book reviews, and of course, your prayers. We also ask that you respect our beliefs and follow the guidelines of the book club. We hope to receive your valuable input, opinions, and reviews that build up, rather than tear down our authors.

WHAT WE BELIEVE:

—We believe that Jesus is the Christ, Son of the Living God.

—We believe the Bible is the true, living Word of God.

—We believe all Urban Christian authors should use their God-given writing abilities to honor God and share the message of the written word God has given to each of them uniquely.

—We believe in supporting Urban Christian authors in their literary endeavors by reading, purchasing and sharing their titles with our online community.

—We believe that in everything we do in our literary arena should be done in a manner that will lead to God being glorified and honored.

—We look forward to the online fellowship with you. Please visit us often at *www.uchisglorybookclub.net*.

Many Blessing to You!

Shelia E. Lipsey,
President, UC His Glory Book Club